KEEP KARMA

AND

CARRY ON

To Sue

Enjoy.

Lots of love

Sue xxx

SUE CEE

First edition independently published in the UK in 2023.
ISBN (Hardback): 979-8-3770080-6-4
ISBN (Paperback): 979-8-8381374-6-3
Typesetting design: Matthew J Bird

A CIP catalogue record of this book is available from the British Library.

For further information about this book, please contact the author at: suelclarke899@gmail.com

To Natalie, Lucy and Michael

ONE

"That woman cannot be Mother," Claire gasped in horror. She was suddenly aware that her jaw had dropped wide open and quickly shut it. Unconsciously, she pulled her twins closer to her and held their hands tightly.

Moments earlier *that woman* had emerged from Arrivals at Terminal Three at Heathrow Airport. She was a suntanned, middle-aged woman with long blonde dreadlocks piled high on her head, dressed in harem pants, a loose cotton tee shirt, and sandals. She was arm in arm with a dark-skinned, black-haired, younger man dressed in white cotton trousers and a tee shirt. They were both laughing and briefly kissed each other. Claire had initially dismissively glanced at her, thinking to herself "Bloody Hippy. Should know better at her age. And with her toy boy," but then reeled in shock and horror when the woman dropped the carpet bag and colourful coat she was carrying and shrieked

"Claire?"

Time seemed to slip into slow motion as the woman started to run towards Claire, arms outstretched. What had happened to her mother, Jayne Velazquez, over the past three years? Where was the dumpy, plain, sour woman, embittered by life as a single parent, that Claire had dropped off at the airport three years ago to go on a repeatedly extended holiday to Thailand?

Claire had been in touch with her sporadically over the past three years, but only by email. Claire still remembered so clearly the shock she had at the first email from Jayne just before the end of her two-week holiday, saying how she loved Thailand and that she had cancelled her flight home and was staying there for another month. A string of emails had followed, putting back her return date, until it was obvious that Jayne was going to stay in Thailand indefinitely and was going to travel to Bali and Sri Lanka on a *spiritual quest* with a couple of people from the Community where she was now living. Claire had stared at the email open-mouthed. Her angry, atheist, money-hungry mother had suddenly become spiritual.

When she had told her husband, Sebastian, at dinner that evening he pontificated.

"It won't last. Probably some dodgy Thai bloke involved somewhere along the line. Once he has fleeced her of everything she has, she will be coming home with her tail between her legs. One of the problems with premenopausal women who go swanning off to other countries to *find themselves*. Easy prey."

That was three years ago.

And now she was back.

She ran up to Claire and wrapped her arms around her, hugging her close, as much as Claire's heavily pregnant abdomen would allow. Claire was almost suffocated by the powerful, heady scent of Sandalwood. The woman felt strong and muscular under her thin tee shirt and nothing like the flabby woman Claire had seen through Departures three years ago. The younger man had picked up the carpet bag and coat and was standing silently with his bag in one hand and the woman's bag in the other. After bear-hugging Claire for several minutes, the woman stood back and looked Claire up and down.

"My lovely Claire. You haven't changed a bit. How are you keeping? We have so much to catch up with."

Claire stared in disbelief at her mother and could scarcely recognise her. She had lost a massive amount of weight, was slim and lithe and she moved effortlessly although she used to be clumsy and uncoordinated. The once mousy, short hair was now long, blonde, and twisted into dreadlocks, tied with multicoloured ribbons. Her ears were ringed with studs, and she had a nose ring and eyebrow bar, although Jayne had always said how she hated piercings and tattoos. Glancing down Claire could see the head of a snake tattooed on her ankle which disappeared up her leg into her harem pants.

"Sorry about the delay through immigration. Bloody fascist bastards. Insisted on a whole-body search. Looking for drugs. Right pervs. Even made me take my yoni egg out."

Claire looked puzzled

"Yoni egg....?" she queried out aloud.

A couple of people who were walking by at this moment and overheard suppressed their sniggers.

"Google it," her mother replied.

Turning to the young man she said

"This is Satish. He is my guru…and friend."

The way they both laughed and looked at each other indicated he was more than *a friend*. Claire looked at him properly for the first time. He was shorter than her mother and his skin was almost black, which showed his Tamil descent. His deep brown eyes were kind with a spark of humour. Claire guessed him to be about her own age of twenty-five. He put his hands together and bowed his head in greeting.

"Namaste." His voice was soft and lilting.

"Pleased to meet you," she mumbled.

She suddenly felt ashamed of her forty-five-year-old mother being partnered with a man in his mid-twenties.

The twins standing at Claire's side had remained quiet up until now, still in shock at seeing this strange woman who was nothing like a grandmother was meant to be. She was certainly not like Tasha's Granny (who was actually her Great-Granny and eighty-five years old). This woman's smell was of heady, exotic perfumes instead of the lavender and wee smell that Tasha's great granny had. Her clothes were strange and colourful, instead of grubby pink and pilled, and she had a handsome young man with her instead of an old, grumpy man, as Tasha's great granny had. Abigail spoke first.

"Is this Granny? She doesn't look like a granny. Why doesn't she smell of wee?" she asked in an uncharacteristically timid voice.

The strange woman turned to her, bent down, and spoke.

"Yes, I am your Granny, but I don't want to be called Granny. Or Nanny. Or Grandma. I am Serena."

Claire looked at her mother, puzzled.

"Serena?"

"Yes." Serena stood straight and looked her directly in the eye. "Jayne Velazquez is no more. I am Serena now. A new person. Healed. Restored. Reborn. So, I have a new name. My full new name is Thai for Serenity and Focus. But it is a bit of a mouthful, so I am calling myself Serena."

Claire shook her head, still trying to take it all in.

"And so much thanks to Satish." She gave him a doe-eyed smile as she took his arm again and pulled him close.

"He has taught me so much."

There was a definite suggestive tone to her voice. He smiled enigmatically. Serena turned to the twins and bent down to their level again.

"Now. You were so small when I left. Which one is which, and how am I going to tell you apart?"

They were almost carbon copies of each other. They both had large blue eyes and long blonde hair. Serena thought they were pretty but too doll-like. Being dressed in identical coats and dresses made it even harder to distinguish which girl was which.

"I am Abigail," said the one with slightly longer hair and a slimmer face.

"I am Olivia," said the other one.

"OK. Abigail and Olivia. It is lovely to see you again. You are going to be lovely young ladies."

They both pretended to be coy.

Serena could see straight away that they were both a handful and spoilt. She remembered that their birthday was in September – six months away, and they would be five. She also remembered that the baby was due on 30th April – just over five weeks away.

"Now what do I have for you in my bag?"

Serena delved into the shoulder bag that was slung over her back. Slowly and deliberately, she brought out two painted wooden elephants.

"We sell them at the elephant sanctuary where I live," she said.

Claire noticed the use of the present tense with some relief. Her mother had only come back for a visit and not to live back here.

"This one is called *Swy* which means *beautiful* and this one is called *Saylm* which means *breeze*. I carved them from life. *Swy* is my favourite. But then….. so is *Saylm*.

The girls gingerly took them and stared at them as though they were the strangest things they had ever seen. The painted wood felt so different to their, mostly pink, plastic toys and they could not see where they could put batteries in them.

Serena straightened up and smiled at Claire.

"And how are you doing? How is Junior? Do you have a name for him yet?"

"I am fine. Tired, running around after the twins all day. He is doing well. We are trying to decide between calling him Percival, or St John."

Serena winced inwardly.

"Nice. Difficult choice."

She stifled the desire to laugh.

Serena took Satish's arm and asked "OK. What is the plan? I am famished. They didn't have any vegetarian food on the plane. We ordered it but the order got lost. We had to make do with just a bread roll or two."

Claire was suddenly flustered at the new turn of events with Satish being with her mother. It was clear that he was going to be tagging along with her. Claire blushed at the thought of her mother having a lover under the same roof as her. She could already imagine how her neighbour next door would react.

Hesitantly she asked

"Er. What plans does Satish have?"

"Oh! He is with me."

When Serena saw the hesitant look on Claire's face, she put her hand to her forehead and continued

"Didn't you get my email a couple of weeks ago? I asked if it would be ok if he came too, but I never received a reply. I was going to send another one as the email system is not that reliable. I am sorry - life was a bit hectic just before we left, and I forgot to email you again. I have to walk two miles to the local village to send emails, so it takes a big chunk out of the day. One of our newly arrived elephants escaped and wreaked havoc in the local village. It took us nearly a week to get her back. Don't worry – Satish can bunk in with me to begin with. He has some speaking engagements booked in London. And he wants to go to Birmingham to see his poorly aunt and see some of his cousins and try to raise some more money for the Community. We need a new and larger kitchen, and we want to make some more enclosures for the elephants. And…. we want to start another Community in Sri Lanka. Satish can be near his family again. He comes from Sri Lanka."

The gulf between the lives of the two women seemed immense. Claire thought of her normal, well-organised, comfortable life which, usually, ran like clockwork. Unless the girls were in full tantrum mode, of course. Sadly, this was occurring more and more as they both tried to assert their unique, individual personalities over each other and over their mother. Life was normally predictable and secure. Serena's life seemed exotic and mysterious, accentuated by her colourful clothes, scent, and jewellery. Claire suddenly felt dowdy in her black trousers and billowing black maternity blouse. She was painfully aware that her hair needed washing, was beginning to show random grey hairs, and she desperately needed a new set of nails as her current ones were chipped and fading. Large bags under her eyes showed the late night and lack of sleep after the massive tantrums from the twins the night before. She had not had time nor energy to put on the façade of being the perfectly manicured woman that both she, and Jayne, once had been.

"Let's get home. I expect you are cold after coming from your tropical paradise. I have some beef stew in the slow cooker."

As she said these words what Serena had said about the food on the plane sank in fully. Serena also looked worried.

"We are vegan," she said. "I did write in one of my emails how I could no longer support violence in my diet."

Claire had read it at the time and snorted her contempt.

"I wonder if she still swats mosquitos when they are biting her," she had said aloud to Sebastian. He too had laughed contemptuously. She also took a sadistic delight in telling Roger, her mother's half-Spanish, ex-husband and her father, and his wife Melanie, when they had come for a steak dinner the next night. Roger had choked on a mouthful.

"Jayne – vegan? Never. Missus Oh-I-like-my-very-rare-steak-with-a-Band-Aid herself. I expect it will last as long as her lover does – assuming that is why she is still there. She won't keep it up."

Now Claire was faced, not only with an extra unexpected guest but a large pan of useless stew and nothing much else in the cupboards after a week of the girls playing up and not having time even to go online to shop. Serena read her expression.

"Not to worry. I guess you have takeaways nearby. We will get a takeaway tonight and sort food out for us tomorrow."

They walked back to the car, paid for the parking, and got in. Serena insisted on sitting in the back next to the girls so she could get to know them. Satish sat in the front, shivering in his thin trousers and shirt. Claire put the heated seat on for him and turned the heater on to full. Satish sat in silence, taking in the strangeness of this new land. It felt so hard and lacking in spirit compared to his hometown in Sri Lanka and his adopted country of Thailand. So much concrete, with so little greenery, compared to the remote, lush forest surrounding the community where they lived. Bangkok was manic, noisy, and polluted but elsewhere the pace of life was slower in Thailand. Here everyone seemed in a mad rush. The negative energies around him threatened to overwhelm him and he focussed inwardly to maintain his calm. Claire was glad of his silence as she began to process the last hour.

It was although she had lost her mother altogether and a new person had appeared, claiming to be her mother. Obviously. she knew it was her. The tilt of her head when she laughed. Her blue eyes, which now sparkled with joy, and her fair hair, which was now so light and sun-bleached and twirled into the largest dreadlocks Claire had ever seen. Her voice had the mixture of South London where she had lived so long and West Country from her birth town of Bristol. However, mixed in now was an undertone of an Asian timbre. Several times she had spoken to Satish in another language. Claire did not know whether it was Thai or Tamil.

Claire smiled in the mirror at Abigail when she asked Serena if they had hairbrushes in Thailand as she obviously could not have brushed her hair for a long time. Claire had thought about reprimanding Abigail for being rude, but Serena had just laughed and said she liked not having to brush her hair as brushing your hair hurt. Abigail said she hated having her hair brushed and she wanted to have her hair like Serena's.

"Can I mummy? Can I?" she squealed.

"Over my dead body," Claire thought to herself. She also smiled at the thought of how Sebastian would react to the rather strange new version of her mother. She then worried that he might throw them both out, thinking about his reputation as a local Councillor, and Chairman of the local Neighbourhood Society. By-elections were approaching. The CEOs of some of his biggest clients lived in the same area of Twickenham and he would not want any hint of anything scandalous or rebellious in his household. However, Serena was still her mother, albeit a very different version from the one she had known all of her life.

Because of the delay getting through immigration, they hit the rush hour traffic. Claire was grateful that her mother was keeping the girls entertained with stories of the elephants and her travels to Bali and Sri Lanka. Satish had fallen asleep with his head resting on the window and was snoring very softly. As the traffic was in gridlock, Claire sneaked a good look at him. She decided that he was rather handsome, and she could see why her mother had fallen for him. His lips were full and sensuous, his wavy, black hair was tied up in a knot on the back of his head, and he had a prominent Adam's apple. His strong masculine scent, mixed with an aroma of exotic spices was exciting and arousing, so Claire had to force her attention back on the road. Serena caught her eye in the mirror and smiled. Claire looked away and reddened. How was she going to cope with this new woman/mother and her gorgeous man?

TWO

Eventually, the twins ran out of questions about the elephants and sat in uncharacteristic silence. On the slow crawl back to Claire's house in Twickenham Serena reflected how enormously her life had changed since she was last here

She had left for Thailand on a cold December day three and a bit years ago with just a suitcase. Her last evening in England had been with Claire and Sebastian and their two very demanding toddlers. Claire had been surprised but fully supportive when her mother had said she was taking a holiday to Thailand, although Claire had been worried about her travelling on her own. Her mother never had time for friends so there was no one she could go with, and life had been incredibly stressful for her. It was time she had a proper holiday. Serena remembered the feeling of relief she had when she got on the plane and thought that for two weeks she was leaving behind the demands of her boring job in a solicitor's office, trying to be a grandmother and support to the work-widow Claire and finding some time for herself. Every week had been the same treadmill. Five weekdays commuting to the City and then spending weekends to and fro-ing to

Claire's to help with the twins. Sometimes Roger and Melanie called in when she was there, which she hated. Roger left her for Melanie when Claire when five years old and married Melanie immediately after their divorce.

When Claire was nineteen Sebastian started working at Roger's financial company, and he and Claire had an instant attraction for each other, despite a ten-year age difference. Their relationship became intense and passionate very quickly.

When Claire's surprise pregnancy was announced Sebastian's father had insisted on their getting married as he was about to become an Assistant Bishop and did not want any scandal in the family. There had even been veiled threats of disinheritance from what would be a hefty legacy if they did not *do the right thing*.

Serena hated that Roger had made Sebastian a partner in the same financial advice company and had announced it at Claire and Sebastian's wedding. She hated that there was a cosy relationship between the two couples, from which she felt excluded. Roger was able to spend obscene amounts of money on his grandchildren whereas Serena was counting every penny.

Serena had always felt defensive and inferior around Melanie, who was dark, slim, and muscular and called herself a personal trainer. Serena would have loved time to go to a gym and get fit, but time and money did not allow it. Roger was fifteen years older than Serena and he had been her boss in her first job as an administrator in a financial consultancy. In hindsight, she could see she had been naïve and easy prey for the early thirties over-sexed, single man, who had smouldering Latin looks and a dazzling smile. A few nights at his flat had resulted in her pregnancy with Claire and a rushed wedding. Her life had become increasingly miserable from then on until she went to Thailand. However, Serena realised with relief that now her anger and jealousy felt as distant as the lush forests of Thailand felt in this maze of brick and concrete. She saw she was looking at her old world with new eyes. None of all this mattered anymore.

Satish awoke, yawned, and stretched.

"I am so sorry," he mumbled with a wobble of his head, and continued

"So rude of me. Please forgive me."

Claire shot him a smile.

"You're tired. Don't worry. We have plenty of time ahead to get to know each other."

"I shall look forward to it."

His voice was gentle, warm, and fluid, and once again Claire felt uncomfortable about the effect that he was having on her.

She pulled into the parking bay outside their house, surprised that there was one vacant at this time of the evening. Heaving herself out of the car she announced

"Home."

Satish got out and nodded.

"Very nice."

The row of cross-gabled Victorian houses with large bay windows, neat front gardens, and each with a car parked outside, was a vastly different world to the thatched hut he shared with Serena in the Community. As they walked up the Minton-tiled path to the front door, he felt a surge of homesickness. The air here was heavy with the smell of petrol fumes and a roar of jet engines overhead heralded another arrival at Heathrow Airport. He longed for the peace of his home and the heady scent of frangipani and the jungle, and the call of the myriad of birds that lived in the trees. Here he could only see the occasional pigeon flying over.

Serena stepped into the familiar stripped pine hallway and dumped her bag down and took off her coat. It had not changed since she had left it just over three years ago. Suddenly it felt as though Thailand had never happened and that she was in a time warp. Catching a glimpse of herself in the mirror on the wall, with her dreadlocks and sun-tanned face, she knew Thailand had been for real, especially when she caught Satish's eye in the mirror, and he winked and smiled at her. She took in afresh her surroundings. The Berber carpeted stairs ran up in front of them and to the right was the door to the living room/dining room extension. The hallway ran past the stairs to the kitchen door. Monochrome prints from a popular furniture store hung on the walls, which were covered with expensive, pale, cream silk wallpaper. What once had appeared so tasteful suddenly looked boring and lacking in originality.

"Hang it on the hook there," Claire indicated while she took off the girls' coats.

"Tea?" Claire enquired.

"I have my own here." Serena delved into her bag and brought out a paper bag containing some dried flowers and handed it to her daughter.

"The bastards at customs thought they were drugs. Frangipani tea is wonderfully happy making and good for digestion. Just pour some boiling water on the flowers and leave it to stew."

The mention of the word stew put Claire back into anxiety about food and the large container of beef stew simmering in the slow cooker. Sebastian had said he would be at a work meal tonight so would be back late. She would have to freeze it. Then she remembered she had already frozen it once and had just reheated it.

"Damn it" she muttered quietly to herself, feeling annoyed at the new version of her mother and her inconvenient diet.

Serena and Satish went into the large all-in-one living/dining room, which could be separated by folding doors. They politely admired the newly stripped floorboards and large, colourful rugs scattered about. They then curled up together on the large sofa under the bay window. Claire felt excluded by their soft, intimate whisperings in a language she did not understand. Serena quickly noticed her unease and asked if there was anything she could do.

"No. Thanks. Entertain the girls for me."

Abigail and Olivia had already appeared with armloads of books and plastic toys, which they dumped unceremoniously in front of Serena and Satish.

"Read us a story!" Olivia demanded.

Serena picked through the books, trying to find one that was not garish or made horrible noises as she turned the pages.

"I will tell you a story instead," she said.

Olivia protested

"But I like looking at pictures. I need pictures. I can't make them up in my head like Mummy says I should."

"Everything you can imagine is real. That's what Picasso said," Satish told them in his soft voice.

Olivia stared at him.

"Who's Pick Arso?" asked Abigail.

"A famous painter who painted very different pictures and said people can imagine whatever they want, and it will be true."

Olivia snorted and looked at him suspiciously, saying

"That's silly. If I make up a picture of a dinosaur in my head, will it really be here? I don't think so."

Satish smiled to himself.

"If you believe it so, it will be so."

His enigmatic tone was lost on the little girl.

Serena realised she was fighting a losing battle with trying to tell a story but was determined she would engage the little girl's imagination another day.

"OK. *Dana Dolly Goes to Town* it is."

She reluctantly picked up a garish, plastic book and opened the first page as the two girls climbed up on the settee next to her. Silently she wondered how long it would take the plastic in the book to decompose and how badly it would contaminate the earth.

Back in the kitchen, Claire was leaning against the worktop trying to work out how to proceed. Hurriedly she had read the labels on all her biscuits and cakes and could only find a packet of Rich Tea biscuits that did not contain animal products. She put them out on a separate plate and found some flapjacks and mini cookies for the girls. Taking a deep breath, she carried the tray of drinks and biscuits through to the living room. For a moment she was captivated by the sight of her strange-looking mother cuddled up to her two daughters on one side and the handsome stranger on her other side. Gently she put the tray down on the low pine table in front of the settee and sank into her armchair. As she lowered herself down into the chair, she became aware that Satish was quietly observing her. He nodded at her and gently said

"If I may be so bold to say, I can see your energy vibrations are very low. You appear unsettled. Can we do anything to help you?"

"Thank you. No."

Her tone was slightly abrupt and immediately she regretted it. She passed the drinks to each of them and then offered them a biscuit. They both declined. Claire felt a surge of frustration and rejection. Satish just smiled sadly at her. Serena had finished reading the story and the twins were demanding she read it again.

"Maybe later." She could not bear to go through the inane story again.

A rumble from her stomach reminded her of their lack of food.

"Do you have any takeaway menus?"

Claire went to haul herself to her feet. but Serena held up her hand.

"Just tell me where they are, and I will get them."

Following Claire's instructions, Serena went into the kitchen and found assorted menus in a top drawer of the kitchen units. She stood and took in the gleaming black and chrome cupboards and black marble worktops. Thoughtfully, she ran her fingers along the hard, shiny surfaces and looked at the black slate floor. Although it all felt oppressive, the kitchen was flooded with light from a massive bank of halogen lights on tracks on the ceiling. How different it was from the Community kitchen which had a mud floor and tea chests for storage. How she suddenly longed for that again.

Snuggling up with Satish again, she flicked through the menus and found Indian vegan food. Opening her phone, she dialled the restaurant and asked for their choices.

"Please cook it in oil and not ghee."

Suddenly Serena paled.

"Oh shit." Putting her hand to her mouth, she said. "I don't think my bank card will work here. I forgot to tell them I was coming back to the UK. Sorry…." she said to the man at the other end of the phone. "Hang on…."

Claire was already getting to her feet.

"Don't worry. Use mine."

With obvious irritation, she dug into her handbag and handed the card to Serena, who quickly read out the details, reaffirmed the address, and handed the card back to her daughter. Serena smiled sweetly and said

"I will repay you as soon as I have sorted out my bank. I will ring them tomorrow."

"Don't worry. This is on me," Claire replied reluctantly, still annoyed she had perfectly decent food that was going to go to waste.

"Do you mind if I go ahead and feed myself and the girls?" she continued.

"Not at all. They are busy in the takeaway tonight and food will be about an hour. Could I take a bath? I feel vile."

"Go ahead. You know where it is. Towels are in the landing cupboard. Help yourself to smellies."

Serena smiled her thanks and then turned to Satish.

"I need a massage. I ache after being cooped up in that plane for so long."

She held out her hand and he willingly took it and let her lead him out of the room. The broad smile on his face told Claire all she needed to know, and she felt uncomfortable and bustled around and snapped at the girls to hide her embarrassment at her mother's blatant behaviour.

Forty minutes later they reappeared. Serena was smiling and red and shiny from the hot bath and Satish had a look of deep contentment on his face. She had changed into a flowing dress, and he was in clean, white, cotton trousers and shirt. Claire was feeling frazzled and exhausted after battling with the girls. They had decided their granny was very cool and they wanted to be like her and not eat meat. Claire had ended snarling at them that surely they did not want the poor cow to have died for nothing. Guiltily they ate their meal in silence, and they were just finishing as the other two came down from their bath, giggling and teasing each other in the unknown language. Claire almost felt annoyed with the strange atmosphere of utter calm, joy, and unflappability that surrounded Satish and her mother.

"Can we be let in on the joke?" she snapped.

Serena and Satish looked at her in amazement. At that moment, the doorbell rang, and Serena went to answer it. She came back into the dining room with two brown bags emitting pungent aromas.

"Rice. Tarka Dhal, Sag Aloo, Nan, Poppadoms...."

"Poppydomes!" shrieked Olivia. "I want some. I want some."

"I ordered extra," smiled Serena. "I know they are always popular."

Serena and Satish sat in the places allocated to them and spooned out their meals. Satish let the girls try his dishes, but they screwed up their faces in disgust. He laughed with his tinkling laugh.

"You will have to like curry if you come to visit us in Thailand. Our food is very spicy."

Claire felt a strange mixture of relief and sadness as she realised, once again, that her mother's visit was temporary.

"Tell us more about the Elly Pellies," Abigail insisted.

While Serena and Satish ate their meal, they regaled the girls with stories of runaway elephants and how they had rescued them from cruel owners and circuses.

"Never ride elephants. They treat them very badly." Satish warned them, his deep brown eyes full of sadness.

"I want an elephant. Can I have one Mummy, please, please….." Olivia whined at her mother.

"It could live in the garden. Pleeeeeese," piped up Abigail.

"Don't be ridiculous." Claire bit back at her. "We don't have room. What would we feed it on? And who would clean up its poo?"

"Maria would. She cleans our toilets. She can pick up elephant poo."

"Maria is our cleaner," Claire told Serena and Satish in explanation. She continued "I think Maria would want a lot more money from us to clean up elephant poo. Now go and get ready for bed. It is nearly eight o'clock."

Both girls huffed and shrugged their shoulders and for a moment wondered about disobeying their mother. They both saw Serena smiling at them and giving a slow and gentle shake of her head.

"Go to bed and I will come and read you another story."

"Yeeeeaaaah." The twins thundered up the stairs.

"Thanks." Claire sank down into her chair again. Wearily, she continued

"They can be little buggers at bedtime. Sebastian always likes them in bed by the time he gets home but tonight he won't be back until at least eleven."

Half an hour later the girls were tucked up in bed and happily dozing off, having had Dana Dolly's adventures read to them another five times. Serena felt she never wanted to read the story again and made a mental note to make the book disappear. She went downstairs to find Satish and Claire sitting talking together in the living room. A rush of relief filled her as she saw that, finally, her daughter was feeling at ease with the man she loved.

"What an interesting life Satish has had," Claire exclaimed. "He knows so much. And travelled so much."

Serena felt a warm glow of pride and sat down next to him, curled her legs under her on the settee, and snuggled up to him. Claire thought how three years ago her mother would have just plopped down on the sofa and would not even have been able to cross her legs. Now she moved with the grace of a dancer.

Over the next hour and a half over a glass of wine, they filled each other in about what had happened over the previous three years. Claire and Sebastian now felt they had finally done all they wanted to the house, which they had bought, cheaply, just after their hasty wedding, to *do up*.

Sebastian was now working ridiculously long hours, but he wanted to retire early, so did not mind the seventy to eighty-hour weeks. Being ten years older than Claire, he wanted to retire in fifteen years, at fifty, so he could have some time to enjoy traveling together and to spend time in their cottage in North Devon. Every school holiday he took time off to drive them down there, where he spent most of the time sleeping and leaving Claire to entertain the girls. It was obvious to Serena that Claire was still feeling like a work widow. The dark shadows under her eyes and the lack of spark in them told their own story. Serena recognised the state of sheer exhaustion that many mothers of young children face. She asked about Maria. She was told that Maria had been acting as a nanny and cleaner for the past two years and had more or less saved Claire's sanity.

"She is from Spain. I don't know what I will do if she has to go back there," mused Claire.

Serena filled Claire in with tales of her travels in Thailand, Sri Lanka, and Bali. Initially, she had been on a standard package holiday at a beach resort in Thailand but had gone for a massage at a local masseur. She had told her about the community called the Lotus Light Community which ran an elephant rescue sanctuary, deep in the jungle. Serena had already visited the touristy elephant project and had been sceptical about the legitimacy of their work. She did not think the elephants were being treated very well. However, the Lotus Light sanctuary was completely different. The elephants were happy and well treated, with no tricks or rides involved. The Community itself was imbued with a deep peace and gentleness that she had never encountered before. She had already become enchanted with the country and its gentle, smiling people. She had there and then decided to spend a bit more time in Thailand and stay in the community, as a volunteer space had become vacant. Booking out of her hotel, cancelling her flight back to England, and emailing Claire suddenly gave her a sense of freedom she had never known before. It was as though a massive weight had been lifted from her shoulders. She no longer felt she was competing with anyone. Gone were the feelings of inferiority she had when she was around Melanie, who had always been so immaculately turned out in the last fashions, whilst she had to make her clothes last year upon year, working as a single mother and sole breadwinner. Melanie could afford expensive haircuts and her make-up was flawless, while she had felt guilty that she had slipped in her own standards after Claire's birth and had not kept the model-like figure that Roger had married. However, Serena no longer wanted these things in life. She smiled at the realisation that these things had no hold over her, even now she was back in England.

Claire nodded silently as her mother spilled out feelings that she had never aired before to her daughter, but she did it with a certain detachment and peace. Realising how her mother had felt around Melanie made Claire feel guilty about being so welcoming to her stepmother and made her wonder a little bit if she had been instrumental in pushing her mother away to the other side of the world.

Serena continued with her story.

"I'd been at the community for only a week when I realised it was where I wanted to live for the rest of my life. Here I have a brochure about it."

She rummaged in her patchwork bag and brought out a cheaply photocopied brochure and handed it to Claire. Folded in three it had very grainy photos of the basic bamboo huts and the communal eating area, which was an open-sided, thatched structure with a basic kitchen at one end. On the back of the brochure were photographs of some of the elephants. Claire pondered on the contrasts between Serena's home in the Community and the listed, Cotswold, Tudor manor which housed her in-laws, and her own sought-after property in West London.

Serena continued

"I found such healing, love, forgiveness, and joy there. There was such peace yet vibrancy. My whole life and being were changing. I suddenly had a massive meltdown. I couldn't stop crying. I cried for days. All the hurt from my life surfaced. I was a wreck. But the Community was wonderful. Bit by bit they helped to put me back together again. I knew I'd changed forever. Six months later Satish joined us as a teacher and mentor. We knew we were soulmates immediately."

She smiled at him warmly and squeezed his hand.

"He's been a spiritual teacher since he was twelve. He's an old soul and so wonderfully wise. His wisdom and learning even as a child astonished all those around him. Knowledge far beyond his years. He's written several books."

She gave him another loving look and continued

"Oh, Claire it's wonderful. We have a proper elephant sanctuary. We take them away from cruel people who use them for rides and doing tricks. The poor things are so traumatised when we get them, so it takes a lot of time and love to make them whole again. We also have rescued monkeys and illegally traded birds. It's called The Lotus Light because the Lotus Light is the light that shines from a thing of beauty that has grown up through the deepest darkness. All of us living in the Community have come from places of deep hurt or darkness and we have reached up through the murky waters of our lives to the Light."

Claire inhaled sharply at this unusual talk from her once hardened atheist mother. Satish interjected, having seen the scepticism on Claire's face.

"We are an open community of spiritual seekers. The only rules are that everything is done in love for the greater good. There is no violence to any living being and we do not judge others. We do not follow any hard-line doctrine. We just ask that members follow the path of love and the greater good. We spend time in prayer and meditation together and do everything communally. Although we as a community do not hold to any one religion, we do have two large stone Buddhas at the end of our road. This is to placate the Thai authorities, who generally leave us alone. New members have much reading to do when they join. They need to read all the major spiritual texts. We start them with whatever are the spiritual texts for their culture, and they read the rest of them after. For Westerners it is usually starting with the Christian Bible, Jewish texts, then the Koran, the teachings of Buddha, the Vedas, and Upanishads of Hindu, and we finish with the Kama Sutra."

Claire was sipping her drink and nearly spat her (non-alcoholic) wine out in surprise. Satish smiled in amusement at her reaction.

"Our bodies are holy as well. We thank God for the pleasures they give us…and each other."

He looked sideways at Serena with a seductive smile. Claire reddened at the thought of her mother reading the Kama Sutra, and even worse, putting it into practice. She also wondered if she could get a copy for Sebastian, as their love life had become non-existent of late.

Gradually the talk wound down and exhaustion and jet lag began to take their toll on the travellers. Claire showed them to their room. Plodding up the stairs she said

"I'm afraid Sebastian has turned the attic into an office so you can't sleep there anymore. We've made the room at the front, next to the girls' room, into the guest room."

Serena and Satish were relieved to see that the bed was a double one. Claire had already put out more towels, flannels, and spare dressing gowns.

"Please make yourself at home, and don't rush to get up in the morning. The girls have nursery tomorrow and Sebastian will be off to work early. I have my Pre-Birth Group in the morning. I'll pick the girls up from nursery at mid-day. Help yourself to breakfast. If you want to go out, I'll leave a spare front door key on the top in the kitchen. Maria will be in at ten to clean."

Serena turned and gave her daughter an uncharacteristic hug. Claire found herself overcome with emotion at this and turned away before Serena could see the tears that had sprung annoyingly into her eyes. Wishing them a good night she hurried from the room.

After loading the dishwasher and putting washing in the machine, Claire decided she would have an early night. She was exhausted physically and mentally, but most of all emotionally. There was a great deal to process. She was sound asleep when Sebastian crept into their bedroom at eleven thirty and climbed into bed. In her sleep she was aware of his presence and automatically turned over and snuggled up to him, slowly rising back into consciousness.

"So, has the Angry Old Bat arrived then?" Sebastian asked in a low voice.

Claire, even in her dozy state, felt a prick of annoyance at his unkindness about her mother.

"Yes."

"And….how is she? Any mellower from her extended holiday? Has her presumed lover, whoever he – or she - is, dumped her yet?"

Claire was now fully awake, and she sat up and turned to Sebastian leaning on one elbow.

"She is different. Very different."

"What do you mean?"

Sebastian was facing her in bed, his interest piqued.

"Oh. Just you wait. You'll see in the morning. She has gone very weird. She has *found herself*. She has changed her name to Serena. And…. by the way…. she has her mid-twenties Sri Lankan lover with her. He's in the spare bed with her. Night night."

She leant over, kissed Sebastian on the cheek, turned away, laid down, and went to sleep. Sebastian lay back in a state of shock and spent the next half an hour staring at the ceiling.

"Bloody hell" he muttered.

THREE

Sebastian woke up just before his alarm was due to go off at six. As he lay on his back, he became aware of a distant humming sound. He strained his ears to hear where it was coming from and realised it was from downstairs. Next to him, Claire stirred and slowly woke up. He said

"I think the bloody water system is playing up again. Can't you hear it?"

Sleepily Claire sat up and listened.

"Oh, hell. I thought Steve had fixed it. We'd better go and turn the boiler off and on again."

They pulled on their robes and went downstairs. As they got to the bottom of the stairs, they realised that the humming sound was coming from the dining room rather than the kitchen where the boiler was.

"What the hell….?" Sebastian muttered.

He pushed open the door and went in, followed by Claire. They both stopped suddenly in surprise at what they saw. Serena and Satish were sitting cross-legged in front of the open sliding patio doors, and the rays of the rising sun were just caressing their heads. Serena was dressed in skimpy shorts and a bikini top. For an embarrassing moment. Claire thought Satish was naked but realised that he was wearing a small, white loincloth, suspended by a thin cord around his waist. Both had their eyes closed, heads thrown back, and were humming a single, long note. Sebastian was mesmerised by the sight of his now slim and toned mother-in-law with blonde dreadlocks piled high on her head. The low sun on their wispy hairs gave the illusion of a halo around her head. Never had he seen someone with a look of such utter bliss on her face. He swallowed and pulled his robe a little tighter around himself.

Claire could not contain herself.

"Mother!" she exploded. "What the hell are you doing? It is freezing in here. And the neighbours can see straight in."

She stormed over to the doors and slammed them together, locked them, pulled the curtains together, and turned to her mother. Serena was sat looking sadly at her daughter.

"We were greeting the sun. We do it every morning. We normally do it naked but didn't think that would go down too well in Twickenham. We follow it with a yoga session but today I told Satish – no headstands."

Claire was rendered speechless. Sebastian was feeling a mixture of amusement, anger, bewilderment, and, to his horror, a certain attraction to this unusual woman who was his mother-in-law. She and Claire were busy staring each other down. Claire was red with anger and embarrassment and Serena's face was filled with a look of sadness and love. Sebastian could safely have a good look at this changed woman. He noticed the serpent tattoo on one leg that started at the ankle, coiled around her sun-tanned leg and the head disappeared into the leg of her shorts. On the other leg, the serpent emerged from the leg of her shorts, and it snaked its way down her leg to her ankle. He felt revulsion, intrigue, and arousal at this powerful image.

Serena uncurled her legs and rose to her feet. Claire also noticed both tattoos.

"What the hell are those?"

"They were part of my healing," Serena replied gently. "They ground me. One draws power from the earth to my feminine energy and the other grounds me back down again."

"What bullshit! Get some clothes on."

Claire reddened further at the sight of the now-standing Satish dressed only in his pure white loincloth, which was in stark contrast to his sleek, dark skin. She now understood why her mother had prohibited him from doing a headstand and forced herself to look him fully in the face and nowhere else. Flustered she then turned to go through to the kitchen.

"Get yourself decent before the girls come down. I'm making tea."

She slammed the door of the kitchen behind her, leaving a bemused Sebastian standing in front of them. Satish cleared his throat, put his palms together in a prayer position, bowed his head low, and said

"Please forgive us for any offence. We merely wish to start the day by giving gratitude for all the wonderful gifts we are given."

He kept his eyes downcast and his hands together until Sebastian muttered something about it not having done any harm but…well…it was a bit of a surprise, as it was not the usual way to start the morning here in Twickenham, and the neighbours would start talking, but never mind – it was over now. Relieved Satish straightened up, and then bowed reverently.

"Thank you for your forgiveness. I am Satish. I am very pleased to meet you at last. I have heard much about you."

"I'm Sebastian," Sebastian grunted.

He did not know whether he should try to shake Satish's hand or put his hands together as Satish did and do a little bow, so he ended up vaguely waving them around.

"Now let's get some breakfast. Please could you get dressed before the girls come down."

However, it was too late. The angry voice of their mother had drawn them downstairs, and they came into the dining room and stopped in their tracks at the sight of the semi-naked, dark-skinned man in their dining room. They stared at him open-mouthed and then both burst into fits of giggles. Satish looked at them inquisitively.

Abigail pointed at his dark torso and giggled behind her hand.

"Why is my body so amusing?" Satish was confused. This made the girls giggle even more. Gently Serena took Satish's arm and led him back upstairs, saying.

"Don't ask."

As they left the room Serena could hear the girls giggling about Granny not having many clothes on, but she was not as wrinkly as Tasha's granny. And she had snakes painted on her legs, which made her cooler than Tasha's granny.

Silently Serena and Satish dressed and sheepishly went back downstairs, having given time for the family to settle down.

Breakfast was strained. Every time the girls looked at Satish and Serena they started giggling together behind their hands. Claire was still angry and flushed. She was particularly annoyed that she kept thinking back to the initial sight of Satish sitting in the sunshine and thinking he was naked. Even more annoying was the warm sensation it gave her in her body when she thought of it. Sebastian was feeling bemused by it all. Only Serena and Satish seemed to be on an even keel. They ate peanut butter on toast with great enjoyment and drank their frangipani tea, while Claire toyed with her poached egg on toast and let her latte go cold. Sebastian tried to rescue the situation by asking Serena and Satish about their plans. To his annoyance, they were vague. He was already planning how he would get them out of the way before he had the Chairman of the local Council Selection Committee and his wife round to dinner on Saturday. He only had three days to do it.

Sebastian left for work and Claire herded the girls upstairs to get dressed and ready for nursery. Serena and Satish cleared up the breakfast things and Serena started washing up. Claire came down and told her not to.

"We have the dishwasher. You don't need to wash the plates."

"But it is better for the earth," Serena replied.

Claire snorted. "Doesn't get them as clean."

Crestfallen, Serena started stacking the dishwasher.

"Leave that. Maria is paid to do it."

Serena straightened up and gave a defeated smile.

She and Satish were relieved when Claire shooed the girls out of the front door and told them she would be back at about one o'clock. Blissful silence and peace descended on the house. They looked at each other longingly.

"Do you fancy another bath?" asked Serena, having already found out that the bath was big enough for two if they didn't make too many waves in it. She had already realised how much she had missed a good soak in the bath, having to rely in Thailand either on dips in the muddy river, or tepid showers from the homemade shower system.

"We need to do some negative energy clearing as well." She took his hand and led him towards the stairs.

Claire felt immense relief to get away from her mother and toyboy – as she called him to herself. Or was he a con artist? She stopped the thought "But he is rather gorgeous" in its tracks and forced herself to focus on driving. She dropped the girls at nursery and then realised she had three-quarters of an hour to fill before going to the Pre-birth Group. Normally she went for a coffee before the group with her friend, Bethany, but she was on holiday. So, instead, she bought a coffee from a Costa and parked on the edge of Richmond Park. Her mind was a jumble of emotions. The effect Satish was having on her was unsettling. Relations between her and Sebastian had become very stale, and she had put some of the blame on him for always being at work and being too tired to give her attention, but she also knew pregnancy had taken its toll on her looks and energy. Added to this, with the constant battles with the twins and their demands, she had very little time for her once strict beauty and fitness regime. She was wondering if there was any spark left in their marriage. There was something very masculine and powerful about Satish with his quiet but strong presence. It highlighted what was lacking in her marriage. She could see why her mother was so besotted with him and envied the joy between them. However, she found it downright embarrassing the way her mother was behaving; like a love-struck, sex-starved teenager, verging on a nymphomaniac. Whenever her thoughts started going towards her mother, she found her mind shot away from the subject. It was all too much to take in.

"I wish she had stayed in Thailand," she muttered to herself.

Her Pre-birth Group was an oasis of calm in her usually frenetic schedule. She had no whining twins to contend with and no plans to be thinking through. Laying down on her yoga mat and listening to peaceful music, she suddenly had an insight into the new life that her mother was trying to lead. However, she quickly dismissed it when her critical mind suggested that Serena was too old for such *touchy-feely* stuff and needed to get real again, although another part of her felt that maybe she was being too harsh on her. On the other hand, she had turned up with an extra visitor unannounced and caused nothing but embarrassment and havoc since her arrival. These constantly conflicting emotions were battling within her, and she forced them out of her mind. The calming music mellowed her and by the end of the session, she had decided to be more accepting of the new woman that her mother had become. Maybe she would ask her for tips on how to be calmer herself. She then drove and picked the girls up from nursery and they came out bearing finger paintings they had done.

"This is my Elly," Abigail announced proudly.

Claire enthusiastically admired the splodge of colours, which were only vaguely elephant-shaped.

"This is Satish," Olivia said. Her splodges of colour were mostly very dark brown and black and were definitely in the shape of a human figure, but right in the middle was a blob of pure white. Claire realised she might have a lot of explaining to do with the nursery teacher.

Stopping at the local small supermarket Claire bought bread, hummus, salad, and cheese for lunch. Fortunately for once the girls were easy to take round the supermarket and did not demand sweets. All they wanted was to get home and see if Granny and Satish were still there.

"She is called Serena, not Granny," Claire reminded them.

"But I want to call her Granny," Olivia demanded. "No one else has a Serena. They all have grannies."

When they got back to the house, Claire was first struck by a strange, slightly pungent aroma and saw that there was an incense stick burning in the hall.

"What the…..."

She licked her finger and snuffed it out. Then she heard Maria's laughter coming from the living room. When she went in, she saw, with irritation, that Maria was sitting in her chair, feet curled up under her, clutching a cup of coffee and laughing at something Satish or Serena had said. They were sitting holding hands on the settee.

"What's this?" Claire snapped. "Have you finished all your chores, Maria? You are not paid to sit around all day."

Hurriedly she got to her feet and deferentially said "I'm sorry, Missus Jackson. I was only having a short break."

"It's our fault," Serena interjected. "We told her to have a minute. She's been working hard. I'm happy to help her make up any lost time. Don't be too harsh on her."

"And what's that horrible smell?" queried Claire. "I don't like joss sticks. Makes the place smell like a hippy's drug den."

Satish wobbled his head deferentially and said quietly

"We were doing some negative energy clearing. There was much anger this morning and we wanted to negate it and put positive energy back."

Claire snorted and angrily extinguished the joss stick stuck into the pot of the large fern on the sideboard.

Maria was standing in the middle of the living room waiting to ask a question and as Claire turned to look at her, she raised her eyebrows

"Yes, Maria?"

"Would you like me to iron?"

"Of course," was the tart reply. "You should have got it all finished by now."

Maria went to defend herself but thought better of it.

"I will do it now."

Claire turned back to Serena and Satish.

"She's paid to work, not gossip. I've bought lunch."

Angrily she turned to go back to the hall but saw the twins standing in the doorway, having witnessed the whole exchange. Suddenly she felt ashamed.

"You two. Go and wash your hands and faces before lunch."

The afternoon was a bit easier. At two-thirty Serena and Satish offered to take the girls to the local park, which Claire accepted with gratitude, but told them they should not be out too long. It gave her a chance to plan dinner for Saturday night when the Chairman of the Council Selection Committee and his wife were coming over. Sebastian was hoping to be selected again as one of the party's candidates for the local Council elections next year, with a view eventually of standing as an MP. However, a financial scandal in the Council that had vague connections to his father-in-law's firm had made it all unsure. Both Sebastian and Roger had been exonerated, but, as Sebastian kept saying to Claire "Mud sticks." Claire knew she had to impress Sir Percival Sanderson and his wife, Chloe, and it was going to be a monumental task. However, there was also the problem of her mother to contend with, and she had no idea what she was going to do with her and Satish. Their veganism alone was going to be a problem, leaving aside how they behaved and looked. They must be the Opposition's secret weapon she decided. She turned her focus back to the menu.

"Venison," she announced to herself. "I shall do venison. And I will make my hazelnut and coffee souffle for dessert."

It got to five o'clock and there was no sign of the girls or Serena and Satish. Slightly worried she scrolled back through her phone messages until she found the one she had received from her mother whilst she was waiting for her at the airport. It had had a number she did not recognise but the message had said "We are held up in immigration. See you soon. Me." That was how Serena had always signed off her messages, which always annoyed Claire. Claire suddenly focussed that Serena had said *we* in her message, but, at the time of receiving it, she had dismissed it as meaning all the people on the flight and not that she had someone else with her. She made a mental note to enter her mother's name against the number. She wondered for a moment what name she would put the number under – Mother, Serena, Jayne? She had never called her Mum, only Mummy when she was very young, but that would not be suitable now.

Having found the number, she rang it. Satish answered.

"Hello. Satish here."

"Hi. This is Claire. Is everything OK?"

Her voice was taut and sharp. She could hear the girls' screams of delight in the background.

"Oh, everything is perfectly fine. We are having a lovely time."

"It is five o'clock!"

It was obvious that he did not understand the hidden meaning of her statement. Claire took a deep, long breath.

"It is getting late. Can you bring them home now please?"

"Oh, most certainly. We will do so now."

Ten minutes later the front door burst open, and the twins spilled in, smelling of outdoors, muddy, hair in a mess and Olivia was clutching a plastic bag full of rubbish.

"We saws a load of taddypolls," Olivia exclaimed.

"Tadpoles, and we *saw*, not *saws*," corrected Claire. "You are filthy. What have you been doing?"

She was already worrying whether the mud would come out of their brand-new wool-blended coats. Abigail's eyes were bright and excited, and her cheeks were pink and glowing.

"And I went as high as I could on the swing. Satish is good at pushing."

"You shouldn't go too high. It is dangerous."

Claire took satisfaction in seeing the crestfallen expression on Satish's face.

"And we picked up rubbish. We are *our bit*," Olivia pronounced as she waved the plastic bag, not quite sure what *doing our bit* meant, but it sounded good.

"Serena said we should do kind things to the earth."

Claire inhaled slowly and told the girls to go and get cleaned up and change before their father got home. For once he was going to be home early. He had promised Claire an early night. She was looking forward to it with a mixture of trepidation and excitement.

"And put the rubbish in the dustbin."

Serena went to say that they wanted to recycle what they could but thought better of it when she saw the anger on Claire's face.

"More negative energy clearing needed," she thought to herself.

While Maria had been cleaning in the morning Serena had raided the kitchen cupboards and had found the ingredients to make a bean and vegetable stew for her and Satish. They said they would like to eat with the girls rather than wait until later. The girls had pulled pork and vegetables. Claire left some in the oven for Sebastian and herself when he got home. Once again, the twins wanted what Serena and Satish were eating but Claire told them there was not enough to go around.

"But there's lots left in the pot," Abigail protested. "We don't want to eat piggies. They is our friends."

The look on her mother's face stopped her from arguing any further. Sebastian arrived home halfway through their meal and was surprised to find the girls still eating their tea. Claire rolled her eyes at him.

"Don't ask."

She made a mental note to emphasise to Serena and Satish the importance of sticking to the girls' daily routine and daily timetable.

Once again, Serena read stories to them, but, somehow, *Dana Dolly Goes to Town* had totally disappeared and, instead, Serena read them a book of animal fables that they had picked up in a charity shop on the way to the park. Satish sat quietly in the corner of their bedroom, making appropriate animal noises when required by the story. Both girls still giggled when they looked at him, but had decided that he too was really cool, just like their granny.

Shortly afterwards they went to bed too. Sebastian snorted

"We know what they want to do. Like bloody rabbits."

He looked over to his wife, flopped down on her chair and his voice softened, and he said suggestively.

"Are you ready for an early night?"

She nodded.

However, once in bed, they both felt strangely inhibited. Claire was still uneasy about having her mother and lover under the same roof as she and her husband. Sebastian seemed to have noticed this too, and once in bed, they just started discussing Saturday.

"I am going to do my venison," she announced proudly.

He was silent for a moment.

"Isn't that rather…. common….now?"

In a small voice, she continued "And my hazelnut souffle….?"

Sebastian's silence gave her the answer she needed. And did not want.

"Well, what do you suggest then?"

Her deflation was turning to anger.

"I don't know. You're the cook. And make sure you get the proper olives this time for the canapes. Last time we had people over you didn't get the ones in Extra Virgin Oil with Rosemary and Organic Jalapenos. You just got plain ones."

Claire did not bother trying to defend herself by telling him everywhere was out of anything but plain olives, due to a strike by Mediterranean olive pickers.

He continued hesitantly

"But the bigger problem…"

Claire knew what was coming.

"…is your mother and her lover boy. We really cannot have them here on Saturday. You must talk to her. Or arrange for them to be out of the way. It could totally scupper my chances of being nominated again if they're here."

Claire sighed.

"I know. I'm at a total loss with them both. I just want my old mother back…. snappy, frumpy, and all. I can't cope with this new one."

She left unsaid the difficulty she was having with her feelings towards Satish. Sebastian showed uncharacteristic tenderness and wrapped his arm around her and drew her close.

He said

"It is almost like she has…… died, but sort of…. hasn't. It feels like Jayne has gone. But she is still your mother on the outside. Though she looks totally different. But inside…. she is like some damn new age, hippy….up-her-own-arse *spiritually aware, not willing to accept her age* old bag. As for Satish. He seems a decent enough chap on the outside, but I do wonder about his motives. Maybe he thinks she is loaded, or something. He will fleece her and then bugger off."

"Exactly," Claire agreed. She was relieved that they agreed on something. She continued

"I will think about something else for dinner Saturday. I need to sleep. Today has been rather stressful again."

She pecked him on the cheek and turned over to try to sleep. Her brain would not shut down. And she could not get the image out of her mind of Satish sitting, half-naked, in the sunshine.

FOUR

The next morning Claire and Sebastian found Serena and Satish down in the dining room again at six o'clock, sat cross-legged in front of the closed patio doors but fully dressed this time. Their humming was so quiet that it could only be heard up close.

Claire decided they were not doing any harm and went to put the breakfast things out on the island in the middle of the kitchen. She had insisted on the island, feeling that any kitchen worth having had to have a central focal point and somewhere where, in theory, the girls could sit and do homework while she cooked. However, it had meant redesigning the extension and moving the adjoining wall between the kitchen and the dining room over to make less room in the dining room and more room in the kitchen. She now had a large, long, thin kitchen with space at one end and the island looking out over the garden at the other. It felt all wrong. So often she had to admit to herself that her design for the extension of the house had been completely misguided and she had ended up with something that was not what she wanted. Deep down she wanted to move again but knew Sebastian would hit the roof at this, having spent over a quarter of a million pounds on upgrading this house. Once again, this morning, she felt a deep irritation at the kitchen and wondered what Sebastian would say about taking the island out. And redecorating at the same time. Her friend Alicia had just had hers done in the softest, pale yellow and she loved it. Her tolerance levels were already low when the girls appeared for breakfast. They were pushed to the limit when Abigail, worriedly and a bit too loudly, after eating her breakfast, asked

"Mummy. Is Granny OK?"

"She is called Serena, not Granny. Why?"

Claire felt a sudden concern for this weird woman who was her mother.

"Well, she kept making rather funny noises last night. It sounded like she couldn't breathe properly."

Olivia interjected

"Bit like Tasha's Grandpa when he has smoked too much."

Abigail interrupted her.

"And she was making squeaky noises and funny moans. She woke me up."

"And me."

Claire turned away hastily so they could not see her face reddening. She reddened even further when she saw Satish standing in the doorway. He quietly walked into the kitchen and pulled up a barstool to sit at the island. Claire waited anxiously to hear what he was going to say.

"She is fine. She is more than fine. She is very happy. And those noises were happy noises."

To stop this conversation in its tracks and prevent any more questions, Claire snatched the empty cereal bowls from in front of the girls and told them to get ready quickly as they had to be on time for nursery. As they obediently, for once, disappeared down the hallway and up the stairs, Claire turned to Satish and hissed

"Can you two just tone it all down a bit, please!"

He looked at her blankly. She did not want to have to spell things out to him, so decided it was time to have a chat with her mother. However, it could not be that morning as Claire had remembered she was going to give a friend financial advice and was going straight to her house after dropping the girls at nursery.

Serena appeared a few minutes later.

"OK. You two," Claire said to Serena and Satish as if they were a pair of delinquent children. "I will be back about one again. Please let Maria get on with her work. Please don't light any more joss sticks. And the girls have their piano lesson this afternoon so there won't be any *expeditions* in the local park. I need to go shopping for Saturday, which I'll do while the girls are at their lesson. So, you'll have to amuse yourselves."

She quickly pushed away the thought of how they might "amuse themselves."

Serena put her hand gently on Claire's shoulder and looked her in the eye.

"Don't worry about us. I've spoken to my bank, and they have sorted my card out. I can draw money on it now, so we're going to go and buy some food. We can't expect you to feed us all the time. We also want to give you some money for our keep."

Claire felt back footed by her mother's sudden generosity. She had only ever been used to a mother who counted every penny and constantly pleaded poverty. Although she did not know how much money Serena had got for her flat, she knew that there could not have been much left over after the mortgage and credit card bills had been paid. Often, she had wondered, and worried, about how she was making enough money to live. She and Sebastian had more than enough money in the bank, but she felt she should accept this offer from her mother. Claire's face softened.

"Thank you. We'll talk about it later. I'll see you at lunchtime."

When Maria arrived shortly after Claire's departure she hurried to start working to make up for lost time from the day before. Several times Serena or Satish would go to talk to her but stopped themselves. Many rueful glances passed between the three of them. At nine-thirty Serena and Satish went out to find the local shops. There was an extensive but expensive health food shop on the high street. Serena gasped at the prices and decided they could not afford them. Going next door to the greengrocers was equally as exasperating. Serena decided that a trip to Southall market was needed, where they could buy all that they needed, along with all the exotic herbs and spices she could ever want. She knew her frangipani tea was getting low. Checking her watch, Serena calculated they just had time to get a bus to Southall, get their shopping and get back for lunch.

Once they arrived at the bustling market they stocked up on grains, beans, tofu, fresh herbs, and vegetables. None of the stalls had frangipani tea, but Satish spotted a small shop that had a sign that said, *Herbs for sale*, with a window full of pipes, posters about *Freedom*, with the backdrop of a green, yellow, and red flag. They entered and it felt as though they were entering a cave. The shop had a heavy, pungent smell hanging over it and the counter was piled high with various kinds of smoking paraphernalia. Serena immediately thought they had gone to the wrong place and went to turn around to go back out when a deep voice came from behind the counter, startling both Serena and Satish. A large Afro-Caribbean man, with the longest dreadlocks Serena had ever seen, stood up.

"How can I help? Sorry to make you jump. I was just looking for my lighter."

Serena hesitated. The man continued

"I love your dreads. They look real good on you."

"Thanks," Serena mumbled, not sure how to continue. Hesitantly she said

"We saw your sign, saying *Herbs for sale*. I wanted some frangipani tea. It is so lovely and calming. I don't suppose you sell it?"

"Sorry, no. But I have some other herbs that can make you happy." He nodded towards the smoking equipment. Serena immediately understood what he was implying.

"Oh, no. We don't smoke. I just wanted some tea to help us relax and make us a bit happier than we are feeling right now."

"Wait there. I have just the stuff. My own special herbal mix. You can make a tea out of it, but I tell you what. The best thing is to make some brownies or a savoury pie and pop a tablespoon full in."

Serena hesitantly asked "What's in it?"

"Ah!" The big man smiled the biggest smile Serena had ever seen, showing gleaming white teeth with a gold tooth right in the middle. "That is my special secret. I only sell it to special people like us." He patted his dreadlocks. "It is far better than your frangipani tea. Nothing bad in it. All good organic herbs. Locally grown too."

Serena and Satish looked at each other, but the big man was not to be deterred and he went out to the back of the shop and came back with a paper bag sealed with tape.

As Serena paid for the herbs, which were more than she expected, the man beamed at them. "You don't need too much. Enjoy and be happy."

As Serena and Satish left the shop, they both felt uneasy about their purchase, but both decided that he seemed such a nice man so it must be alright. Loaded with their bags they started looking for the bus back to Twickenham.

They arrived home at the same time as Claire and the girls. They dumped their bags in the kitchen and were about to start unpacking when Claire said to leave it for now as Maria had prepared a salad for them all. There was ham and egg for Claire and the twins and more hummus and a tin of mixed beans for Serena and Satish. As they sat down to eat, Claire's mobile rang. Her face fell as she listened to the loud, pompous voice on the other end.

"OK. Can't be helped. I hope you are better soon," Claire said.

With an irritated sigh, she put the phone down next to her on the table.

"That was Missus Delange…. the piano teacher," she explained to Serena. "She badly sprained her wrist this morning and has to cancel lessons this afternoon."

The girls squealed with delight and Abigail started dancing around the dining room singing

"No plinky plonks. No plinky plonks."

"Abigail!" her mother reprimanded her. "You are very lucky to have lessons. So many little girls would love to have piano lessons, but their mummies and daddies don't have enough money. Just be more grateful."

Abigail pouted and sat down at the table again. Claire closed her eyes and sighed.

"I so needed to go to the butcher's. And to order flowers for Saturday."

"Don't worry," Serena smiled. "We will look after them this afternoon. You take as long as you want. Treat yourself while you are out."

She saw the look of hesitancy on Claire's face.

"Don't worry. We won't take them to the park. We'll amuse them here."

Claire had a gut feeling she was making the wrong decision, but after a moment replied

"Thank you. That would be lovely."

Once the lunch dishes were cleared away, Claire thanked her mother once again, and with unease, put on her coat and left.

The girls sat wide-eyed and waited to hear what Serena and Satish were going to do with them that afternoon.

"Do you like cooking?" asked Serena.

They both looked hesitant.

"Mummy never lets us do any. She always says she can do it."

"Would you like to learn?"

The girls' wide eyes and squeals of delight told Serena all she needed to know. Before they could start cooking Serena had to unpack their shopping. Tofu, fresh herbs, and vegetables were put in the fridge. She found some empty jars into which she emptied brown rice, lentils, mung beans, and the dried herb mixture, and put them away in the cupboard. They then started the cookery lesson.

Claire spent a wonderful afternoon enjoying her *me* time. She decided she would go to the butcher's and florists last of all and would treat herself to a slice of walnut cake and a cup of Lapsang Souchong in a local teashop. As she relaxed in one of the comfortable chairs and happily sipped her tea, she began to think to herself that having her mother with her was not such a terrible thing after all. The girls seemed to love her, to the point that Claire began to feel slightly ousted in their affections. However, eventually, Satish and Serena would be getting on a plane back to Thailand and she would quickly be able to re-establish her superiority in their lives. She then went to her favourite boutique and spent an obscene amount of money on a new maternity dress for Saturday night. It was bright yellow, with a bold flower design. The colouring contrasted with Claire's dark hair and complexion which she had inherited from her father. His Spanish genes had come through to her and made her look the complete opposite of her fair-haired, usually pale-skinned mother. She ordered a colourful Spring bouquet from the florist, to be delivered on Saturday, along with a smaller bouquet that she would give to Chloe. Having decided to ignore Sebastian's snobbery, she ordered the venison, but also a couple of guinea fowl as a backup if he dug his heels in about her choice of menu.

She was feeling satisfied with her afternoon as she pulled up on her road. Today she had not been so lucky and had to park a long way down the road. Lugging the bags up to the front door, she unlocked it, and as soon as she stepped inside the door, she had a sinking feeling. The girls' laughter was heard coming from the kitchen. Satish was telling them a funny tale from his native Sri Lanka, complete with silly voices and animal noises. She could hear Serena's joyous laughter. Dismissing her foreboding she walked along the hall and pushed open the kitchen door. A sight of devastation hit her.

Serena, Satish, and the girls were all sitting cross-legged in a circle on the floor. In the middle of them, on the slate floor itself, was a pile of flour with a well in the middle of it. As she entered Serena was in the process of pouring water in the middle of the well in the flour. Judging from the blobs of dough and flour embedded in the slate floor around them and splattered on the black cupboard doors, this was not the first batch they had made. Claire stood dumbstruck. Suddenly she found her voice

"What. The. Bloody. Hell, Are. You. Doing?"

"We are making Chopootis," said Abigail jumping to her feet and holding up hands and arms covered in dough.

"Chapatis," snapped her mother. Glaring at Serena, she continued

"For goodness' sake Mother you should be doing it on the worktops, not on the floor. It is disgusting. Look at the mess!"

Serena looked at her angry daughter and refused to be drawn into arguing. She simply stated

"The girls could not reach the worktops."

Claire was ready to explode with rage.

"Look at the floor. It is a total mess. It'll never come clean. And so unhygienic."

"It is how we make our chapatis at home."

"Surely not on the floor!" Claire was horrified.

"Oh, we do use a board. But I couldn't find one big enough and Maria had cleaned the floor thoroughly this morning, and we are going to fry the chapatis, so we thought it would be ok."

Once again Claire was rendered speechless. Both the girls were now proudly showing their mother how they had dough right up to their elbows and Claire could see it was also in their hair. It would be a nightmare to get out.

"We like cooking!" said Olivia, picking up a small chapati she had made earlier and holding it out to her mother.

Claire could see the dough was grey.

"Did you wash your hands first?" she snapped.

The blank look on the faces of the group gave her the answer. Claire felt a bit nauseous.

"Don't you dare eat them. They are disgusting. They are a health hazard."

Even in her anger, Claire felt a prick of conscience at seeing the crestfallen look on her daughters' faces.

"Get cleaned up. And get this floor clean before Sebastian comes home."

She turned and left the kitchen, slamming the door behind her. Serena looked sheepishly at the girls.

"I don't think your mummy is very happy with us."

"Don't care," Olivia pronounced. "She is just a grumpy pants."

She went to give Serena a floury hug.

"You can be our mummy instead. You are much more fun."

"And you can be our daddy." Abigail snuggled up to Satish.

Carefully Serena untangled herself from the little girl's doughy embrace.

"I don't think your mummy and daddy would be happy to hear you say that."

"Don't care!" said Olivia. "It is true."

Serena and Satish exchanged glances, and not for the first time Serena felt a twinge of sadness that she and Satish would never be able to have their own family. Her early menopause had eliminated the chance of their own children.

Serena said they needed to clean up and put the chapatis in the fridge ready to cook later. She was not going to let her daughter ruin the little girls' excitement at learning a new skill, even if the chapatis might not be edible. Serena had decided she might accidentally overcook the grubby ones to inedibility and take the blame.

Serena's hopes that the dough would come off the floor easily were soon found to be misguided. However hard they washed, scrubbed, and picked at the floor with toothpicks, there was still a patina of flour and embedded dough on the rough slate surface. Serena decided a slate floor for a kitchen was a stupid idea. Claire stayed upstairs out of their way for an hour but when she came back downstairs, she was horrified to see that there was still clear evidence of the cooking lesson on the floor. Serena apologised, saying they had done all they could to hide it, but not to worry as it would fade in time. Claire pursed her lips, took a deep breath, and told her not to worry. She could not face another argument with her implacable mother.

When Sebastian came home and immediately noticed the strange marks on the kitchen floor, Claire just shook her head and said firmly "Don't ask."

Sebastian knew better than to ignore her warning. Claire had already decided that the next morning she would sit down with Serena and Satish and give them some home truths.

"I have a migraine coming on," she said to Sebastian. "They are upstairs at the moment and say they are cooking a curry in a bit. They say we can all have some and they are making a mild one for the girls. But be careful of the chapatis. They need a health warning. The girls have already been bathed and hair washed."

She did not elucidate further but left Sebastian looking puzzled while she went to lie down.

"Tomorrow," she decided "is Showdown Day."

FIVE

Claire awoke the next morning feeling angry and depressed. Sebastian had told her that he did not like her new dress and that she needed to get something a bit more *tasteful* for Saturday night.

"Don't you decide you are changing your image as well!" he had snarled as she had twirled around in it just before they went to bed the night before. "It's far too garish. You look like a bloody sofa."

He had also insisted that she did not cook the venison but would have to make do with guinea fowl.

She also remembered that she had promised to meet up with her best friend, Becci, whose birthday was that day.

"Damn it," she muttered to herself.

It was the time when she had wanted to confront her mother.

"I'll see if the girls can play with Tasha this afternoon. I'll confront them then," she said to herself.

The twins had both been nagging all week to see Tasha's new puppy. Claire sighed at the thought of the inevitable constant demands that would come for them to have a puppy as well. Cecil, their old big black furry tomcat, would not take too happily to that idea. Pleased with her solution to the problem, she got out of bed with a new resolve. Quickly she texted her request to Tasha's mum, who replied immediately and said the girls could come for lunch. Claire sighed with relief.

As she was later getting up, she had to rush a bit more than usual to get the girls ready for nursery. Serena and Satish were nowhere to be seen. As she passed their bedroom door, she heard suppressed giggles. Irritably she tapped on the door. Serena answered wrapped only in her flimsy wrap, her eyes glowing, and her face flushed. Satish was in bed with the sheets pulled up around him.

"I'm out this morning." Her tone was frosty. "Are you in this afternoon? I want to talk to you both."

Serena was a little taken aback.

"Of course. We want to sort out what we can give you each week."

"No. It's not about that. I'll see you later. I'm taking the girls straight to their friend's house for lunch. I'll see you after."

She walked purposefully down the hall to the stairs.

Serena closed the door softly.

"What was that all about?" she asked Satish, who sat looking mystified. She continued "It can't be her period, we know that!"

As they both giggled, she climbed back under the sheets again and into his waiting arms.

Claire met her friend, Becci, at their favourite coffee shop, ordered them coffee and cake, and gave her the gemstone pendant she knew she wanted, a pretty, handmade card, and a bunch of tulips – her favourite flowers.

Becci thanked her and then looked long and hard at her friend. She could see the simmering anger on her face.

"OK," she said. "What is it? Spill!"

Claire had the sudden urge to burst into tears but fought it back. Taking a deep breath, she said

"Mother!"

Becci's eyebrows shot up in surprise.

"I thought you were looking forward to seeing her again."

"Oh! I was. I was expecting my old mother to come back from Thailand. Not some bloody menopausal hippy who has gone all weird and *spiritual*."

She made signs with her fingers to indicate apostrophes.

"And with a bloke my age in tow."

Again, her brain had to stamp out the thought "but he is rather gorgeous."

Becci was shocked at the venom in her voice and realised that perhaps her birthday celebrations were going to turn into a counselling session. It would be good practice for her as she needed some extra experience to pass her counselling certificate. Surreptitiously, she turned her phone to record mode and hid it under a napkin behind her mug. She had a feeling this would be a good conversation to write up.

Claire spoke nonstop for over half an hour, giving Becci every tiny detail of what had happened since she had picked Serena and Satish up from the airport. Becci sat, as any good counsellor does, nodding, making affirming noises, and only speaking to clarify a point or two. At times Becci had to suppress laughter at the antics being described. When Claire finally ran out of steam and realised that her latte had gone cold, Becci took a deep breath and said

"Wow!"

"Wow. Is that all you can say?" Claire snapped at her.

Again, she felt the tears pricking in her eyes.

"Sorry."

Becci lent over and put her hand on Claire's arm.

"I feel for you. It must be so difficult to deal with such a change in a person. Especially someone as central to your life as your mother."

Claire pulled away and got a tissue from her bag and wiped her eyes, and replied

"We've never been very close. She was always working or being miserable or snappy. She was such a perfectionist. Nothing ever felt good enough."

Silently Becci reflected "like mother, like daughter."

"But now," Claire continued "she's some touchy, feely away-with-the-fairies hippy. She and Satish are like a pair of rabbits on Viagra. As for the questions the girls keep asking such as why is Granny making panting noises in bed? She has turned into a raving nymphomaniac I can't handle it."

She put her face in her hands and started to sob.

The couple at the next table looked across in interest at her raised voice and smirked at each other, having heard every word. Becci squeezed her arm.

"I think there are a lot of emotions mixed up in all this," Becci said gently.

Claire snorted and got another tissue from her bag to blow her nose.

"Firstly," Becci continued, "there is the separation from your mother, and then she comes back such a different person. She's changing and growing in many ways. That in itself is going to be an upset. She's challenging so much of your belief system. And those of our society. After years of hard work and surviving, she's going through a bit of a mid-life crisis. She's doing the rebellious stuff she never did as a teenager."

Claire looked up and almost shouted

"I'm the one who is meant to be rebellious. It's kids who rebel. Not my bloody mother. It is all wrong."

A couple of the other customers at other tables turned around to look at her after her outburst.

"Well, it is," Claire continued miserably "Your parents should always be normal and sensible. They shouldn't be going off doing weird things."

Becci said nothing. She knew she had to treat her friend carefully if she were not to damage their friendship beyond repair. Taking a deep breath, she asked

"Do you think you are a bit jealous of her? Especially with her new man with her?"

She had already picked up from the way Claire spoke of Satish that there was another agenda there.

"What do you mean?"

Claire looked at her with annoyance. Becci took another deep breath, realising she had waded in a bit too deep.

"They say if we don't learn from history, we are doomed to repeat it. Your mum married her older boss, young, pregnant, and rather naïve. She had you early – unplanned - not that I think she regrets it."

Becci hastily tried to retrieve the situation when she saw Claire's hurt and shocked expression. Hesitantly, she continued "You did the same. You've almost totally relived your mum's history."

She put her hands up in the air as if surrendering.

"I'm not judging here. I know you are very similar to how your mum used to be. You want everything to be perfect and ordered. You want the good things in life and will work hard to get them or support your fella to do so. You're following the belief system she had, even though she didn't have the chance to stay with your father and be rich. Then she disappeared out of your life. Now she appears again, and her new belief system and the one you grew up with are totally different. She has rejected everything that she, and you, held dear. It's a threat to your belief system. No wonder you feel angry and upset. It has turned upside down all the securities you had about your shared beliefs and also the relationship with your mum."

Becci sat back in her chair feeling proud of herself and her insights and was already imagining the positive feedback she would receive from her tutor when she had written up and presented this case. However, she did not dare to go into the dangerous territory of Claire's obvious infatuation with Satish and her failing relationship with Sebastian.

Claire dabbed her eyes, thought for a while, and then sighed "I suppose you're right. I just wish she didn't have to be so bloody annoying. And happy all the time. It is so irritating."

Claire suddenly realised just how jealous she was of her mother's happiness and easy-going attitude to life. It had only served to highlight the misery of her own life. Becci patted her friend on the arm, and then picking up her phone, switched off the recording, while Claire sat dabbing her eyes with a tissue.

"Let me get you another latte," Becci said.

It was a cheap price to pay for a good case history.

Back at the house Serena and Satish felt they could do nothing right and so decided to stay in bed all morning. They could hear Maria vacuuming along the hallway outside their door. She knew not to go into their room, so they felt cocooned away in their own little world. She only did a couple of hours on a Friday, so she left at midday, and Serena and Satish emerged from their bedroom and made lunch. Claire reappeared at about two, having decided to stop for a quick lunch with Tasha's mother. She had arranged for Tasha's father,

Tom, to drop the girls off home at five. Claire was abrupt and business-like when she walked into the living room and found the couple, as usual, sat curled up together on the settee. She was annoyed to see Cecil had climbed onto Serena's lap and she was stroking him. No one ever was approached by Cecil. He was not a lap cat. Even Claire only occasionally persuaded him to sit on her lap, and that often ended up with him scratching her.

"Right." She pulled her chair closer to them. "We need to talk."

Serena and Satish exchanged glances. They knew it was going to be bad.

"Things have got to change. I welcomed you back here and I'm glad to see you, Mother. However, I did not expect another person to be with you. Especially not someone so…."

She had to shut her brain off from thinking and her mouth from saying *gorgeous*, and suddenly lost her flow.

"unexpected," was what came out instead.

Satish's liquid eyes widened in hurt and surprise.

"I will go if you want me to. I am sorry to be a burden."

He put his palms together, saying

"Please forgive me. How may I make amends?"

Claire felt a rush of regret at her words.

"Forget it. You're here now. I'm glad you are making my mother so happy. However, please could you both be a little more…discreet. Make sure you are fully clothed at all times. The girls are not used to seeing half-naked men wandering around. If they say anything else at nursery, we could have Social Services banging on our door in no time. Their teacher has already asked me about the drawing Olivia did. I told them we'd gone swimming and she had never seen an Asian man in his swimming trunks before. It was all rather awkward and embarrassing."

She took a deep breath and continued

"The girls have a strict routine every week. We want to give them every chance in life, so that is why they have piano and ballet lessons, and extra coaching from time to time. They need to learn to behave like young ladies and not animals. So, don't go putting any weird and wacky ideas into their heads. We don't want to spoil their future prospects."

Serena and Satish sat in silence, not reacting to her tirade.

"And your appearance, Mother. Please could you be a bit more…. normal? Get some sensible clothes. Look more like a woman of your age and not a bloody hippie. We have some very important guests coming to dinner tomorrow and I really don't want to introduce them to my dreadlocked, tattooed, and pierced mother. It is Sebastian's future here at stake. I very much doubt your politics are the same as his anymore, given how you are carrying on, but you must respect his beliefs while you are under his roof. You are staying in his house, after all. So, can you either stay out of the way tomorrow evening or make yourself look more presentable? Put a scarf on your head. Cover up your tattoos. Wear some sensible clothes."

Claire suddenly felt guilty at the hurt expression, shock, and disbelief on her mother's face.

"I'm sorry," she added limply "I just want the best for Sebastian and my girls."

Serena sat in astounded silence, and Satish took her hand and squeezed it. Tears pricked her eyes and a tear rolled down her cheek. In an almost inaudible voice, she replied

"I'm sorry you feel like this. I don't apologise for who I am now, although I do apologise if some of my behaviour has offended you. We'll leave as soon as possible. We'll try and be out of your way by tomorrow afternoon. I'm sure we can find a hostel somewhere."

Claire felt overwhelmed with guilt and suddenly realised that, annoying as she might be, she did not want her mother to go. Also, if she went, it meant Satish would go too.

"No. No," she said. "Stay. I....oh bloody hell.... can you just be a bit more normal tomorrow, please? I had three years without you. I don't want to lose you again."

Serena got up from the settee and went and knelt in front of her daughter, who was now crying fully, and took her hand.

"And I want to be here for the birth of my grandson. Don't worry about tomorrow. We'll go out. There is a talk on Tantra and Awaking the Kundalini Power we want to go to in central London. We'll be out all evening."

Claire's immediate thought was that she hoped that they were not going to be noisily putting it into practice once they got home. The repentant look on her mother's face reassured her that she would behave, for now.

"Would you like tea?" Claire pulled herself to her feet and felt strangely deflated. Although in her mind it was her mother who was in the wrong, somehow, she felt that she was the one who was in the wrong. She felt even worse when she saw the look of hurt and sadness still in Satish's eyes.

The girls returned at five and came squealing through the front door.

"Where's Serena? Where's Satish? We want a puppy if we can't have an elephant. Can we? Can we?"

They stopped in confusion at the heavy atmosphere hanging over their house. Both girls noticed the red blotches around Claire's eyes and demanded to know whether she had been crying. She told them sometimes when ladies are carrying babies in their tummies, they get sad and cry easily. She reassured them there was nothing to worry about. The girls wanted to know where Serena and Satish were. Claire told them they were resting, but she felt guilty that after their talk the couple had gone back up to their room and not reappeared. She had heard quiet sobbing coming from their room when she went upstairs a little bit later, and Satish's gentle voice trying to calm her mother down. The very subdued couple reappeared to help prepare tea, but they went back to their room immediately after.

The girls sat in total confusion after finishing their meal.

"What's wrong with Gran…Serena?" asked Olivia. "Don't they love us anymore?"

Claire felt even worse than she did earlier.

"Just a little bit of a misunderstanding. Don't worry. Everything will be fine tomorrow."

The girls did not have a story read to them that night and they too went to sleep sad and worried that Serena and Satish did not love them anymore and that they would not get a story the next night either.

SIX

When Claire awoke the next morning, the guilt set in immediately. She wondered if she had been too harsh with her mother. However, Sebastian had not been helpful. He thought Claire was being too soft and told her that Serena was *her mother* so she had to deal with her. He also wanted to know whether she was going to take her dress back and change it for something more *tasteful*. They decided he would take the girls to their ballet lesson in the morning, and he would drop Claire off at the shop to change it.

Breakfast was a subdued affair and, judging by the size of the bags under Serena's usually bright blue eyes, she had not slept much. She and Satish ate their breakfast in almost total silence, just replying in monosyllables to questions from the twins. The girls exchanged worried glances.

"We're going out for a while this morning," Serena eventually said. She continued "Then we will get out of your way for this evening. Don't worry. We won't be here when your guests arrive."

It was now Sebastian's turn to feel guilty.

"No need to rush out."

However, as he said these words, he imagined the reaction Sir Percival would have to his mother-in-law and her lover, and he did not press the point any further.

The household went their separate ways, with the expectation they would all be back for lunch. The girls had dressed in ballet clothes with their hair scraped up into buns on top of their heads. In their pink tutus and tights and diamante tops, they no longer looked like the rebellious twins that Serena and Satish had come to love. They both felt a deep sadness at these clones of what *good little girls* should be. The family went off to ballet and shopping. Claire changed her dress for a plain black dress with a cowl neck.

"That's more like it!" Sebastian pontificated when she showed it to him.

"Now we need to get home and start preparations for Sir Percival and his missus."

"What's that smell?" asked Sebastian as they entered the house.

There was a strange smell, like burning hair. Claire shrugged and took their shopping through to the kitchen. The large sliding door to the garden was open, and she could see Satish had a stick in his hand and was prodding something that was burning in the fire pit. Intrigued she went out. The sight that met her stopped her in her tracks. Serena was sitting on the grass with her back to her. She no longer had her dreadlocks. Instead, her hair had been cut off into a very short pixie cut, and dyed rainbow colours. Satish was burning her dreadlocks in the fire pit.

"What the…...?"

Claire strode out into the garden and her mother turned a tear-stained face to her. Claire looked at her in disbelief.

"You look like something out of a Gay Pride march. Look at you!" she sneered contemptuously at her mother in her multi-coloured coat and with her rainbow-coloured hair.

"So?" said Serena. "Would that matter?"

The pursed lips and the expression on Claire's face indicated that it would.

Satish looked straight at Claire and said

"Do not judge, so that you may not be judged yourself. So it says in the Holy Bible."

Claire was furious.

"Don't go quoting the Bible at me. How dare you? You and your….your….weird ideas."

Serena turned back to watching Satish.

Claire would not be ignored.

"And just what the hell are you doing Satish?"

Serena answered for him without looking at her,

"Growing my dreadlocks was part of my journey to growth and wholeness. I'm so sad to let them go, but I must move on to the next part of my journey. We felt it appropriate to hold a ritual and burn them."

Sebastian and the girls had joined them by now and were standing listening, not knowing quite how to react.

Olivia went up to Serena, sat down next to her and put her arms around her. and lay her head on her shoulder.

"Well, I like your pretty hair, even if Mummy doesn't."

Abigail copied her sister and hugged Serena from the other side.

"Me too."

Claire knew she was defeated and returned to the kitchen. Sebastian shrugged his shoulders at Satish and followed his wife into the house. He thought that Serena's hair was rather fetching, and he had not realised until now just how pretty his mother-in-law was.

The household quickly descended into a state of anxiety as Claire started to panic and prepare for the arrival of their guests. She refused the help offered by Serena and Satish.

At five o'clock Serena and Satish came down to the kitchen, all ready to go out, with their coats on. Claire was taken aback once again to see her mother's short hair. She was in a frenzy preparing food for the dinner party at six-thirty, with the Sandersons arriving at six, and had already decided it was going to be a disaster. Serena could see her daughter was struggling and again offered to help. Part of her longed for her mother's help, but Claire knew that it would mean she and Satish missing their talk and therefore staying in that evening. She also knew Sebastian would never forgive her if she did not get her mother out of the way.

"No. Thanks. I will be fine. Go and enjoy yourselves."

Her mind quickly veered away from the thought of Satish listening to a talk on Tantra and awakening his serpent power. She hoped her red cheeks would be taken as being caused by the cooking. As the happy couple went out of the front door arm in arm, she felt a pang of jealousy.

It seemed that everything that could go wrong did go wrong. One of the guinea fowl turned out to be going off and was inedible. She sliced her finger badly as she was chopping onions and had to find a plaster, with blood pouring out of her finger. The girls decided they would have a massive squabble over what to watch on the TV and when she phoned upstairs to Sebastian in his attic office to ask for his help, he refused to come down. He was writing preparatory notes for his proposal for standing as Councillor again, which he wanted to show Sir Percival that evening.

She put the oven on and put a pan of goose fat in to heat up for the roast potatoes and the meat. Just as she stood upright again, she felt a sharp pain in her abdomen and her waters broke, flooding over the kitchen floor. She doubled over, screaming for Sebastian. Instead, Abigail came running in. As she saw the indelicate sight of her mother bent over, standing in a pool of liquid she put her hand to her mouth and screamed in laughter. She ran out of the room squealing in amusement.

"Mummy's done a wee wee. Mummy's done a wee wee. All over the floor."

Olivia came in to see and burst out laughing.

"Just. Get. Your. Daddy!" Claire screamed at them, between pants.

A sudden contraction hit, and she grabbed the worktop and started breathing deeply. This time Sebastian did come downstairs. The girls had run up to him shouting

"Mummy's done a big wee wee all over the kitchen floor."

He strode into the kitchen to see his wife doubled up again and desperation on her face.

"He's coming early." Claire's voice was full of panic and fear.

Another contraction hit. A minute of panting gave her a little relief.

"Bloody hell!" Sebastian said. "Eh... ambulance.... eh my phone is..... upstairs."

"Use mine! By the microwave!" Claire snapped.

In her confusion and panic, she could not remember her pin. Eventually, she got it right and Sebastian managed to open the phone, only to realise they could have phoned the emergency number without the pin. Sebastian put it on speaker, while he frantically started rubbing his wife's back, desperate to do anything.

Once the ambulance controller had got their details she apologised and said

"We will get someone to you as quickly as possible but there has been a pile-up on the M4, and all our ambulances are involved there."

"Shiiiiiiiiiiiiit!"

Claire doubled up again.

The girls stood in wide-eyed horror at their mother's distress.

"Phone Serena. Get her back here. Pronto."

Sebastian rang off from the ambulance controller and phoned Serena, but it went straight to Answerphone. The last thing Serena expected that evening was to have a phone call from her daughter, so she had turned it off to save the battery.

"Phone Maria."

Maria agreed to come straight away to look after the twins.

"Go and watch Peppa Pig!" Sebastian barked at the girls who were terrified by their mother's sudden weird behaviour and shrieking. The girls backed out of the kitchen with their mouths open

He redialled 999 and was put through to the same controller as before. She had already tried to hurry up an ambulance, but they were still all busy with the pile-up. The conversation was cut short by another scream from Claire. Sebastian started rubbing her back again, but Claire snapped at him that it was totally useless what he was doing.

"Hello. Hello. Are you alright?"

Sebastian realised the call was still connected to the controller. At that moment Claire shrieked

"He's coming. I can feel him coming."

"Can't you get anyone here? My wife is actually giving birth right now."

"I am sorry, but we have no one available right now. Let me talk you through it. Where are you?"

Sebastian snapped back.

"I've already given you the address. In Twickenham. Didn't you take any notice?"

The controller took a deep breath.

"I mean… where are you in the house? Is your wife lying down or standing?"

"She's standing, or rather hunched over, in the middle of a lake of amniotic fluid in the middle of the kitchen floor," was his sarcastic reply.

"Can you take her to hospital by car?"

Sebastian remembered the two strong craft ales he had drunk after lunch and the monster Scotch he had poured himself as he was writing his notes in his den.

"I'm afraid I'm over the limit."

Claire, between contractions, looked at him in anger and disbelief.

"You're….. whaaaaaaat?"

Her anger was cut short by another contraction.

The calm voice of the controller cut across her screams.

"OK. Can you time the contractions, please? I'm putting this out as a red alert to our team. Someone should be with you shortly. Now, sir, is there anyone who could take you to the hospital?"

Sebastian thought about Missus Handley living next door, in her nineties with seven cats and who was as blind as a bat. The Smithsons living on the other side were away on holiday. Despite having lived on this road for five years, they did not know anyone else, as their lives had been too busy and wrapped up in work and the twins.

"No," was the abrupt answer.

Olivia's face peered around the door.

"Daddy. I'm scared. Is Mummy going to die?"

"No, I'm bloody noooooot!" Pant pant "Just get out."

Olivia scuttled away. At that moment there was the sound of the key turning in the front door and Sebastian and Claire were relieved to hear Maria's sing-song voice calling out.

"Hola. Where are you?"

"In the kitchen."

Maria stopped in her tracks at the sight of her usually immaculate and fractious employer doubled up and with soaking wet clothes, bright red in the face, and hanging on to the kitchen worktop. Her first reaction was to laugh but quickly stopped herself. Instead, she said

"I was at a house on the next street helping at a party. They let me come straight away."

"See to the girls. Keep them out," Claire snapped.

"Hello, hello," went the phone. "Is there someone else there with you?"

Sebastian grabbed the phone.

"The maid."

He felt proud being able to say that.

"Is she able to drive you to the hospital?"

"She couldn't even drive a bloody donkey, let alone a car," sneered Sebastian, who, for some reason, disliked Maria but was grateful she kept the house clean.

"Get your wife comfortable. Lay her down on the floor."

Suddenly Claire gave a long and piercing scream.

"He's coming. I can feel his head's coming."

All the well-rehearsed panting and breathing she had learned at the Pre-Birth Group was forgotten.

"Lay her down," the controller ordered again.

Sebastian helped his wife to the floor and grabbed some towels and dishcloths from the laundry bin to put around her.

Claire gave one longer groan and push and then he was born, with a pair of black, lacy thongs on his head. Carefully Sebastian picked him up and removed them.

He panicked.

"What now?"

The calm voice of the controller asked

"Is the baby breathing?"

A lusty yell affirmed this.

"OK. Lay him on his mother's stomach. The crew is nearly there."

Sebastian's brain racked through all the scenes he had seen in films where a woman had given birth.

"Don't I need to boil some water…..or something?"

"A little bit late for that now, sir. Would you be happy to cut the baby's cord? You will have to wait then for the placenta to come."

Sebastian carefully placed the bright red, angry, squalling bundle of flailing arms and legs on Claire's stomach. He quickly counted the fingers and toes and made sure his son was well endowed. He breathed a sigh of relief.

'Definitely a little boy!' he thought to himself proudly.

Claire's eyes misted with tears as she started gently stroking her son. He was still tiny and covered with lanugo and looked more like a tiny monkey than a human baby. Claire felt a flood of disappointment, compared to the perfect births of the twins, who had been beautiful from the moment she first set eyes on them. Their births had been a well-crafted and peaceful affair, with soft music, a birthing pool, aromatic oils, and electric candles.

The voice on the phone called out "Is the baby ok?"

At this point, the doorbell rang, and Sebastian could hear Maria going to answer it. He had never felt such relief in his life as when he saw two paramedics appear in the kitchen doorway. One of them had the name Clare emblazoned on her uniform. Claire noticed this and felt annoyed it was not spelt correctly. Clare knelt beside her and took over from Sebastian, cutting the baby's cord and waiting for the afterbirth. Maria had found a clean towel to wrap the baby in and asked if Claire had her bag packed for the hospital. She was told where to find it, so Maria went off to fetch it. The girls had crept in quietly, having realised that the ambulance had arrived, and as soon as Abigail saw the screwed-up, red face and hairy body of the baby she screamed

"Mummy's had a monkey."

She ran down the hallway screaming.

"It's a monster. It's a monster baby."

Olivia also peered into the kitchen, wide-eyed and she too screamed and ran after her sister. They stopped and started hugging each other in the middle of the hallway, crying and screaming.

Their screams were suddenly obliterated by the sound of the smoke alarm. Sebastian, having become aware of the pinging sound of the fat still heating in the oven, had opened the oven door and the sudden rush of oxygen had caused the fat temporarily to ignite, setting off the smoke alarm.

At this point, the doorbell went again. Maria hurriedly answered it.

"Oh, bloody hell," sighed Claire when she heard Sir Percival's voice booming, almost as loudly as the smoke alarm.

"Hello my dear, Maria, isn't it? Here we are. Six o'clock on the dot," he said, looking in amazement at the still-screaming twins. He continued "Oh, what a to-do young ladies," and then looked towards the kitchen door. "What a din! Whatever is going on?"

Claire will never forget the clear voice of Olivia telling him, between sobs, that Mummy had done a big wee wee in the middle of the kitchen floor and had just had a monkey and not a baby, and now the house was about to burn down. Sebastian stood in the middle of the kitchen with his head in his hands, surrounded by the mess of his son's birth, two paramedics still bustling around, the screaming of the smoke alarm, and felt his political career crumble into dust.

SEVEN

At twelve-thirty Serena and Satish crept up the path to the front door and quietly let themselves in. The talk had been inspiring and uplifting in many ways, and they were keen to put some of the teachings into practice as soon as possible.

As the front door creaked open and they tiptoed into the dark hall they immediately knew something was wrong. Although they expected the guests to have departed by now, they thought Claire would still be up and waiting for them. There was a strange smell – a mixture of burnt food and bodily fluids, with an undertone of Dettol. They looked at each other quizzically. Then they saw the crack of light under the kitchen door. Creeping along the hallway Serena quietly called out

"Hello?"

She was so surprised when a harassed-looking Maria opened the kitchen door.

"Oh! Missus Serena."

She collapsed crying into Serena's arms and sobbed "Missus Jackson has had the baby. On the kitchen floor. And ruined dinner."

Her body was wracked with sobs. Satish pulled up a chair for her to sit down, and the couple looked at the sight of devastation in the kitchen. There were pans of food spread over the kitchen worktops. Some of the food was half-cooked, some of it was burnt and it was all left forgotten on the side. Bloody towels and tea clothes were piled in the corner. Maria had been trying to scrub the floor with Dettol to get rid of the aftermath of the birth. At least she had managed to erase the evidence of the chapati-making session.

"Where are the girls?"

Serena knelt next to Maria and gave her a piece of kitchen towel to dab at her eyes.

"Upstairs in bed. They were too scared and upset to go to bed for a long time. They think the Mistress has had a monkey and not a baby."

Serena and Satish exchanged glances.

"He was all hairy," explained Maria. "And ugly."

She looked shocked at what she had just said.

"Oh. Please forgive me. I shouldn't say such horrible things."

She started crying again.

Serena put her arm around her and asked her where Claire and Sebastian were.

"Hospital. He was too early. He should've waited another month. Oh Missus Serena I do hope he is going to be okay."

Serena suddenly felt guilty that she was not here when her daughter needed her most. This was compounded when, switching on her phone, she saw the lengthy list of attempted calls and texts, which got increasingly more demanding and frantic in tone. Quickly she texted "We are back home now. Maria told us what happened. Are you both okay?"

A couple of minutes later the phone rang and Sebastian's strained voice said

"Hi. We're at the hospital. There have been a couple of post-partum complications. I'm staying here with Claire."

"Oh, I'm so sorry," whispered Serena sadly. "I wish I'd been here."

Sebastian felt guilty at having insisted that his mother-in-law was *out of the way.*

"Give her my love," Serena continued. "And congratulations. Is there anything I can do?"

Serena felt sorry for Sebastian as she heard his weary reply.

"No. Thanks. If you could look after the girls that would be great......"

"No problem. You concentrate on Claire and the baby. Does he have a name yet?."

"We have decided on St John."

Serena cringed.

Serena and Sebastian agreed that a taxi should be called for Maria so she could go home. Sebastian did not want to have to pay a sleep-in rate for Maria, especially when he had his mother-in-law there who would cost nothing. When Maria protested that she should finish cleaning up, Serena refused to let her do it, telling her she would see to it and Maria had done more than enough. She needed to go home and rest. Serena and Satish finally collapsed into bed at four-thirty after cleaning the kitchen and the oven, sorting out which food was salvageable, and then comforting the twins when Olivia woke up crying after a nightmare that giant baby monkeys were chasing her. The techniques they had learnt at the talk that night were forgotten for now.

At half-past eight, Serena and Satish were downstairs in the kitchen, hollow-eyed and exhausted, giving the girls breakfast. They heard the front door close, and an equally exhausted-looking Sebastian came into the kitchen.

"Daaaaaadddyy!" The girls jumped off their chairs, abandoning their cereal, and ran to their father's arms.

"Is Mummy getting a proper baby from hospital? We don't want a monkey for a brother," demanded Olivia.

"He is not a monkey," snapped Sebastian. "Sometimes when babies are born too soon, they have some hair on them. It will fall off soon."

Olivia wrinkled her nose in disgust.

"How are Mum and Baby doing?" asked Serena gently.

Sebastian sat down.

"Okay, thanks. All a bit of a shock. St John is a month premature, and he has had a bit of trouble breathing properly. However, he's in the right place and there is nothing to worry about. Claire is going to stay in for a few days to have a rest and for the staff to make sure St John is all right. He had trouble feeding but I'm sure Claire will soon sort him out. I've come to collect a few bits and grab a bit of sleep if that is okay. Do you have any plans? Or can you look after the girls for me?"

Serena assured him she would be delighted to do so. Already she was planning various activities they could do with the girls. Sebastian went to have a few hours' sleep before going back to the hospital and Serena and Satish started planning with the girls what they would be doing for the day. The idea of a trip to the local stationery shop to buy materials to make welcome cards for St John was greeted with whoops of delight.

"Mummy doesn't let us do sticking," Abigail said with a pout. "Too icky and messy."

Sebastian re-emerged at lunchtime to find the dining table covered in cards, glitter, and glue but could not be bothered to protest. Abigail held up her card which clearly showed a finger-painted figure which looked suspiciously like a monkey, but it was difficult to be sure. The fact that it was in a tree added to the suspicion. Olivia had just done loads of colourful splodges. Both girls had used a tube of glitter each to decorate their cards, and the table, their faces and their clothes, and the carpet, and even Cecil the cat had a light dusting of pink glitter.

"When can we see him? We want to see him now," demanded the twins.

"Maybe tomorrow. He's in an incubator. Claire phoned me earlier to tell me. He's struggling a bit."

Serena could see the concern on Sebastian's face.

"What's an inkybiter?" asked Olivia.

"Somewhere poorly babies are put to keep warm," explained Serena, but the twins still went wide-eyed with worry.

"Don't worry. He'll be fine," continued their grandmother. "Let's write your names on your cards. Then we will have to let them dry a bit."

Sebastian said he was going back to the hospital with some things for Claire and asked Serena if she minded looking after the girls again. Serena realised that she was enjoying spending time with them, so beamed up at him, saying

"No. Take as long as you like."

Sebastian showered and then grabbed a sandwich before heading back to the hospital. Another phone call from Claire had told him that the baby was ill, and the doctors were concerned. He had also packed some items for himself should he end up staying there. However, just as he was about the leave and had gone into the bathroom, the doorbell rang.

Serena answered the front door, knowing Sebastian was indisposed. She was taken aback to see Roger and Melanie standing on the doorstep, with a large bunch of flowers, a magnum of champagne, a huge blue teddy many times bigger than the baby, and a large, blue helium balloon with the words "Welcome to the New Baby Boy" on it. Roger's mouth fell open at the sight of Serena, but he quickly closed it again. He could not believe the change in his ex-wife. Melanie maintained her usual pout.

"Well, well, who do we have here?" Roger's slick voice enquired. He continued "Claire told me you were coming back. Claire texted me to tell me of St John's arrival. We just had to mark the occasion."

On Friday Sebastian had filled him in at the office about Serena and Satish and their goings-on. Roger and Melanie had jumped at the chance to call in to see if what Sebastian had said was true, and they had no interest in Roger's grandson whatsoever.

"Come in."

Serena beckoned them in, suddenly aware that the effect that Roger used to have on her was no longer there. Even despite his appalling treatment of her, she had always in the past felt her chest flutter when she was around him and she always had an overwhelming desire to please him. Every meeting with him, and especially when Melanie was there, had always left her feeling increasingly miserable and more of a failure, but desperately wondering what she could do to change things. She never could, and the angry, jealous spiral deepened and deepened. Now she was amazed at her feelings of neutrality towards him. Melanie tip-tapped in behind her husband, in her high heels and Bodycon dress that left only slightly more to the imagination than Satish's loincloth had. Roger and Melanie went towards the living room as if they lived there and stopped in the doorway to see Satish sitting on the settee under the bay window with a twin on either side, happily listening to one of his folk tales from Thailand. He stopped and Serena introduced him to Roger and Melanie. Roger felt a prick of jealousy when he saw how softly and lovingly they looked at each other and realised just how attractive his ex-wife was now, although he was disappointed not to have seen her dreadlocks. However, he was glad to be able to see the tattoo which tantalisingly peeked out of the legs of her harem pants. He also realised, rather irritated, that he could no longer charm her, and that he had lost his power over her. Glancing at his miserable current wife, he wondered if he had made a terrible mistake all those years ago.

The twins had spotted the enormous teddy and jumped up and ran over to grab it, but Melanie told them, in no uncertain terms, that it was for their baby brother. And, no, she did not have anything for them. The twins settled back next to Satish with pouts on their faces. Satish and Serena exchanged glances.

Roger and Melanie awkwardly sat down on the other settee and Serena felt obliged to offer drinks, which they politely refused.

"We are not staying long. Just wanted to leave something for the baby. How is he?"

At this point, Sebastian came down into the room and, after greeting them, filled Roger and Melanie in with the gory details and how mother and baby were doing. Melanie wrinkled up her nose in disgust. While she was so engrossed in, and being grossed out by,

Sebastian's lurid telling of last night's events, Serena was able to study her. Her straight black, bobbed hair was obviously dyed. She still had her orange, fake tan complexion and her tight-fitting dress showed off her toned body. However, her face showed that she was blatantly having Botox and, as always, her immaculate foundation finished in a ridge around her jawline. Serena felt an overwhelming desire to pick at the edge of it and see if it would all come off in one go, like a mask. Melanie exuded frustration and irritation. Both Serena and Satish did some quiet visualisation and energy protection work on themselves to negate the negative energy coming from Roger and Melanie.

Roger assured Sebastian he would take care of everything in the office if he needed to stay with Claire and not to worry. Melanie did not look impressed as she realised it would be another excuse for Roger not to come home before late evening to their cheerless and sterile marriage.

Roger was feeling frustrated by the afternoon's meeting. He had wanted to come and poke fun at Serena and show his disgust at her antics. He had thought he would still have power over her but realised that she now only had eyes for Satish. He did not know how to relate to her, and, even worse, how to regain his power over her. The conversation became increasingly stilted. Serena had squeezed herself between Abigail and Satish, and he had his arm around her, and she had her arm around Abigail, while Roger and Melanie sat bolt upright side by side on their settee with no body contact. It was to everyone's relief that after an hour Sebastian looked at his watch and told them he had to get back to the hospital because Claire was expecting him over an hour ago.

Roger and Melanie quickly took their leave, saying they would wait until Claire was home before they visited again, and that Sebastian should call if he needed anything. Sebastian gathered his bags and said goodbye to Serena, Satish, and the girls, and followed them out to their car.

Once they had gone, Serena and Satish looked at each other knowingly, and then said to the girls

"Would you like to go to the park? But only if you don't tell on us if we give you big pushes on the swings."

The girls squealed with delight but pouted when Serena made them put on old clothes and their slightly too-small coats that were now tatty. The expedition to the park was spoilt by Abigail falling off the swing and cutting her knee badly. Satish had to carry her back from the park, and it looked dramatic with her blood on his white cotton trousers. On the way back from the park there was a call from Sebastian. The baby was a bit better, so Claire did not need Sebastian there, and he was coming back for the night as it was difficult to find anywhere to sleep in the hospital. Serena realised she would have some explaining to do about Abigail when Sebastian got home. Fortunately, the girls were in bed when he came home. Serena felt relieved. Sebastian said he had an important work meeting in the morning that he had forgotten about so needed a good night's sleep. It was not a meeting that Roger could manage as it was with one of his dedicated clients. Sebastian was worried about leaving Serena and Satish to look after the girls, but Serena assured him it was no problem, and that she would get them to nursery in the morning as usual. As Claire was in a private room in the hospital, Serena could visit her while the girls were at nursery. Satish was content to spend the morning reading and writing in the house. Sebastian began to feel a twinge of appreciation for his mother-in-law. He and Serena and Satish were grateful when bedtime arrived and they could all fall, exhausted, into bed.

The girls behaved well in the morning and Serena walked them to nursery before going to the hospital. She was shocked to see Claire looking haggard, with large bags under her eyes and her skin sallow. The nurses brought St John to her to try and get him to feed from Claire, as she had not been able to get him to feed yet. He was a tiny, crumpled, jaundiced, hairy little creature with a pouty face. The doctors still did not know if he had any long-term health problems or negative effects from his premature birth, but short term he had a chest infection and was still in the incubator, only coming out to attempt to feed.

Once again, he did not seem to understand what was required of him, and Serena could see the bitter disappointment on Claire's face. She seemed irritated with the baby and gave up very quickly.

"Just give him a bottle," she snapped at the nurse.

"Missus Jackson. Please keep trying. It is important for him, especially as he is prem. Your milk will build up his immunity."

Claire almost snatched him back from the nurse and once again thrust her nipple into his mouth. Once again, he did not respond as he should do.

"See. He has no idea. Just give him a bottle."

Sadly, the nurse took him away.

Serena took Claire's hand and for a minute thought that Claire was going to snatch it away from her. Tears filled Claire's eyes.

"I just don't want him. I don't love him. He's ugly. He's stupid. I never wanted him in the first place. He was a mistake. But I didn't want an abortion."

Serena was shocked at the venom in her daughter's voice.

"You're tired. It was all so unexpected and quick. I'm sure you don't mean it. He's only a baby. He'll grow and I'm sure he'll be beautiful. You'll come to love him."

She remembered the girls' cards in her bag but thought better of giving them to Claire, as Abigail had resisted Serena's attempts to persuade her to do another card, which did not look quite so much like a monkey. *'Perhaps'* she thought to herself *'that card would not be helpful right now.'*

Claire said she wanted to sleep so Serena said her goodbyes and that she would be back the next day. Her heart was heavy with her daughter's rejection of her grandson, and she wondered what she could do to help Claire love him. She was surprised at her own, incredibly strong, maternal feelings towards the little crumpled being. Could she offer him the love he needed? But for how long?

EIGHT

Roger was not happy. He awoke the next day with a blinding headache due to the several extremely large Scotches he had consumed the night before. Melanie had been giving him the cold shoulder on the way home from Claire's and when he finally exploded at her as to "what was her problem?" she replied

"Jayne – or Serena as she calls herself now. You were nauseating in the way you were hanging on her every word. She's just a sad menopausal woman who is being conned by a toy boy."

Roger was taken back by the hatred in his wife's voice. He did not know how to respond. He realised he felt very protective towards Serena in the light of his wife's venomous attack against her.

When they had got back to their Docklands flat after visiting Claire's house Melanie had immediately gone off to their home gym to work out. Roger had sat dejectedly on their new leather sofa and started pouring himself drinks. It was true what Melanie had said. During that hour in Claire's house, he had found himself being increasingly beguiled by his ex-wife, even though she did not appear to see the effect she was having on him. Satish was an enigma to him. On one hand, he initially appeared so young and naïve, but there was also something about him that made him wise beyond his years. The deep love and the connection between him and Serena were something Roger had never felt for anyone, especially not either of his wives. Roger, usually masculine, controlling, and powerful, suddenly felt completely emasculated. He was also intensely irritated. Knocking back another Scotch and soda, he had vowed to fight back. At this point, Melanie had appeared from their gym room sweaty and glowing. Normally he would have found her desirable and many times before he would approach her to try to coax her to the bedroom, usually only to be rebuffed as she wanted to go straight to the shower. This time, she just looked like a sweaty, angry woman trying to beat back the inevitability of aging. She had hesitated, suddenly aware of a shift in the usual pattern of his behaviour.

"Are you alright?" she had demanded.

"Yeah. Just stressed. I am working from home tomorrow. Sebastian has a new client of his coming into the office. An American heiress who is settling in this country. She wants some more investment advice. Going to give him free rein in the office and board room. Do you fancy going out for dinner tonight?"

"Maybe. Let me get showered."

Roger had sunk back into the soft settee and put his hand into his pocket to find his mobile phone to ring around a few restaurants. To his annoyance, it was not there.

"Bugger."

Then he had remembered he had taken it out at Claire's to look at a message and had put it down on the arm of the settee. He did not remember picking it up again.

Melanie had spent longer than usual showering and getting dressed. When she returned, she was in her jogging bottoms and comfortable sweater.

"I have some filled pasta and salad we can have for dinner. I don't feel like going out."

The reality was that she did not want to try to kid Roger that they could have a romantic time together and she wanted to catch up with a series on TV that she had been watching. Roger had retreated to his home office and started plotting.

When morning arrived Roger still felt ill at ease, which was not helped by his headache. Melanie disappeared before he was up, having said the night before that she had two new clients arriving early at her gym. He switched on his computer, and it pinged up a reminder for a dental appointment for the next day. Irritated he realised he was already booked with a client at that time, and he would need to phone to cancel it. Then he remembered again he had left his phone at Claire's. The realisation that he had to go back to get it filled him with excitement. It would be a chance to see Serena again, as it was obvious from the conversation the day before that she and Satish had no plans for the week and they did not seem to be in a hurry to do anything.

Roger almost leapt from his computer chair, switched off the computer, and hurried to shower and dress. He shaved carefully, sloshed on his new, extremely expensive cologne, and, looking at his reflection in the mirror, wondered if he should quickly cover over with hair dye the grey hairs that were showing in his black hair. Thinking that maybe they gave him a distinguished look, he decided he would play the suave gentleman, bordering on the Silver Fox. Breakfasted, dressed, and feeling ready for battle, he went to the underground car park where his vintage Jaguar was parked. He told himself that the Jayne of old would soon re-emerge to overcome the Serena she had become. He remembered the envy in her eyes when he and Melanie used to drive off from Claire's whenever they had a *family* get-together on Claire's birthday when she was a child. Smirking he roared out of the underground car park and set off for his conquest.

Fortune was with him. He found a parking spot right outside Claire's house and he felt it was a good omen. Ringing the doorbell, he swept his hand through his hair, hoping it would be Serena answering it again. However, it was Maria who answered.

"Oh. Good morning, Mister Roger," she said, obviously surprised to see him.

"Good morning, Maria. I left my phone here yesterday."

"Oh. Si. I found it this morning under the edge of the settee. But I couldn't ring you to tell you."

She chuckled at her own joke and waved her hand for him to come through to the living room. Roger felt ridiculously excited as he went into the living room, expecting to see Serena. To his disappointment only Satish sat on the settee, cross-legged, tapping away at a notebook.

"Morning." Roger felt deflated.

Satish looked up and gave a blinding smile.

"Good morning, Roger. Nice to see you again."

For a moment Roger thought that he was being sarcastic but Satish's kind, open face showed he meant it. Roger spotted his phone on the coffee table and went to retrieve it. He was desperately wanting to ask where Serena was but did not dare in case it was too obvious that he had an interest in her. Satish somehow knew this and explained

"Serena has taken the girls to nursery and then she was going to visit Claire."

"Oh."

Roger tried to hide his disappointment and sat down in Claire's favourite chair. He did not want to go away without a small victory. To his relief Maria offered him a coffee which he jumped at, hoping that if he managed to drag it out long enough, Serena might come back before he had to leave. Satish said he would have green tea. Roger got the sense that he was interrupting Satish in important work, but that Satish was too polite to say anything. Satish typed a few more words and then shut down the notebook and put it to one side.

"Work?" Roger enquired.

"Oh. I am writing a book."

Satish's face did not give much away.

If it had been anyone else Roger would have made a joke, asking if it were another 50 Shades series and asking whether he was going to become filthy rich through it, but thought it was not appropriate.

"What is it about?" he asked instead.

"Energy, healing and protection."

Roger suppressed a snort, knowing that to gain ground with Serena he needed to keep Satish sweet.

"New Age stuff. I don't understand much about it. All a bit beyond me," Roger replied neutrally.

Satish smiled and wobbled his head in acknowledgment.

"It is ancient Eastern teaching. Only now is the West catching up with Ancient Wisdom and calling it New Age."

Roger was unaware that Satish had already read his vibrational state, his emotions, and his intentions. Satish had also mentally put a wall of light around himself and Serena as protection against Roger and his scheming. On an unconscious level. Roger felt Satish's impenetrability and lapsed into silence until Maria brought in the drinks. She was relieved to see Roger had found his phone. She enquired about Melanie, and Roger had to stop himself from giving a nasty reply about her being her usual snappy self.

"She's fine, thank you."

Satish had been sitting in self-containment but realised he had to engage with this irritating man who used to be married to the woman he loved and adored.

"What work do you do?" he enquired, already knowing full well what Roger's job was.

"Oh, making obscene amounts of money helping others make obscene amounts of money, and then hiding it from the taxman."

Roger laughed but realised just how unimpressive that was to Satish. "It gives me a buzz," he added limply.

Satish nodded. Roger felt he was up against a wall of inscrutability with Satish. Changing the subject was a safe way to continue, he decided.

"So, what are your plans while you are here?" *'Apart from scrounging off my daughter'* Roger continued in his mind.

Satish smiled and replied

"I am going to visit my relatives in the Midlands. I have an aunt who is not long for this world, and I wish to see her before she passes. I have a few lectures to give and some people to meet. My book needs to be with the publisher by the end of next month to complete my trilogy. Also, we wish to raise funds to open a new community in Sri Lanka. That is my country of birth, and I would like to be near my family again. It will be like our community in Thailand, where we are combining care for our fellow creatures with care for people. We have many people to meet to tell about it."

For a moment Roger wondered if Satish was trying to extract a donation from him, but the open expression on Satish's face showed Roger this was not the case. He wondered if Satish would even accept any money from him and he felt annoyed that this strange man could make him feel so inferior and irrelevant; a feeling he was not used to or liked.

They both heard the front door opening and the chattering of two excited little girls. Roger suddenly felt his heart pounding as he heard Serena's voice calling out. How melodious it sounded now, when once it sounded harsh and nagging, just as Melanie's voice sounded now. Serena bounced into the living room but stopped when she saw Roger. He could see she was not as happy to see him as he was to see her.

"Roger!"

Her tone was surprised and slightly uncomfortable.

"I left my phone here," he explained ruefully, suddenly feeling foolish. Hoping to gain ground he continued "Satish has been telling me all about the wonderful work you two are doing."

Serena looked at Satish's confused face and shrugged her shoulders. Boldly she went over to Satish and kissed him lingeringly on the lips. Roger felt a surge of arousal at this open sign of affection. Serena curled up next to Satish at the end of the settee, only a metre or so away from Roger, just as the girls burst into the living room, squealing "Satish. Satish. Tell us more about your Ellies."

They stopped when they saw Roger. Olivia spoke for them both in a subdued voice

"Oh. Hello Grandad."

Serena was amused to see Roger wince at this aging moniker. He tried to appear bright and held out his arms to them.

"Come and tell me about your morning."

The look that was exchanged between the twins showed that this was not normal behaviour for their grandfather. Instead, they scurried over to Satish's settee and sat down on the other side to Serena and Satish. Immediately they told him all about the taddypulls they had seen in the fish tank at nursery.

"Tadpoles," Roger interjected.

The girls just looked at him and turned back to Satish, who started to talk about elephants. Deflated Roger asked Serena how Claire was doing. Serena sighed. She did not want to share with him her concerns about both Claire and the baby, especially not about her fear that Claire was rejecting St John.

"She is tired and finding it all a bit much," she answered truthfully, not able to give the bare-faced lie that Claire was fine, and all was well. Roger nodded as though he understood and cared.

Serena suddenly began to feel unwell. She was aware that her breathing was becoming laboured, and her face began to itch and swell around her nose and mouth. Satish stopped in mid-tale as he became aware of Serena's discomfort. She began scratching her face and breathing more deeply, which seemed to make her feel worse. Satish asked if someone could get a glass of water and Roger obliged. However, as he came back and lent down over Serena to give her the glass, she broke into a massive coughing fit. The smell of his cologne was overpowering. Red blotches were breaking out on her face and hands. Satish looked worried and helped her sip water. Roger loomed over her, feeling concerned. With tears streaming from her eyes, Serena looked up at him and apologetically said

"I'm sorry Roger, but I think I have had an allergic reaction to your cologne. I have this reaction to strong smells."

Wanting to say childishly "I know when I am not wanted," Roger instead apologised and suggested that he left. Serena was now gasping and asked Satish for her EpiPen which was upstairs in their bedroom. He hurried upstairs to find it. Sheepishly Roger let himself out of the house and went home, feeling even more emasculated.

Sebastian, on the other hand, was having a much more *successful* day. Up until now, Sebastian had managed to keep Roger from meeting his *new client* as he wanted to keep the lie going that she was a frosty middle-aged widow. In fact, at their first meeting two months ago, Eleanor Ellis had turned out to be a highly attractive, tall, curvaceous, blonde woman with a lovely, deep Southern Texas drawl. She was two years younger than him and had been divorced thrice and widowed once. As she had admired the original artwork hanging in the office, they immediately found they had common ground in liking the same upcoming and eccentric artists, which led to a discussion about their tastes in music and literature.

"Oh. My. Gawd," she had drawled "You are so like me! We are like two bitties of corn on a cob."

After an hour and a half of social chatter, they had got down to business, and she was very happy with Sebastian's suggestions for her investments. However, as lunchtime soon arrived, Sebastian had found himself inviting her to an insanely expensive restaurant over the road. She had happily accepted. Over lunch their fingertips had got closer and closer, until they were holding hands over the crisp, white, linen tablecloth, eyes locked on each other. By the end of the afternoon, they had found themselves in her luxurious hotel suite, sipping champagne in her eight-foot bed. Claire, children, and suburban living were part of another universe – one which Sebastian no longer wanted to engage with or suffer. He was in the universe to which he felt he belonged. He had felt that in Eleanor he had finally met his soulmate. And she said she felt the same about him. The last two months had been filled with the most passionate affair Sebastian had ever known.

Today had followed the usual pattern of her visit to the office, a public farewell in front of the secretaries, and then half an hour later Sebastian followed her to her hotel room. Today he finally accepted that he had met the woman of his dreams and he knew his life would never be the same again. It was time to move on from his unfulfilling existence.

NINE

Claire flopped back on her pillow and sighed. St John still did not get the idea of latching on, and her frustration was growing and growing. She was also angry that Sebastian had not been in to see her yet and it was now nearly five pm. She knew he had an important meeting at work but that it should have finished at lunchtime. From previous conversations with him, she had guessed it was with a frumpy American divorcee or widow. Irritated she took her phone out of her bedside table and rang him. He took a while to answer. He sounded slightly drunk and a bit defensive with his slurry hello.

"It's me. Are you coming to see me today? Mother came earlier. I need some more chocolate and maternity pads."

She thought she heard a stifled female giggle at the other end of the phone.

"What's going on? Who are you with?" she demanded.

"Nothing. Just one of the secretaries messing about."

Eleanor pulled a pretend offended face at this, which made Sebastian have to stifle a drunken laugh. He tried to hit her with a pillow but missed.

"She's working late," Claire snapped. "Your secretaries are usually out of the door by four-thirty. Are you coming or not? And can you bring me those things in? Please."

"Of course, my love. I'll see you shortly. Love you. Goodbye."

He hung up, leaving Claire feeling very unsettled and not believing a word of what he had said, especially as he never usually ended their phone conversations saying *Love you* as so many couples seemed to do.

When he arrived an hour later, she thought better about grilling him about what he had been doing. It was obvious he had been drinking, which he brushed aside as having been the result of celebrating St John's arrival with St John's namesake – St John Boughton-Smythe who was the retired founder of the company. Claire had smelt champagne on his breath and not the usual beer, wine, or whiskey that he drank. The baby had been wheeled into Claire's room again in the hope that he would feed from her, and Sebastian picked up the crumpled little being and held him in his arms. He too felt a distinct lack of affection for him, realising the contrast to how he felt about the girls when they had been born. Two conflicting, and equally bad thoughts passed through his head. Part of him wished St John had never been born but on the other hand, Claire would now be too distracted with a new baby and the

Terrible Twins to see that he was engaging in another exhilarating and torrid affair. St John had been the result of making up after Claire had discovered his last affair with one of the secretaries, who was immediately sacked after their liaison came to light. He suddenly heard that Claire was speaking and giving him a list of things to do at home and he had zoned out.

"And don't forget to check that Maria is ironing the girls' clothes properly. Please tell my Prebirth Group that I will not be going again. How is Serena coping with the girls? Is she getting them to nursery on time? Don't forget their piano lesson this week. They missed it last week and they will get behind. I hope to be out before their ballet on Saturday. Though it is nearly Easter so they might have broken up now."

Sebastian nodded and grunted in acknowledgement to each item on Claire's verbal list, but mentally he was still languishing in Eleanor's warm bed, surrounded by her overpowering scent, and flushed from their afternoon together in her bed.

He realised Claire's tirade had stopped and she was looking at him sternly.

"Are you ok?"

"Yes, yes. Just some hard negotiations today. I just keep running over them in my head."

He nearly spluttered out laughing at his double entendre. This emboldened him. He continued "It was a very creative meeting though. I learnt a lot of new things. I got wrapped up in some pretty intense stuff."

He hesitated for a moment and forced himself not to laugh.

"I think there could be some very interesting ongoing business with my new client. Pushing new boundaries. Developing links across the pond. Deepening our special relationship between our two countries."

Claire looked at him suspiciously.

"And just who is your client?"

Sebastian chastised himself inwardly for being foolishly brazen. He hurriedly added "She is your typical thrice-divorced American harridan and the last hubby died of a heart attack. Not surprised with her looks. Right old hag."

Again, he had to suppress a laugh, knowing that the mental image he was trying to conjure up was the opposite of reality. He continued

"More money than she knows what to do with. It will pay for us to have a few good holidays though."

Claire seemed reassured by this, although two weeks in their Devon cottage was nothing to get excited about, and neither would it cost much money. Sebastian handed the baby back to her and felt that he had better escape from this potentially dangerous situation, with him on a high after his day with Eleanor and Claire very much feeling vulnerable and on the lookout for trouble.

"I need to go home and crunch some more numbers," he said quickly. "I need to get them to Elea…. Missus Ellis before midday tomorrow."

In reality, he desperately wanted to crunch her phone number in his phone and tell her how he was going to accept her invitation to go back for a drink to *wet the baby's head.*

"You have only just got here," Claire complained.

Guilt got the better of him and he agreed to stay a little longer, but all the time he had one eye on the clock as it slowly ticked around towards seven o'clock when he knew Eleanor would be back from a shopping trip to the West End. She had teased him earlier with her talk about how she liked black lace and wanted to buy some to show off. At one minute to seven, it got too much for him.

"I need the john," he said. "It is downstairs. I might as well go home. I will come tomorrow. Oh, nearly forgot. Here are the items I got you. I will try and get away for a bit in the morning and pop in to see you."

He knew that Eleanor was meeting an old friend for morning coffee at Fortnum and Mason's so this would be the ideal time to visit Claire. He bent down and kissed his wife and then the fuzzy head of his son, who was now nestled in her arms. Claire was still puzzling over his use of the word *john* – an Americanism that he usually hated.

Breathing a massive sigh of relief, Sebastian scuttled down the hospital corridor and once outside pulled out his phone. He looked up Edward Evans on the list and rang the number. The soft seductive voice answered.

"It is me," he breathed. "I'll see you around eight-thirty."

"Well, that is just dandy. I have some new purchases I would like to show you….."

He felt his breathing increase in speed and depth.

"I can't wait."

"Me neither."

They hung up. Sebastian wanted to shower and change but knew that he did not have much time. If he put his foot down on the accelerator he could get home, shower, change, and get back to Eleanor's Mayfair hotel by eight-thirty. He knew he would have to lie to Serena and Satish and fob off the twins with an excuse as to why he was going straight out again. When he arrived home to his other life, he felt a pang of guilt. Serena was so understanding when he explained he had an important dinner meeting with a client that he had forgotten about, but Satish did not appear to believe him. He just looked at him, but even more unsettling, he also seemed to look around and through him as well. The twins were disappointed that he was going out again. Sebastian profusely thanked Serena for looking after the twins, cooking their tea. and now having to get them to bed. However, with her putting them to bed it was not the usual battle that Claire had with them. Sebastian realised it was due to the funny stories that they looked forward to once they were in bed. He breathed another sigh of relief when he closed the front door behind him, ran a hand through his blond hair, and took his car key from his pocket.

"Now for some fun," he told himself.

Once the twins were in bed, Satish and Serena curled up together on the settee. Serena could immediately see that Satish was unsettled and asked him what was wrong. He hesitated with his answer.

"I do not wish to meddle. This is your family. I think Sebastian was lying tonight. His energy was bad. Carnal. Muddy."

He looked apologetically at Serena, who sighed deeply.

"I felt the same," she said. "I don't trust him."

That lack of trust was deepened when Claire phoned just before she tried to settle for the night, saying she wanted to say "Goodnight" to Sebastian. but his phone was switched off. Serena said he had another meeting tonight. but Claire sounded puzzled.

"He was supposed to be working from home tonight.," she said quietly. Serena felt awful as she heard just how hurt her daughter sounded. She tried to reassure her.

"He seems very forgetful at the moment. You try and sleep and give little St John a kiss and a hug from me."

Serena hung up with a heavy heart. When she woke up the next morning and saw that Sebastian had not been back home all night her heart was even heavier.

TEN

Sebastian slowly surfaced from the deepest sleep he had had for many months. Several bouts of intense sexual acrobatics and the sharing of a magnum of Champagne had just about knocked him out. He became aware of the lack of another body in the bed next to him and he could hear Eleanor showering. He felt smug, devious, and like a naughty boy getting his own back on his overbearing mother figure – who in his life was now Claire, replacing the role that his strict and intolerant mother had had when he was a rebellious teenager. It was with no little horror that he understood just how he detested Claire and how he had no respect for her anymore. Claire had spoilt and monopolised the twins, so he felt no fatherly feelings towards them, and he was getting sick of feeling that he was just in the role of breadwinner and nothing more. There was no partnership left with Claire. He had no life left in Twickenham. This was the life he deserved, in a luxurious hotel room with a gorgeous, rich, exciting woman who had taught him things he never knew were possible with the human body.

"Well honey, with four husbands and a few lovers on the side, I have had plenty of practice," she had drawled to him. "Now, let me show you something else......"

Sebastian also realised that he would have some explaining to do to his mother-in-law as he knew that he had to go home to pick up important paperwork. If he timed it right, he could go home while Serena was taking the girls to the nursery. For a moment he felt bad that he was leaving everything to her, and he felt a prick of disappointment that he would not see her that morning. This was a surprise to him as previously he had had no time for Jayne, remembering that he had not blamed Roger for ditching her for Melanie. As he lay in the bed thinking about her, the memory of her sitting, scantily clad, in the sunshine came back to him, and the way the tattoos snaked up her legs, and he felt the familiar warmth beginning to seep through his body. At this point, Eleanor came out of the shower room, her hair wrapped in one fluffy towel and her body in another, and she walked over to the bed. She pulled back the sheet and, looking a little surprised, said

"OK big boy I can see you are feeling ready for some more action."

Half an hour later Sebastian extricated himself from Eleanor's clasp and said he had to go but promised he would return that afternoon. Just how he was going to juggle work, seeing Eleanor, and visiting Claire was going to be a massive challenge.

Claire woke that morning with a nagging feeling that things were not right. Her night had been broken by several nightmares and by the nurses bringing St John to her regularly to see if he could feed on her. However, her breasts were swollen and tender and the doctor had been muttering about mastitis. She phoned Sebastian but it went straight to Ansaphone. She phoned Serena and asked if she could speak to Sebastian, but Serena sounded evasive, saying she had not seen him yet this morning.

"But it's eight o'clock. Surely he must be up by now!"

Serena's silence made her uneasy. She continued

"Ask him to phone me. How are the girls? Are you coping OK? Do an online shop if you need to. I'll transfer some money to your account if you need it. Is Maria doing her work properly? Check the calendar on the fridge. I can't remember what the girls have on this week. There is a birthday party they have been invited to, but I can't remember when. Might be easier to cancel it – I am sure you won't be able to go and buy a present and a card and get the girls there." In her mind, she wondered what her friends would make of her strange mother and lover and did not want to be the subject of bitchy gossip.

Serena replied to each one of these points calmly and positively. It was as well that Claire could not see her face because, inwardly, she was in turmoil. Both she and Satish had concluded that Sebastian was being unfaithful again, and they were deeply saddened that he would do this while Claire was so vulnerable. It would not take a genius to see the cracks in the relationship between Sebastian and Claire, and Serena was sure that there was also an unfamiliar perfume clinging to him when he had returned the previous night. Fortunately, it had not given her an allergic reaction as Roger's cologne had done.

Serena asked if the twins could visit their mother yet, but Claire was not enthusiastic about it.

"Let me see how the baby does today."

Serena noticed the lack of his name in her conversation.

The twins were very subdued at breakfast, picking up Serena and Satish's low moods, and also missing their parents.

"When is Mummy coming home?" asked Abigail, her eyes wide and sad. "Can she leave the monkey behind? We don't want it."

Serena sighed and put her arm around her granddaughter, pulled her close, and laid her head on the little blonde head. She suddenly felt overwhelmed, sad, and at a loss as to what to say.

"Mummy is coming home soon. And your baby brother will be beautiful when he comes home. He just looked a bit funny when he was born. I know you are going to be a really good big sister to him."

"And where's Daddy?" Olivia demanded. "He's not here."

Serena and Satish exchanged glances.

"I expect he is working. He works very hard you know."

"I want Daddy!" Olivia wailed.

"I want Mummy!" Abigail wailed.

Both girls started crying and it took a long time to calm them down. Serena decided that skipping nursery might be a wise move and that giving the twins some fun activities at home would be better for them. Immediately the girls cheered up.

"Serena. Can we make chapypooties again?"

Olivia skipped around the kitchen.

"Er. Not a good idea. I don't think Mummy would like that."

Satish suggested they did potato printmaking.

"We make printed cards in our community which we sell to raise money for the elephants. We use wood to make the blocks to print from, but I think we could use potatoes instead."

Serena checked the calendar on the fridge and saw that the party was the next day. There was plenty of time to get a present and a card, as she did not want to disappoint the girls when they were feeling so insecure. It would take their minds off their parents' absence and their baby brother.

Satish found a bag of large potatoes in the cupboard and set about carving elephant shapes on the flat sides of halved potatoes. They still had some paint and glitter left over from the cardmaking session on Sunday. Serena cleared up the breakfast things and phoned the nursery, saying the girls were too unsettled to go today. The teacher was very understanding and said that today was the last day before Easter. Serena suddenly realised with horror that the next weekend was Easter weekend, and it was obvious that Claire had forgotten all about it and was not able to organise eggs and cards.

"I hope the Easter *family* meal tradition has been dropped," Serena muttered to herself, thinking that the last thing she wanted was to spend most of Easter Sunday in the company of Roger and Melanie.

Satish had the girls happily printing away in the kitchen when Serena heard the front door open. She went to the door between the kitchen and the hallway and saw Sebastian about to creep up the stairs. Closing the door behind her, she approached him. By the open-mouthed look of shock on his face, it was obvious he did not expect to see her and was not happy to do so. Serena kept her voice level.

"Is everything ok? We didn't hear from you last night. We were worried when you didn't come home."

Serena was aware she sounded like a mother catching her teenage son creeping in after an all-night party. She had to control the anger she felt rising within her, despite all her attempts to contain emotion.

"And Claire has been trying to get hold of you. She's worried."

Sebastian stopped on the first stair and looked down at her with suppressed fury in his eyes.

"I had too much to drink last night. With a client. I had to stay over."

"Really?"

Serena had a now uncharacteristic tone of sarcasm in her voice and continued "Your wife needs you right now."

"She is in good hands."

"She needs YOU!"

He snorted.

Serena was glad to hear that Satish had put music on loudly in the kitchen so the girls would not hear what was happening.

"Your daughters need you."

"They don't need me. You seem to be doing a pretty good job at taking over here."

"I have no choice. Claire is my daughter, and the twins are my granddaughters. I care for them. Which is more than you do."

Serena surprised herself with the venom in her voice and realised that now it was all out. There was no going back.

Sebastian stood back down from the stair and drew his face close to Serena's and snarled in her face.

"That is bloody fine coming from you. Pissing off to Thailand and shacking up with some bloody toy boy. Just when she could have done with your help. You disgust me. Someone of your age with someone young enough to be your son."

Serena held his now hateful stare.

"And why is it different from a man having a younger woman? Claire is ten years younger than you. I am fifteen years younger than Roger, but no one batted an eyelid. Hypocrite!"

Serena felt emboldened by her outburst and continued "Who is she? And don't deny it. I have a sensitive sense of smell. I can smell a different perfume on you."

Sebastian took a deep breath and stepped backwards.

"I don't know what you are talking about. It's none of your bloody business anyway."

Serena stepped forward.

"Oh yes, it is. This is about my daughter and her family. And you are not going to mess her up. Just because you always think you have something to prove."

"Shut up you old whore."

Sebastian turned and raced up the stairs. Serena broke down into sobs and sat on the bottom stair, her head in her hands. Satish, although engaged with printmaking with the girls in the kitchen, had intuitively picked up on her emotions, and told the girls to continue printmaking while he just popped out to see Serena. When he saw her sobbing on the bottom stair, he gently led her into the living room and sat with his arm around her, stroking her hair.

"Satish. What have we come back to?" she sobbed. "I feel so bad I lost it with him. I know he is seeing someone. He doesn't love his family. I feel so helpless."

Satish hugged her tight and rocked her, gently humming, and then said in his gentle voice

"We were called back for a reason. We must follow the path for which we are destined. And part of that path is to bring healing wherever we go. There is much bad energy here. We must do some serious healing work."

For a moment Serena wondered if everything was beyond that now, but she just meekly nodded. They sat clasped to each other, losing track of everything as they hugged and hummed and quietly chanted. Their cosiness was suddenly broken by one of the girls calling out in the hall

"Daddy's here!"

To which there was the thundering voice of Sebastian shouting

"What. The. Bloody. Hell. Do. You. Two. Think. You. Are. Doing.?"

Satish and Serena uncurled themselves from the settee and hurried out to the hall. There they saw the twins, with paint and glitter up to their elbows, paint-covered potato halves in their hands. Sebastian was standing on the bottom stair, his face bright red and furious.

"We made an Elly Train," said Olivia proudly.

All along the hallway, on the pale cream, silk wallpaper, some low down and some as high as the twins could reach, was printed a long string of multi-coloured, glitter-covered elephants.

E L E V E N

Sebastian left to visit Claire, having attempted to wipe one of the elephants off the wallpaper with kitchen paper. It just left a horrible bright pink smear, so with a sigh, Sebastian realised the elephants would have to stay – for the time being. The thought of explaining what had happened to Claire filled him with doom and dread. The girls were puzzled by their father's outburst as they thought the hall looked much prettier with pink, blue, yellow, and red elephants trotting in a line, some as high as they could reach and others along the skirting board. Once Sebastian left, Serena and Satish burst into fits of laughter, tears streaming down their faces, clutching their sides. The girls looked bemused.

"Your father's face…." stuttered Serena amidst guffaws of laughter. "I thought he was going to explode."

"I don't think Daddy liked our Ellies," Olivia said sadly.

"I hope Mummy does," said Abigail.

Neither Serena nor Satish wanted to tell the little girls the truth. Although they both rather liked them.

Claire was surprised to see Sebastian so early. He arrived shortly after the medicine trolley had been round and before the doctor's rounds. He seemed evasive. She had wanted to ask him where he had been but felt too weary for another fight. She was cheered up by the hand-made chocolates and fashion magazines he had brought her. Not wishing to be seen buying them, he had grabbed a couple of new copies that had been left in the waiting room downstairs. All the time he was there she could see he kept surreptitiously looking at his watch. Eventually, it got too much for her.

"If you need to be elsewhere don't mind me."

"No. No. I just have to keep an eye on the time as I have a meeting later. Another busy day ahead."

The glint in his eye said volumes. Claire decided she could not be bothered. If he was straying again, then good riddance. She did not have the energy to play his games anymore. She closed her eyes and told him she wanted to sleep. Silently he left the room.

Claire felt very differently when her mother arrived. She was glad to see her and held out her arms for a hug. Serena was taken aback but reciprocated. Satish agreed to spend the afternoon looking after the twins, reading books, and telling stories, not allowing the girls anywhere near paints or glitter, while Serena visited her daughter. Serena was delighted to be able to get to the hospital.

"How's it going?" she asked gently.

Claire sighed.

"He's still not feeding from me. I just don't feel I can be bothered with anything. I think something is up with Sebastian, as well."

A tear slid down her face. Serena took her hand and assured her a few days of rest would make her feel better, and she was possibly getting the post-baby blues.

"I felt awful just after I had you. Bursting into tears over nothing. But once I was home, I felt fine again."

This had not been true. Once she had arrived home as a new mum with Claire in her carrycot Serena had felt overwhelmed and pushed into a corner. Roger had made it obvious he believed all baby-related matters should be managed by the mother and had shown no interest in his daughter. Shortly afterwards he started the first of a string of affairs.

The door opened and the doctor appeared with his entourage. He held up his hand and a lackey dropped a file into it. He scanned it quickly and then asked

"How are we today Missus Jackson?"

Only then did he see Serena was there and was about to ask her to leave when Claire asked if she could stay.

There was a brief discussion about the mastitis which had caused Claire discomfort during the night, with the decision taken to put her on antibiotics. He wanted Claire to stay in for at least a few more days. What he did not say was that all the staff showed concern about Claire's lack of interest in, and, indeed, annoyance with, the baby. They wanted to see significant maternal bonding before releasing them, as well as ensuring he was healthy enough to go home. He had improved overnight but there was still rattling in his chest. However, St John had now taken a bottle and was feeding happily with the nurses. Claire felt relief. Serena felt sad. After the doctor left the nurse brought St John in for Claire to have a go at bottle-feeding him. She held him for a while as he guzzled greedily and then held him on her shoulder to wind him. However, it was all done with a certain sense of detachment. After he had posited on Claire's shoulder, Serena took him while Claire cleaned herself up. She cradled him in her arms, and he looked directly up at her with his little, dark, almond-shaped eyes. A feeling of extreme love and protectiveness suddenly overwhelmed her. It was deeper than anything she had ever felt for Claire or the twins. His head had morphed into the proper shape now, and he had already lost much of his lanugo. The yellow jaundiced skin was now a healthy pink. He no longer looked like a monkey but a sweet, helpless little baby. As Serena looked deep into his eyes, she whispered to him

"You are an old soul. I can see it."

It looked as though he smiled at her, but Serena knew it would only be wind. Whatever it was, a deep connection had just been formed between them.

On the way back to the house Serena stopped at an artisan and handmade toy shop to buy a present for the party the next day. Claire had been touched that Serena did not want to disappoint the twins, and had told her that Aliciana, whose party it was, liked dolls. Serena found a beautiful handmade rag doll with long plaits at the shop but gasped at the price tag. Satish had given her money from the sales of his latest book, which was now creeping its way up the bestseller chart. Realising she had no idea where else to buy a present at such short notice, Serena parted with the money. She also found a funny card of elephants dancing, which seemed appropriate, with the twins' love of elephants and the fact that Aliciana was one of their friends from ballet. However, she decided it would be tactful not to let Sebastian see it.

Back home she was relieved to find that nothing untoward had happened. The girls enjoyed the bean burgers she made for tea and Abigail said she had changed her mind about wanting Mummy home as she liked having Serena as her mummy, and she did not want to have to share her with her monkey brother.

Sebastian came home at eight o'clock, saying he had eaten and had work to do in his office. The girls were already in bed, and once again had asked for their father. Serena felt sad at their unrequited love.

Sebastian's day had improved rapidly after he left Claire. He went to the office to work until around two-thirty his phone rang, and a soft drawl said

"Hi Honey. Ready and waiting."

Eleanor told him that she had met with her old friend who had invited her down to Henley-on-Thames for Easter. Eleanor had been torn about going but the friend knew of a wonderful dinky little cottage that would be perfect for her to buy, but she needed to see it right away before it was snapped up.

"She has got first refusal on it for me as long as I see it before Saturday," she breathed as she licked Sebastian's ear. He felt he could cope without her from Friday to Monday, but not much longer. There was the likelihood of Claire returning home at the weekend, so he knew he had to be at home.

"We had better make up for lost time in advance then."

Wednesday arrived and Serena was astonished to realise it was only a week and a day ago that she and Satish had landed at Heathrow. So much had happened and so many emotions had bombarded them both. She had noticed that Satish seemed to be withdrawing into himself and, when asked what was happening, he replied

"I feel overwhelmed with bad energies here and I don't feel strong enough or in the right place to heal them. It is wearing me down. I need my energy to write."

Serena sighed.

"I'm sorry my family is such a load of basketcases. "

Satish looked puzzled.

"Nutcases. Mad. Screwed up," she continued.

He sat looking downcast, before saying "I feel there is worse than that. I feel darkness. I feel deceit. I feel there is so much lust, pride, and anger. Most of all I fear it is going to turn out very badly. And I cannot change it."

Serena took his hand and kissed it.

"Always the healer. Sometimes sadly things seem beyond healing," she said in a low voice.

The morning was spent playing with the girls in the garden while Maria cleaned. Early afternoon arrived and it was time to take the girls to Richmond to their party. Both Serena and Satish were pleased to be going somewhere away from the overpowering bad vibes of the house.

The girls moaned when they said they were walking. Satish told them how he had to walk five miles to school every day when he was a boy. The twins looked at him open-mouthed.

"We will get a taxi back," Serena promised, knowing the girls would be tired out by the end of the party.

After much whining about their feet being sore and their shiny patent leather shoes pinching, they arrived at a large, semi-detached house groaning under a massive wisteria plant that rampaged all along the front of the house. A leggy blonde woman answered the door and looked blankly at Satish and Serena but then squealed

"Abigail and Olivia! Aliciana was just asking where you were. And you are?"

She looked approvingly up and down at Satish but was a little less welcoming in the way she looked at Serena, with her rainbow hair and tie-dye clothes.

"I am Claire's mother, Serena and this is Satish. She had her baby boy on Saturday, so I am doing grandmother duties while she's in hospital."

"Oh! How wonderful. We must celebrate. I already have the Pinot Grigio open. Come in. My name is Sophia."

They went into a large lounge/dining room where around twelve women were sitting, all sipping glasses of wine, some of whom were already fairly drunk. Through in the garden, Serena could see an open-sided marquee had been set up and a hideously garish clown was going through his (unamusing) routine.

"Go through girls. Aliciana is waiting for you."

However, Olivia just clung to Serena's leg. She remembered that Olivia had a phobia of clowns.

"I think she is better with me for a bit. She doesn't like clowns."

Sophia had already realised what a big mistake it had been booking the clown. Three months ago, she had had a terrible job finding anyone on the list of children's entertainers who had any availability at less than six months' notice. She was so relieved when the final one said they could help and had taken her booking. Unfortunately, they had phoned earlier that day to say that the Disney Princess she had originally chosen had been double booked and the clown was the only available option. When Sophia started shouting that it was not acceptable, they had expressed their regrets about having nothing else available at such short notice. It was the clown or nothing. Reluctantly

Sophia had booked the clown. Already two other children who hated clowns had gone home crying with their angry mothers, who had even had the temerity to take their presents back with them. What had been worse was that the mothers had demanded back the twenty pounds per head charge for allowing their child to attend the party. Sophia had felt angry at this, because, after all, each birthday bag they were to take home had cost fifty pounds to put together, so asking for twenty pounds to attend must be justified. It was with some hesitancy she asked for twenty pounds for each twin from Serena, who looked at her in shock.

"I am sorry. I don't have that much money on me, apart from the taxi fare home."

"Well make it thirty then, if you have it."

Reluctantly Serena counted out the money, which did not leave much for the taxi home. She decided they would ask the taxi driver to take them as far as he could for the money she had left, and they would have to walk the rest.

Serena and Satish were aware of the lull in the conversation and the interested looks from the other people in the room, but they found a couple of chairs next to each other, and politely refused the offered glasses of wine. Serena asked if there was any herb tea, which Aliciana's mother went off to brew, just before she went to ask the clown to leave, as she did not want any more children going home in tears.

Conversations began flowing again as the novelty of Serena and Satish's presence waned. Once the clown had packed up Aliciana came back into the room and Olivia gave her the present. Without a word of thanks, she ripped the paper off it, and then stood staring at the rag doll. Her nose wrinkled in disgust. She prodded its stomach hard several times and then turned it upside down and shook it.

"It doesn't do anything," she protested. "Where do the batteries go?"

She opened the card and again just looked at it as though it was the weirdest thing she had ever seen. Serena and Satish exchanged glances.

Sophia made an announcement.

"Tea is ready. Please come through to the kitchen and help yourselves."

Chairs were hurriedly pushed back, and the throng of hungry and tipsy women surged into the kitchen, but Serena and Satish hung back. Aliciana's mother noticed this and asked

"Are you Keto? Or Paleo by any chance?"

"No, I am Sri Lankan," Satish replied, puzzled.

Sophia shrieked with laughter. "So droll. So droll."

"We are vegan," Serena said quietly. "But don't worry if there is nothing for us."

"Au contraire. It is all vegan. It is the thing to be vegan at the moment. So healthy. No nasty fats and hormones. It's keeping me slim."

When Serena noticed the jars of mayonnaise and sour cream dip to go with the crudities, she wondered if Sophia knew what being vegan really meant.

Neither Serena nor Satish felt at home with the cliquey group of women, several of whom sat blatantly eyeing him up, whilst looking at Serena with obvious disdain. Fortunately, a woman called Katia took pity on them and sat and chatted with them. She adored Thailand and had spent many a happy summer on Ko Samui in a beachside resort. When asked what she thought about Bangkok and the culture of Thailand, she looked blankly at them. When she heard that Claire was likely to be in hospital until the weekend, she offered to have the twins if Serena and Satish needed space to themselves. Serena noticed that she did not say anything about Sebastian helping, so she wondered if other people had seen what she had seen about his lack of care for his family.

The end of the party could not come soon enough. Katia had a seven-seater car and was going home via Twickenham, so her offer of a lift was gratefully accepted. Both Serena and Satish climbed aboard with a sigh of relief, and the expected tantrums from the twins having to leave the party never materialised. Instead, they seemed to want to go home and to have Serena and Satish to themselves.

TWELVE

Once home the girls wanted to go to bed early with a story, which was good news to Serena because she knew Sebastian was going to be working from home that night. Serena dreaded seeing him again. He had kept out of her and Satish's way after the argument, coming back late the night before and scuttling out of the house in the morning, but had said he would be in that evening, but he did not know when. Eleanor had a theatre trip booked with another old friend and she had tried to get another ticket so Sebastian could join them. However, the play was sold out, so she went with just her friend.

Once the girls were asleep Serena did some centering exercises and visualisation of bubbles of light around herself to protect her from Sebastian's bad energies. When he did arrive home it turned out easier than Serena had anticipated. It was as though the venomous words he spat at her the day before had never existed. Serena had been deeply wounded by them, and it took a lot of Satish's good energy, and lovemaking, to negate them. Sebastian seemed almost friendly and amenable, thanking the pair for looking after the girls and taking them to the party. He asked if they needed any more money to do some shopping as he had realised that it was Easter weekend ahead and he did not want to stop the usual Easter tradition of Roger and Melanie coming over to spend time with the twins, and he was hoping that Serena did not mind this. It was usually so they could get drunk and verbally tear down everyone they knew. The sadistic side of him was looking forward to how the new *spiritual* woman version of his mother-in-law was going to cope. He had also picked up through a brief conversation with Roger that Roger had been bowled over by the new, slim, vivacious woman that was his ex-wife. Sebastian also realised that Roger regarded it as a challenge to get her away from Satish, as his ego had been battered by her total disinterest in him. Roger had not told him of the cologne experience.

Another afternoon of passion with Eleanor had also convinced him that he needed to make plans to move on with his life. His marriage with Claire was dead in his eyes, and he had no interest in caring for another squawking baby. Initially, he had not wanted the twins but had warmed to them after their birth. However, now he felt extraordinarily little affection for them and regarded them as *the Brats*. He had none for his son, and when Claire had told him she was pregnant again he had wanted her to have an abortion. She had refused. He felt no connection with his wife anymore. However he had felt a deep and instant bond with Eleanor, and she said she felt the same. A few hints were dropped about there *being plenty of room* in the cottage in Henley-on-Thames if it turned out to be as nice as her friend had said. Sebastian and Claire's house was fully paid for, and Sebastian did not need to take any money out of it, and it had been signed over to Claire as part of an intricate tax *fiddle*. He too had been disappointed in it and had wanted to move but did not dare to admit it to Claire. He knew just how she loved the kitchen. He had also decided that he would call an unannounced truce with Serena by being amenable and not being so blatant with his affair until things were settled with Eleanor.

Serena was glad of the change of atmosphere and thanked Sebastian as he took a wodge of notes from his wallet and told Serena to buy whatever was needed for Easter. He offered to cook a roast for Sunday if Serena could cook something for her and Satish. When he had spoken to Claire earlier, she told him that the hospital was happy for her to come home on Saturday and return Monday. However, St John would have to remain in until he was a bit bigger and stronger. Claire was looking forward to being home for a while, although she would probably go back for an hour on Easter Sunday to spend time with St John.

Checking on the calendar in the kitchen Serena found that there were no piano or ballet lessons, so she set about planning Easter for the family. She was extremely surprised to find she was enjoying it, with plans for baking Easter biscuits with the twins (on the worktops and not on the floor). She also planned to look around the garden to find things to make an

Easter Garden and organising the Easter egg hunt that was now their tradition. Satish was extremely quiet and several times Serena caught him looking deep in thought. Eventually, he came out with what was troubling him.

"I am sorry to say I do not trust Sebastian. He still has a muddy energy about him. I do not believe he is being truthful and straight with us. I see blackness around his heart."

He sighed deeply. Serena was concerned to see how the negativity of her family was beginning to drain him. However, she was juggling planning Easter with looking after the twins and trying to visit Claire. Much as she wanted to suggest he went to visit his family early she knew she needed him and his gentle energy and support more than ever. The next couple of days involved meal planning, online shopping, giving Maria extra hours to get the house ready for Claire's return, as well as day-to-day care of the twins.

When Claire arrived home on Saturday, she was delighted to find a clean, tidy house, well stocked with food and two very happy and well-behaved girls, who were busily making *welcome home* cards for her, without covering the whole dining room, floor, walls and cat with glitter and paint. Sebastian had already told her about the elephant printing episode, but she was so glad to be home that all she did was laugh when she saw them. She was even more delighted to see Satish again, bringing home to her the growing infatuation she felt for him. Another positive thing was Sebastian's attentiveness and seeming desire to look after her. No one mentioned St John. It was as though he did not exist. However, he was very present in Serena's heart, and she felt desolate at the thought of the tiny baby alone in his cot in the hospital, still wired up to monitors.

By the end of Saturday afternoon, Claire was showing signs of exhaustion. Satish offered to do healing on her. Sebastian went to make a sarcastic comment but stopped himself in time, determined that he was going to keep a low profile over the weekend while he quietly arranged his *escape* from his life of drudgery. Instead, he sank back into the settee with a look of disdain on his face.

"Come and sit on this chair."

Satish pulled out one of the dining chairs and placed it in the middle of the room.

Claire did as she was told and shut her eyes, put her hands, palms upwards, in her lap, and relaxed. Satish walked silently around her, eyes shut, and started moving his hands around her, without touching her. She felt warmth flood through her body and what felt like an electric shock from where his hands were. For a second, she opened her eyes for she was sure he was caressing her body, but his hands were a handspan away from her. How she wished his hands were actually caressing her. Sneaking a peek at him, he almost seemed to be glowing. Hurriedly she shut her eyes again and began to feel overwhelmed by his close, masculine presence. She felt emotions and physical sensations that she had not felt for a long time and an overpowering surge of desire. Suddenly he pulled back, opened his eyes, and looked shocked. Claire was mortified. She was afraid that he had read her lustful thoughts. Seeing the look of embarrassment on his face, she knew he had picked up how she was feeling and the fact he had aroused something in her that had been dormant for many months. Feeling her face burning red, she thanked him and said she felt much better. He put his hands together and wobbled his head.

"My pleasure."

Claire suppressed the thought that she would like to give him a lot more pleasure, remembering that she had given birth just a week ago. Satish made his excuses and went upstairs. Serena looked at his retreating back with puzzlement. Claire hurried off to make tea and Serena followed Satish upstairs. She found him sitting cross-legged on their bed, meditating. Silently she sat on the bed beside him. Without opening his eyes, he quietly said

"There is too much misdirected lust in this house. The sexual energies are wrong."

Serena reflected that probably Claire and Sebastian would say that about her and Satish. Hesitantly, she asked

"What do you mean?"

He looked sad and awkward. He took her hand.

"I got such a feeling of awakening energies from Claire. Not healing ones. Devouring ones. She wants me."

Serena was taken aback but was grateful for his honesty. However, he had not finished.

"And Sebastian has sexual energy around him, but it is not for Claire. It is for another person."

Serena nodded silently. Satish was confirming what she had been feeling increasingly. Sebastian was back to his philandering ways. He was an incredibly attractive man, tall and muscular with thick blond hair and piercing blue eyes. Both the girls had picked up his colouring rather than the brown hair and hazel eyes of their mother and grandfather. Sebastian's natural arrogance at having had a privileged upbringing made his conquests feel they were so lucky at being chosen by him to share in his fortunes.

Serena was aware that Satish was looking intently at her. With sudden realisation, she exclaimed

"I hope it is not for me! That's sick."

Satish was gentle with his reply.

"Just a little bit. I see him look at you sometimes in an unwholesome way. But you are not the main person. I think there is someone else."

"Poor Claire. Just when she needs his support the most."

Serena felt the anger bubbling up in her. She wanted to go and confront Sebastian but knew that was the last thing she should do right now, with Claire back from the hospital and St John still in there. Taking a deep breath, she said

"We must keep this to ourselves for now. Claire must know sooner or later, however. Although we don't have much proof do we?"

Satish shook his head.

"I somehow don't believe Claire would take my reading Sebastian's aura as being proof."

Serena smiled.

"No. She is not into our *woo woo* stuff."

Satish looked uncomfortable and squeezed her hand.

"And do not let me be alone with Claire. Her energies are unsettling me. My energies are for you alone."

The look of love in his eyes melted Serena's heart. She twirled the commitment ring she had on her left hand, remembering the touching Commitment Ceremony she and Satish had undertaken after six months of being together. Although not legally married, they had promised each other to live in harmony and exclusivity until either death or spiritual forces parted them. She leant forward and kissed him.

"And mine are for you alone too. Now, we must go downstairs again and act as though all is normal."

However, it was not normal downstairs. Sebastian had witnessed the strange interaction between Claire and Satish and had followed her into the kitchen and grilled her about it. He was trying to throw Claire off the scent of his affair with Eleanor by insinuating that she *had the hots* for Satish. Claire could not deny it to herself but had to deny it to Sebastian. The last thing she wanted was for him to walk out on her now, which she knew he would do if he believed she was being unfaithful, even if it were only in her imagination. In his mind it was normal for men to have affairs, but not for women to do so. Serena found Claire in the kitchen with a tear-stained face and Sebastian having retreated to his attic office. Claire would not tell Serena what the problem was and clammed up completely when pushed on it. Eventually, Serena decided it was hormones and made her sit down as she started to prepare tea for the family.

At that moment, the order from Ocado arrived and Serena spent the next hour trying to cram food into already overstocked cupboards, cook tea, break up a squabble between the twins, and mentally go through the list of things to be done before tomorrow. Suddenly Thailand felt a million miles away. Would she ever see her home there again?

THIRTEEN

Easter Sunday started wet, with threats of possible snow showers. Serena drew back the curtains in their bedroom and looked forlornly out of the window.

"No outdoor Easter egg hunt for the twins today," she mused sadly.

"We will have to hide them indoors," Satish said. "Now come back to bed for a while. We need some positive energies to start the day."

She did not need any persuading. For once they decided they could forego their morning ritual of greeting the sun, which was remaining staunchly hidden.

An hour later the twins could be heard stampeding up and down the corridor.

"Has the Bunny been yet? We wants eggs!"

Reluctantly Serena and Satish peeled themselves away from each other and left their warm cocoon of love and quickly showered and dressed. They found the girls downstairs at the breakfast bar eating cereal and a very hollow-eyed Claire drinking tea in her dressing gown. Sebastian was still in bed. Claire remarked that Roger and Melanie would be with them in a couple of hours, as they wanted to be part of the Easter egg hunt.

Serena felt sceptical as to why Roger had a sudden interest in his grandchildren. "Brownie points," she muttered to herself but then reprimanded herself for unkind thoughts. Serena suggested Claire get herself ready and then bathe the girls.

"And who knows? Maybe the Easter bunny will have come by then?"

Claire picked up on the suggestion and half an hour later the girls were squealing and chucking water around in the bath with Claire supervising them, while Serena and Satish hurriedly hide small, wrapped Easter eggs all around the house. Sebastian appeared at this point, disgruntled at the noise, and complaining how he had a headache and wanted a lie in. Serena had to bite her tongue to stop giving him an acidic reply. Once again, she felt angry that he brought out in her feelings she thought she was strong enough to avoid. Quickly envisaging a sphere of light around her body she continued hiding the eggs.

At eleven on the dot, the doorbell rang, and Sebastian let Roger and Melanie in. The twins were bathed and dressed and skipped downstairs to find their grandfather sitting in the living room with two enormous chocolate eggs, wrapped in pink bows.

"To the best little granddaughters in the whole wide world."

One egg had Olivia written in white chocolate on it and the other had Abagail written on it. No one dared to point out the spelling mistake. Serena suddenly realised she had been so busy arranging everything that she had not bought large eggs for the girls from her and Satish, but had spent lots of money on different coloured, smaller eggs to hide for the Easter egg hunt. She knew this would be regarded as a huge failure in Roger's, Melanie's, and Claire's eyes.

Coffee was made and the girls started devouring their eggs. Eventually, Sebastian stood up from his chair, made it as though he had suddenly spotted something out of the window, and then exclaimed

"I do believe I have just seen the Easter Bunny skipping gaily off down our path! He must have left his eggs behind."

He gave a suggestive snort at the last part and turned and winked at Roger and Melanie, who also snorted at the puerile joke. Satish had been offered the job of saying this part in the carefully choreographed plan but had declined. Whilst he felt peace in his spirit at hiding the eggs, he did not want to tell a blatant lie. The girls squealed with delight and at their father's prompting went off to hunt around the house for the hidden eggs, each girl twirling a small wicker basket in which to put them.

"Don't forget to bring them all back here so we can share them," Claire called to their backs as they ran through the door.

The adults had about twenty minutes of slightly stilted conversation. Claire still looked exhausted and miserable. Sebastian was somewhat aloof and did not look at Claire at all. Roger and Melanie, who were not usually open to emotional atmospheres, knew something was wrong. St John did not get mentioned until halfway through. It was Melanie who enquired how he was. Claire was almost dismissive of him.

"He's ok. Still under surveillance. I can go and see him later if I want."

However, her tone indicated that she was not bothered. Serena felt a stab in her heart. Tears threatened to come but she fought them back. Satish looked at her tenderly and took her hand. He too felt bereft at the lack of love Claire had for her son.

Roger started bragging about some new client he had, who he was going to milk as much as he could. He then put his foot in it.

"And, wow, that new client of yours, Seb. Caught a glimpse of her the other day. What a stunner! What a body! Stinking rich too. No wonder you are keeping her to yourself!"

The visual daggers that Sebastian sent him stopped him in his tracks. He blustered

"Not that she is your type, Seb. Bit too much plastic surgery. I am surprised she doesn't melt under her sunlamps."

The damage had been done. Sebastian's face was bright red. He had broken into a sweat and was suddenly looking down and fiddling with his wedding ring. Claire stared at him open-mouthed, with anger and hatred on her face.

It was at this point that two excited and chocolate-covered girls burst back into the room.

"We's founded the eggies," screeched Olivia.

"And eaten some," Abigail said defiantly, holding up a sticky, brown hand.

"And we found some funny eggs….in Serena and Satish's room."

Olivia proudly produced three highly polished, jade eggs from her basket and held them up for all to see.

"They is too hard to eat. Must be pretend ones."

The adults were mortified. Claire leapt to her feet and instantly regretted it and flopped back into her seat. She did not dare look at Serena or Satish. Roger and Melanie initially looked horrified but then both had to hide their amusement. Sebastian looked bemused and had to quickly suppress the image of his mother-in-law with yoni eggs.

Claire snapped "You shouldn't have gone in their room. I told you to keep out of there."

She had been worried the girls might find a copy of the Kama Sutra, which she suspected her mother had, and she would have a lot of explaining to do to the girls. However, she had noticed that Barbie and Ken had been placed in some interesting positions lately.

Serena had regained her composure.

"Never mind. No harm done. Please may I have my eggs? They are for juggling."

Obediently the girls handed them to her and just to continue with the façade Serena tried to juggle with them but failed miserably, dropping all three on the floor.

"I must keep practicing."

She smiled, stood up, and then took them back to her room.

No one knew what to say next. A heavy silence descended over the room.

Satish watched his partner leave the room and his heart was filled with love for her. He then sat back cross-legged on his sofa and observed the others in the room. Claire had sent the girls out to the kitchen to eat some of the chocolate eggs, having rationed them and told them they could have the rest later. She flopped back in her chair, sighing, and closing her eyes. Satish could see the exhaustion, frustration, and confusion that swirled in her aura. His heart went out to her. If only she could let go a little. He remembered the uptight and frigid woman that Jayne was when he first met her. How quickly, with his tuition and kindness, she had blossomed into the wise and loving woman whom he adored. If only the same could be done for Claire. Maybe that was why he was here, he pondered. Like mother, like daughter. However, he knew his interest in Claire was purely platonic and altruistic. Perhaps if Claire could start to grow, she would understand her mother a little more. Satish decided he would meditate on how he could help her to heal without arousing her obvious desires for him. Feeling satisfied with his thoughts on her, he moved his attention to the other sofa and its inhabitants.

Roger was at one end, Melanie in the middle, and Sebastian at the other end. Roger appeared to have been aroused by the jade eggs as he had a very amused look on his face and kept moving and fidgeting in his seat. Satish could see he was fantasising. This made him feel angry and sick inside. Although Satish was normally above such base feelings as jealousy, he always felt that he had a second claim on Serena. Roger had been her husband and father of their child, something that Satish would never be. The thought that Roger was now interested again in the woman he loved made Satish feel insecure, however much he told himself that Serena had no interest in Roger. Melanie sat poker-faced next to him, fiddling with her watch. Satish observed how tense she was, constantly flicking at her hair, pulling her dress, and crossing and uncrossing her legs. Every so often she shot glances at Roger, carefully avoiding looking at anywhere but his face. Satish mused how different she was from Serena. Serena was bursting with natural energy and health, to the point where she almost glowed. Melanie was toned and tanned, but her image of health was so false. Satish could see her "health" was only limited to her body and did not reach her mind, emotions, or spirit. There was a deadness about her.

Sebastian too was obviously running the event over in his mind, as he had a smirk on his face. He was also wondering if Eleanor had any yoni eggs as well or whether he should get her some. Satish could see so many muddy and unpleasant emotions swirling around in him, and quickly looked away, as it put him out of balance.

When Serena returned, she found them all sat in stony silence. Curling up next to Satish she looked at them all looking at her.

"What?" she asked defensively.

Sebastian held back from saying anything, as he wanted to keep Serena on his side. It was Claire who spat out

"You! You disgust me. Both of you. You two are like bloody rabbits. Do you know how many times I have had to make excuses for the noises coming from your room?"

Claire did a fair imitation of Abigail.

"Mummy, why is Granny making squeaking noises in her bed? Why does she say "Ooo I like that" so often? What are they doing?"

Claire's angry eyes bore into Serena.

Serena sat open-mouthed and her face was full of hurt. Tears welled up in her eyes. Claire had not finished.

"Some Mother you are. Buggering off to Thailand. Don't see hide nor hair of you for three years. Then you come swanning back here with someone who could be your son. At your age. You are forty-five, not fifteen. You're full of all your *woo woo* crap. Like some drugged-out hippy. As for Satish. What's his motive in all this? Money, sex? Do you pay him for it? You two act like sex-starved teenagers. You disgust me."

Roger looked smug and as though he was ready to enjoy the coming fight. He was longing for the serene Serena to crack and the crabby Jayne to reappear.

However, he was to be disappointed. Through her tears, Serena quietly said

"I'm sorry if my new happiness offends you. What I have with Satish is genuine and pure love. I'm happier than I've ever been in my life. If our lovemaking offends you, I'm sorry. I'm sorry I disgust you."

Serena wanted to say that at least their union was pure and honest, unlike what was going on in Sebastian's life, but her higher self stopped her, as she knew that was being vindictive. She continued with a shaky voice

"If that is how you truly feel, we'll leave. I don't want to be where I'm not wanted."

With this, she stood up and held out her hand to Satish, who stood up and put his arm around her.

"We'll make arrangements to go."

They left the room, leaving Claire suddenly feeling alone and frightened. Sebastian too was in a state of shock, having realised that if Serena and Satish left, then he would find it difficult to continue his relationship with Eleanor. Roger and Melanie felt as though the ground had been cut from under them. Roger had been so ready for a showdown in true meltdown style as there used to be between Jayne and Claire. Instead, Serena had back-footed them all with her quiet and apologetic behaviour. Roger realised, with great surprise, that he felt ashamed of his feelings and eagerness for a fight. He suddenly felt like a nobody against Satish's quiet, strong, and gentle presence.

"We had better go," he said, and Melanie agreed, and they hurriedly let themselves out.

Sebastian and Claire sat on opposite sides of the room for twenty minutes, not knowing what to do or say. Then they heard something being bumped down the stairs. Hurrying out into the hall, they saw Satish and Serena bringing down their filled bags and a suitcase. Behind them, the twins were watching with horror on their faces.

Serena said

"We have found a Travelodge. Satish has phoned for a taxi. It is coming in five minutes."

"Oh, shit," Sebastian moaned and retreated to the living room.

His world had once again fallen apart. First his political career a week ago and now his love life. Without Serena here to cover for him he could not continue seeing Eleanor. He heard the pathetic wailing of the twins as they realised Serena and Satish were leaving. Abigail hung onto Satish's legs and Olivia clung onto Serena.

"Nooooooo." They wailed in unison. "Don't go. We wants you."

Claire cursed herself for her outburst and suddenly realised how much she needed her mother. Bursting into tears, she put her head in her hands and pleaded

"Don't go. I'm sorry. You don't disgust me, really. I just felt so embarrassed. Please stay. I can't cope without you."

Serena looked at her distraught daughter and felt compassion for her. However, she knew she needed some space to process everything and regain her equilibrium.

"This is the second time you have told me I am disgusting. I'm no longer going to allow people to put me down or destroy me. I am who I am now. I think some space between us would be good. I'll keep in touch. I will come back, if and when you want me to. But for now, we both need some space."

On cue, the taxi arrived outside, beeped its horn, and Satish and Serena left, after hugging the twins and telling them they would be back soon, and that they were just having a quick holiday. This seemed to pacify them a little bit, and they rushed to the kitchen and brought back two rather battered Easter eggs for them to take away as presents. Serena felt touched by their kindness and did not have the heart to tell them she did not eat chocolate.

As the taxi pulled away Claire returned to the living room, to find Sebastian looking furious.

"Well, that was a clever move," he snapped. "Pissing your mother off like that. Just because you are a frigid cow...."

Once again Claire's mouth dropped open.

"Mummy, what does *frigged* mean?" piped up a little voice behind from the doorway.

FOURTEEN

As their taxi drew away from Claire and Sebastian's house, Serena immediately wondered if they were doing the right thing. Leaving her daughter at this point was the hardest thing she had ever done. However, she could not stay somewhere where she felt so resented and unappreciated. She told herself that a little bit of time apart would heal them both. Fortunately, the first place they tried to get a room had a cancellation. Satish had been worried that on Easter Sunday so near to Heathrow Airport, they would not find anywhere to stay. They booked into the hotel and felt a sense of relief as they both fell onto the king-sized bed. Serena decided to have a bath, and once she was half-submerged in the bubbles, Satish started to give her a neck massage. As his hands started to wander down her body, she felt for the first time ever that she did not want to make love to him. Gently she took his hands and looked him in the eyes and said

"I'm sorry."

He could see the deep hurt and trauma in her eyes, and he withdrew his hands, having to curb his growing desire.

"I will make you a drink," he said, and reluctantly left the bathroom.

Once dressed again Serena sat on the bed and pondered about their future, and what they should do now.

Back in Twickenham Claire had immediately regretted her outburst at her mother. She felt ashamed of her cruel words and reflected on Sebastian's hurtful comment about her being a "frigid cow.". Was it true? Admittedly she had not felt any intimacy with him for some time, but she had put it down to her pregnancy. Maybe she was driving him into another woman's arms. She also recognised her jealousy of her mother with a younger, attractive lover who was so obviously besotted with her. Going to make herself a coffee in the kitchen, she saw the large joint of lamb sitting on the side and remembered how Roger and Melanie were supposed to be staying for lunch. The Easter Garden Serena and the girls had made in one of her baking dishes was in the middle of the island. A plate of decorated Easter biscuits was placed next to it. It was a painful reminder of the Easter Day they had planned, which had now fallen apart. Sebastian had disappeared upstairs to his office, and the girls were sitting with their noses in their Ipads, watching Peppa Pig. Suddenly Claire felt so alone.

"I'm so sorry," she whispered into the air as if the words might somehow magically transmit themselves to her mother. Not knowing what else to do with herself she started preparing the lamb and heating the oven. Opening the fridge and seeing the nut roast that Serena had prepared made her cry. All she wanted right now was for her mother to reappear in the kitchen and start helping her with her quiet and gentle efficiency.

Up in his office, Sebastian sat in his swivel chair and thought long and hard. Without Serena here to support Claire, he could not leave her. Not immediately anyway. He would have to put his plans with Eleanor on hold. He was scared she would cool off and he so wanted to keep the momentum of their affair going. With her away visiting friends for the weekend, he had some time to think things through, but he could not see how they could keep seeing each other once she was back if he had to be looking after the twins and if Claire had to go back into hospital with St John. He decided to phone Eleanor, but it went straight to Ansaphone. He decided against leaving a message in case anyone who should not hear it overheard it.

In the hospital, Doctor Shakti looked in concern at the tiny figure of St John Jackson lying in his cot, still connected to monitors. He sighed and turned to Nurse Billington.

"Any contact from his mother today?"

She looked at the notes in her hand and slowly shook her head. Doctor Shakti pursed his lips and thought for a few minutes.

"This little man needs some physical contact and affection. Have you tried phoning her?"

The nurse informed him that she had tried several times, but Claire's phone was turned off. Doctor Shakti looked angry.

"How could she? With her son in hospital? So vulnerable. I fear this little chap is at risk. Do we have the grandmother's number? I feel she has more connection with him than his mother does."

Nurse Billington looked through her notes and nodded.

"I will phone her and ask her to come in," she said.

Serena and Satish had spent the last hour discussing what they should do and had agreed that perhaps they should go and visit his family in the Midlands sooner than originally planned. Serena was reluctant to leave London while Claire was so helpless but realised that she needed some space from her. Satish phoned his cousin, Anish, in Birmingham, who was delighted that they would be visiting.

"It is a good thing you are coming, Satish. Mother is not good. She is very poorly. I fear she does not have long."

Serena had seen a picture of him, and he could have been Satish's twin. Anish continued

"And bring your lovely lady with you. I can't wait to make her acquaintance."

It was decided they would travel up on the Tuesday after Easter, giving them a whole day free on Easter Monday. With that decided, they went in search of a very late lunch.

Just as their meal arrived Serena's phone buzzed, and she hurriedly answered it when she saw it was the hospital. Nurse Billington's kind tones assured her that there was nothing wrong, but they would welcome a visit from Serena as Claire was unobtainable, and she felt some physical contact with St John would be beneficial. As Claire had not come in then perhaps Serena could give him some attention. In reality, Nurse Billington, with Doctor Shakti's backing, was going to share with Serena her concerns about Claire's lack of maternal feelings and ask what support Serena could give her. Serena said they would go straight over to the hospital once they had finished lunch.

Back in Twickenham Sebastian appeared back downstairs in the middle of the afternoon. Claire had sent the girls upstairs to tell him a roast dinner would be ready at about four o'clock, but he had got bored of trying to find things to do in his office. There was plenty he could do, but he was unsettled and angry at the day's events. He flopped into his favourite spot on the sofa and looked across at Claire, who had her nose in a glossy magazine, but who very obviously was not reading a word of it.

"So, what's your game plan now?"

He could not keep the anger out of his voice.

"What do you mean?" She continued looking at her magazine.

"Well, you have a baby in hospital…..."

"Oh hell!" she interjected. "I'd almost forgotten about him with all this going on. I suppose I should go in and see him."

She was surprised at her lack of guilty feelings. Taking her phone from her bag she switched it on and saw that the hospital had rung her ten times. Quickly she hit the recall button and got through to Nurse Billington, who sounded very frosty.

"Is everything okay?" Claire asked desperately.

Nurse Billington wanted to say "No. Everything is not okay. You obviously do not care a fig for your son, and you shouldn't be allowed anywhere near him."

But she could not say this. It was unprofessional. Instead, she forced herself to say

"He is alright. We are still monitoring him. We wondered if you were coming in today."

"Yes, yes I will. I've just had some domestic problems here. I'll be in about six."

Nurse Billington did not sound impressed with this but could not say anything.

"I'll be going off duty about then. I'll pass your notes to the next shift.", meaning that she would instruct them to observe Claire very carefully and see if there had been any improvement in her attitude to her son. She prayed that Serena would be in before then so she could have a chat with her. Otherwise, she might have to make a phone call to Social Services.

Once she had finished talking to Nurse Billington, Claire looked at her husband and asked if he would look after the girls and get them to bed whilst she visited the hospital.

"Of course," was his reply.

He felt frustrated that he would be tied to the house, but with Eleanor away he had nothing better to do. With that, he said he would check the meat. Without thinking he put his phone on the arm of the sofa. Claire went back to her magazine. A few minutes later his phone buzzed to say a message had come through. Claire leapt to her feet and grabbed the phone to read it. She had heard him going upstairs to the bathroom. It was from someone called Edward Evans. However, the message disappeared before she could read it and, knowing that he would know if she had opened the message, she decided to phone the number back. She had long ago worked out his passcode. Trembling she hit the dial button. Seconds later a husky American voice answered

"Well, Seb honey. That was quick. Success. The cottage is utterly divine. Room for two of us. A love nest if ever I saw one."

Claire did not need to hear any more than that.

"You slut. You are welcome to him!" she spat down the phone, hung up, and flung the phone across the room, where it smashed against the marble fireplace. Sebastian appeared a few minutes later but stopped in the doorway when he saw Claire's face, and his phone smashed in the fireplace.

"You utter bastard!" she snarled. "An ugly old American witch, eh? What an idiot I have been. You can pack your bags as well and piss off to her. Our marriage is over."

Sebastian took a deep breath and thought about going over to Claire and putting his arms around her and telling her she had got it wrong. From the look on her face, he knew that would not work. He had never seen such hatred on her face. Instead, he sighed deeply and sat down where he had been sitting not that long ago before the fateful message had ended his marriage.

"I'm sorry," he said limply. "You know we have not been getting on for some time. I just can't help myself. You know me and attractive women…."

He tried to make a joke but once again the pure hatred on Claire's face stopped him. He continued

"Well, maybe I should wait until you have St John back here. With your mother out of the way, it is not going to be easy. She might have been an oversexed randy old bat, but she was useful."

Claire's defences began to crumble, and she felt annoyed at his insulting tone. She wiped away tears angrily. Once again, all she wanted was for Serena to walk into the room and take charge again. Swallowing hard she took control of herself.

"I'll feed the girls. Then I'll go to the hospital. I don't want to stay there tonight though. I'll ask them how soon he can come home. Then, when he is back here, you can piss off to your American slut."

She got up and stormed out of the room.

After Serena and Satish had finished their meal, they decided that Serena would visit the hospital alone and Satish would start to make some plans to visit people in Birmingham who might be able to help with fundraising for their planned community in Sri Lanka. She felt so sad as she travelled in the taxi to the bright shining hospital. Her heart was aching for the little baby who so needed love but was so lacking it. When she arrived Nurse Billington took her into an office, ordered someone to get her a cup of tea, and shared her concerns about Claire and St John. Serena felt helpless and did not know what to say. Eventually, she had to admit that she had had an argument with her daughter that morning and she had moved out. The nurse went to put her head in her hands but pulled herself up as she knew it was unprofessional.

"I am so sorry. That makes it very awkward. Do you think you'll return there?"

Serena shrugged her shoulders.

"I said I would go back when she wants me to. But I'll not impose myself. However, I too am concerned about St John. It is as though Claire has forgotten about him. I'll go and give him some love."

"Thank you."

Nurse Billington wished to herself that Serena could take him with her, but continued

"He seems to be making improvements and I think he could soon be allowed to go home. But only if there is a bond developing between mother and son. We are very concerned about his welfare and whether he'll be neglected. I might even have to alert Social Services."

Serena went to the nursery, and the nurse on duty disconnected him from his monitors and handed him to Serena so she could hold him close to her. He looked up at her with his tiny, bright eyes and snuggled into her. He now looked normal, with chubby cheeks and the only hair left on him was fuzz on his head. Feelings of love and warmth swept through her, and she started to sing to him and rock him gently. He seemed to be happy with this and drifted off into a peaceful sleep. Serena continued crooning to him, realising with a growing sense of guilt that she felt more deeply for him than she had done for Claire when she was a baby. She fought back tears and cuddled him closer.

"Poor little mite. You have done no wrong. Come into the world just to be neglected and unloved. It is not your fault. I'm so sorry. I'll give you all the love I can, while I am here and while I can."

Serena suddenly became aware of someone standing behind her, and slowly turned, with the tiny baby snuggled up on her shoulder. Claire stood there, tears running down her face, having heard every word her mother had said to the tiny baby. Hesitantly she stepped forward and held out her arms for her son. Gingerly Serena passed him to her, and for a moment he woke but then sensing that love still surrounded him, went back to sleep. Claire had to fight her sobs as she did not want to wake him again and Serena put her arm around her and imagined light and warmth surrounding the three of them. For many minutes they stood as one unit, united in love. Nurse Billington appeared at the doorway but seeing the touching scene, hurried away. She had been delayed in leaving and had heard that Claire had arrived. Now she could leave her shift with a lighter heart.

The next shift of nurses came on and Claire and Serena were summoned to the ward office. Nurse Brown informed them that St John could probably go home mid-week. Claire was welcome to come back in to stay if she wished. She sighed deeply and said that would not be possible. Serena looked at her puzzled.

"I will explain later," Claire said to her, and then to the nurse

"Can he come home any sooner? I don't have cover for my girls."

The nurse studied her notes and said she would speak to the doctor in the morning.

"Mum. Can we talk?" Claire asked.

Serena was taken aback at the familiar term, which Claire never used. It was always "Mother".

"Of course."

They went to the café, but it was closed, so they had to hunt around to find a Costa Coffee that was open. Once Claire had a large latte in front of her and Serena had a flat white made with soya milk, Claire opened up.

"Sebastian is leaving. I am throwing him out. He has taken up with that rich American whore. I can't be doing with it anymore. He will wait until St John is home. I think he planned on leaving me to live with her anyway."

She told her mother about the message and phone call.

"And what is more, he didn't even try to deny it like he usually does. I cannot deal with his selfishness anymore. I realised tonight that I must focus on my children."

Serena inwardly breathed a sigh of relief at her positive feelings towards her children. She wondered about sharing with her daughter the fact that both she and Satish had thought he was having an affair but decided it would not be helpful. It would feel too much like scoring points. She took her daughter's hand and allowed her to save face and not have to beg her to come back.

"You know I am here if you want me. I will do whatever you want. I will come back if you want me to."

Claire had been too proud before to ask her mother to move back in, but relief flooded through her at this offer. Through her tears, Claire nodded and said she was so sorry for being so horrible to her and she would love her mother to move back in, and Satish was more than welcome to come back as well. Serena felt mixed. She had been excited at the thought of going to meet Satish's family and make plans for their return to Thailand, having felt so totally rejected by her daughter. Now she had to change her plans again.

'It must be my karma,' she told herself, but it did feel like she was going backwards. Once away from the house in Twickenham, she had realised just how oppressive and dysfunctional it was.

Finishing their coffees, they returned to their respective residences. Serena felt a deep sadness as she entered the hotel room and had to tell Satish of the change of her plans. He looked disappointed but told her she had to help her daughter. She was her priority. However, if she did not mind, he wanted to go to Birmingham to visit his family and would return to be with her as soon as possible. Serena blinked away tears, but he gently took her face in his hands and kissed them away, and then slowly his kisses found other parts of her body. As she willingly melted under them, she felt a dread that this was one of the last times they would be so lovingly intimate together. She felt everything was about to change.

FIFTEEN

Satish and Serena stayed another day at the hotel, giving themselves space to meditate and plan their next steps. Satish felt it right to go to Birmingham to see his aunt and cousin, and to catch up with old friends. Serena's heart ached at the thought of being apart but knew it had to be so for a while. Serena wanted the day never to end. Cocooned in their room, cuddled up in their bed, they felt safe from the world and the foreboding they both felt. They ventured out to a local Indian restaurant after exhausting the limited vegan menu at the hotel but hurried back as quickly as they could afterwards to a night of desperate passion. As they collected their room key, the expressions on the faces of the reception staff were a source of amusement as they tried to work out what was going on with this middle-aged white woman and her young Asian companion who seemed in such a rush to get to their room. Serena felt so young and alive, and Satish felt complete with the woman he loved by his side.

The following day they reluctantly took taxis in different directions. Embracing each other before they separated, they whispered their love to each other, but they both felt things were going to change from now on.

"I can't believe it's only two weeks ago we landed back here," Serena said sadly as she cradled Satish's face in her hands and looked deep into his eyes.

"I'm so sorry it has been so difficult for you, with my wacky family."

From their conversations, Serena knew that Satish was finding the atmosphere at Claire and Sebastian's increasingly difficult to cope with, and she felt that for the sake of their own relationship, he needed some space. Much as she dreaded being without him, she knew he had to go. His aunt was fading fast, and she knew he would never forgive himself if he did not go to her bedside before she passed from this world. His cousins had also told him some exciting news about possible funding for their community but would only tell him the details face to face.

Satish was feeling more and more estranged from the lively, passionate woman he had fallen in love with as he saw the concerns for her family drawing her away from him. He wondered if she would want to stay in England to support her family, or if she would reach a point where she just wanted to escape back to Thailand with him. Unusually for him, he felt a deep sense of unease in his spirit. Satish sighed deeply as his taxi headed northwards towards Euston station, desperately wishing Serena was by his side and they were heading to the airport to go home. This feeling only deepened as he got out of the taxi at Euston, had to queue to get his ticket, and fight his way onto an overcrowded and late train.

Serena looked out at the dull, grey landscape as her taxi wound its way back to Twickenham and she too longed for the warmth and happiness of Thailand. She wondered whether Satish would find solace in his family and not want to return to the mayhem of her family with all its problems and stresses. Would he even go back to Thailand without her?

Claire waited frantically for the arrival of her mother's taxi. Serena had texted her as she was leaving the hotel, and the next twenty minutes seemed forever, as she peered out of her living room window. The twins kept pestering her about when Serena and Satish were coming back and had been extra noisy and excitable, dancing round and round and crashing into things and breaking Claire's favourite vase. Sebastian had left early for work to be out of the way. A hurried phone call mid-morning from him at the office to Eleanor updated her on the seemingly ever-changing circumstances, but he told her that now he was going to be free to leave Claire, once Serena and St John were back home. He was worried by Eleanor's long silence after being given this news. When he eventually plucked up the courage to ask if everything was okay, she unconvincingly told him it was. The conversation felt stilted after that, and Sebastian began to feel a cold fear creeping into his heart. He began to wonder if she was cooling off.

Back in his home, the atmosphere was buzzing with anticipation.

"They're here!" Claire suddenly burst out as the taxi pulled up outside. Rushing to the front door, she opened it and both she and the twins ran out oblivious to the rain. Serena was paying the driver and turned to be embraced by her tearful daughter. Two excited little girls jumped up and down squealing with delight. Simultaneously they both stopped and looked puzzled.

"Where's Satish?"

Two pairs of worried blue eyes looked up at Serena.

"He has gone to see his cousin. He will be back soon."

The pouts on their faces sent a stab into her heart. She bent down and kissed each one of them.

"I'm going to miss him so much. You two are going to have to keep me busy so I don't get sad."

Immediately she wondered to herself what mischief they could get up to between them.

The house felt so empty without Satish. Even though he was quiet and generally tried to melt into the background, his strong and gentle presence was always felt, and now his absence was breaking Serena's heart.

A phone call from the hospital halfway through the morning confirmed that St John could come home later that day. There had been a conference between Doctor Shakti and the nursing staff, and they had decided that, if Serena could move back in with Claire, they would be happy to let the baby come home. Two more premature births had put enormous pressure on beds, so they were happy to let him go home. Claire confirmed to them that Serena was back with her, so they said she could collect St John that day if she wished. The hospital was also desperate for her to be with her son as quickly as possible after showing bonding with him at her last visit.

After lunch, Claire began to sort out baby clothes and spent time cleaning and tidying St John's nursery.

"Isn't he going to be in with you?" Serena asked tentatively.

"Oh! I suppose so to begin with. I want to get him into a routine as quickly as possible and into his own room. I did it with the girls, so I am going to do the same with him."

Serena felt a deep sadness at the clinical attitude Claire had towards her children. Claire picked up on this and continued

"After all, he is going to have a bottle so anyone can feed him."

Serena kept to herself the thought that Sebastian was not going to be around for much longer and she hated feeding bottles to babies. Sighing she felt her life was beginning to take her in a direction, not of her making. Thailand seemed such a long way away.

In the middle of the afternoon, Claire went to the hospital while Serena entertained the twins. She decided to show them some yoga postures and try to get them to meditate for a few minutes, hoping it might be something to calm them down. However. the sense of calm quickly evaporated when a taxi pulled up outside and Claire got out carrying St John in a carrycot.

"Mummy and Monkey are here," shrieked Abigail.

Olivia started jumping around the living room making monkey noises, and Abigail joined in. Serena reprimanded them, a little more severely than she intended to, so the girls quickly stopped. Serena opened the front door and helped her daughter in with her grandson. He was wide awake and looking normal. The twins peered in at him.

"Have they swapped the monkey for a proper baby?" asked Olivia.

Claire gritted her teeth and then snapped

"He is not a monkey. He never has been a monkey. He never will be a monkey. So, stop saying that."

However, the twins had realised that this was a way to wind their mother up, so they kept making quiet monkey noises as their mother carried their baby brother through to the living room. They looked on with disgust as Claire changed his dirty nappy on a changing mat on the living room floor.

"Don't like boys. They are ugly," pontificated Abigail as she looked at his little naked bottom.

"Girls is better. They don't have dangly bits on their bottoms."

Serena and Claire looked at each other. They realised they had a hard task ahead of themselves to get the twins to accept their baby brother.

Serena spent much of the rest of the afternoon cuddling St John. She was overwhelmed by the maternal feelings that flooded her body, emotions, and mind. With some guilt, she realised she saw echoed in Claire's brusque and clinical mothering the way she had mothered Claire. Then she remembered the cold and clinical mothering she had received when she was a small child. Tears filled her eyes as she realised the joys and warmth that she had missed in her relationship with her own daughter. All the feelings she should have had for her daughter she now had for her grandson. Kissing his little fuzzy head, she vowed she would love him and protect him and fill in where her daughter was lacking.

She thought again of her own mother, whom she had not seen for twenty-five years. Her parents had disowned her when she got pregnant and even though she married Roger, she was still considered an outcast. Occasionally she got news about her mother through her cousin, who had lived in the same small Gloucestershire village where they had moved to when Serena was ten. The only contact between Serena and her mother was when her father died two years ago and Serena got the news through a curt email message from her mother, which also told Serena not to bother coming back for the funeral. It appeared that her cousin gave news both ways, as her mother knew she was in Thailand and had her email address. The pain of the estrangement of her mother was the one wound that had not yet been healed and Serena wondered if it ever would. She mused about contacting her mother and seeking her forgiveness and trying to rebuild their relationship. She looked at the twins, who were now happily drawing and colouring, and again felt a flood of maternal feelings. True they were exhausting and could be rude and undisciplined but looking at their little blonde heads bent over their colouring books, Serena suddenly felt she did not want to be anywhere else in the world at that moment. With a start, she suddenly realised she had not thought about Satish at all for at least an hour. A sudden deep sadness came over her as she remembered once again that she and Satish would never have children together, although she knew he would love to be a father. However, she no longer wanted to bear children and her early menopause made it impossible. She was completely content to be a grandmother to her grandchildren, and through them feel the joy of raising children which she had never felt before. She realised that here she felt complete and sighed a deep, contented sigh. Claire, who had been sorting out a bag of new baby clothes, suddenly looked over at her mother and asked

"You okay Mum?"

Serena smiled at this rarely used name.

"Yes. I am okay thanks. I am more than okay."

Claire could not believe the serene, beaming face of her mother who earlier that day had seen the man she loved disappear, not knowing when he would be back. Once again, she felt that she could not understand her strange but beguiling mother.

SIXTEEN

Eleanor Ellis, also known as Susanna Sanchez, but whose real name was Rachel Robertson, and a multi-millionairess, snapped her phone shut and stared at the plush wallpaper on her hotel bedroom wall.

"Damn it!" she snarled and chucked the phone on her bed and went over to the window.

Pulling back the net curtain she opened the window wide enough to puff smoke out of, lit a cigarette, and perched on the windowsill, watching the traffic below. She had never left the hotel as she had told Sebastian she would be doing. She had not gone to Oxford to meet friends. Instead, she had stayed in London to have a quick and what she had hoped to be a passionate date with a budding young artist who wanted to paint her in the nude, thus ticking off another item on her bucket list. The idea of posing in the nude had been one of her fetishes. She soon cooled off from the idea when he spent most of the time that they were in bed together creepily staring at her, and muttering on about skin tones, and did she fancy being painted in a cubist or surrealist style.

However, the main motive for staying in her hotel was to do some research on Sebastian's firm and make sure that he was the right man to sting. He did not remember meeting her when she was working under the name of Susanna Sanchez. She was the classy brunette waitress in the upmarket wine bar, who served him and his drunk and loud office colleagues when they celebrated a birthday four months ago. How easy it had been to listen in to their conversation and work out where they worked, what they did, and then get their details from their credit cards. She had then phoned their office to make an appointment to speak to someone about investments under the name of Eleanor Ellis, and posing as a rich American heiress who wanted to settle in England. Sebastian had been the person who answered her preliminary calls and was therefore assigned to handle her as a client. He had been almost too easy to seduce. She had then set about her plans to scam him.

Now, this latest phone call from Sebastian had blown all her plans. Things were moving too quickly. True, she had dangled before him the love nest cottage which she supposedly wanted to buy, but it did not exist. It had all been part of her plan. However, she was depending on him staying with his wife until she had completed the first sting. It would be a small amount, to begin with, to soften him up before the big one. She would tell him that her bank card had temporarily been giving problems and she would ask him to lend her a couple of hundred pounds. Paying it back almost immediately would gain his trust. Then she would sting him for the big amount. She already had the story lined up. After putting in her offer on the cottage, someone else would be offering a higher amount for it, and she could not pay the deposit quickly enough to secure it. It would take a couple of days for her money to be released from America and she would be in danger of losing the cottage if she did not pay her deposit immediately. She had done her research on Sebastian's company and had a shrewd idea of the sort of salary he was receiving. He could probably fund her to about sixty thousand pounds short-term. It would be less than a month's salary. She had already skimmed his credit and debit card with a small portable card copier she always carried with her, and her eagle eyes had noted his pins when he flamboyantly used them to wine and dine her.

Throwing her cigarette end out of the window, she went back to bed and took her iPad out of its case. She went to type in Sebastian's bank account but then remembered that he would see if she had been online to check his account. An expert hacker, she had already worked out Sebastian's log-in details for most of his accounts but had refrained from accessing them until the time was right. However, there was one offshore account she had not managed to find the details of, and she believed it was where he kept the majority of his money stashed. She needed to chase Dwayne to see if he had made the cloned bank cards yet, so she could check Sebastian's bank balance at an ATM.

Pursing her lips, she thought a bit longer. A smile crept across her face. Tapping a number into her phone, she leant back against the plump pillows on the bed. The call took some time to be answered, and when it was, the line was crackly and poor.

"Eleanor! What do you want?" a male voice at the other end snapped.

"Oh, now then. What a way to greet your favourite sugar pie."

She put on her ultra-sexy Southern drawl. "Don't be like that with me, Randy."

"Wait a minute. I will go out of the office."

She could hear doors opening and then the sound of traffic.

"Right." His tone was brusque. "What?"

"Well, honey, I could do with a few more Airmiles… on my Sanchez account."

"No! No more. I nearly got caught before putting them on your other account. I could lose my job."

"Aww! Sweetie pie you are my only hope. I need to go to Europe. I only need five thousand miles. All you have to do is to go tap tap on a few keys on your computer…."

"I told you Eleanor I am through with this. No. More."

Eleanor's tone changed. Hardened.

"And how's Sally-Anne doing? Out of her wheelchair yet?"

She heard a sharp intake of breath at the other end.

"You bitch. You know the damage is permanent."

His wife had had a car accident three months after he had met Eleanor in a hotel bar in Texas and they had ended up back in his room. A passionate affair had ignited between them until Sally-Anne had her accident. Ever since then every time Eleanor wanted to travel, she phoned him at his company, which dealt with Airmiles, to demand more miles be put on her accounts, or she would send Sally-Anne the recordings she had made of their lovemaking in the various motels they met up in during their affair.

"Only five thousand miles and I won't trouble you ever again."

"You said that last time."

"Did I?" She tried to sound innocent but knew deep down she was pushing the boundaries. Last time he had told her he was going to come clean with Sally-Anne about Eleanor and put it down to being seduced when he was drunk and lonely on a business trip. Enough time might have passed now that she would unhappily accept it. She relied on him for his care for her and financial support.

By the huffing and puffing from the other end of the phone, she knew Randy was debating what to do.

"Well?" she asked.

Eventually. he replied "OK. The last time. All right? And I am going to tell Sally-Anne about us. I know it will break her heart, but she needs me. It'll be tough, but I know she won't throw me out. Anything to get you out of my hair."

"What hair?" she sniped, knowing that his baldness was a sore point with him.

"You bitch."

"Yap yap. Just do it. My Sanchez account. Or Sally-Anne will find out sooner rather than later."

"They'll be on your account just as soon as I get back into my office. Now, piss off and I never want to hear from you again."

The line went dead.

The next call was to Dwayne who confirmed he had made the cards and could meet her later that day with them.

Going to her wardrobe and taking her suitcase out of it, she opened it and found the two fake passports, one in the name of Eleanor Ellis and the other in the name of Susanna Sanchez, a long, brunette wig and a small case with coloured contact lenses. Opening the one for Susanna Sanchez she sighed and looked long and hard at the photo of a brown-eyed, brunette woman.

Running her hand through her hair, she sighed.

"I do so prefer blonde. It is the real me after all."

Susanna Sanchez's passport showed stamps in and out of Mexico City, Madrid, Houston, and Los Angeles. Her backstories were either as the fictional daughter of a large cattle rancher, who had ranches across Mexico and Texas, or as the Spanish waitress with fake study and work papers, who worked to fund her wanderlust. Smiling Eleanor saw the last stamps on her passport – out of Madrid and into Los Angeles.

"Time to be Susanna again."

She flopped back on her bed and dialled a number.

Oscar Ramirez was slumped back in his chair with his feet on his desk, looking out of the window at the baking Madrid sunshine. Tapping his teeth with his pen, he pondered again about how he was going to reach his crime targets. Everything had been working against him lately and it seemed every time he thought he was going to have a successful lead or an arrest, it slipped out of his fingers at the last moment. His boss had once again made veiled threats about "employees need to show they are worth their salary" and "we can't keep on missing targets" and reminding him of threatened cuts to staff numbers. He used to be so quick and ahead of his game. Lately, things had plummeted. He was sinking into a depression and once in it, he knew he would be completely unable to function again, just as he was a year ago. Carmen, his wife, was pregnant again and with two children under four, life at home was hectic and exhausting. His wife believed he worked in an export business, rather than as a risky crime fighter, and was earning just enough to keep them, whilst in fact on his high salary, he was piling money into a savings account, intending to retire early and enjoy life. However, he was worried that before then his double life would catch up with him. Maybe it was time to get out of this job and come clean and find work that was not so stressful.

His personal mobile rang and made him jump. He stared at the number in disbelief and quickly answered it.

"Hola Querido. Como estas?"

The Spanish was fluent with a twang of an American accent, but the pronunciation of the Spanish was Latin American.

"Susanna! I am good thanks. Where are you?" He tried to keep his voice steady.

"I am planning to come to Madrid in a couple of weeks. I have the 3,000 Euros which you lent me. Thank you so much. I completed my course but had some family issues to deal with. That's why I disappeared so suddenly."

"Don't mention it. I look forward to seeing you."

He leant back in his chair and remembered the amazing nights he had had with her, with her believing he was Eduardo Solares, an affluent businessman, who had taken a fancy to the high-class waitress who had served him in a five-star hotel restaurant where he was dining with his cousin, planning his uncle's seventieth birthday party.

She had been on the radar for a while as a potential fraudster and he was assigned to her case. Little did he know then that she had already been at work on his uncle, having met him at the same hotel two weeks previously when he had visited with some old work colleagues. He had initially kept from his nephew the fact that he had been sleeping with one of the waitresses, who then went on a month later to max out his credit card and disappear. His shame was so deep that it was several weeks before he admitted it to his family and by then the trail had gone cold, especially as he had never found out her name. Oscar had then realised that this waitress and the increasingly notorious fraudster Susanna Sanchez were the same, and it had been a shock to him, having lent her the money to "do some studying" which she said she would repay when she got a pay rise. Oscar had lent Susanna the money with the blessing of his boss, hoping to reel her in as they knew her usual modus operandi. They knew that she would ask for a small loan, repay it and then swindle a larger amount once her victim had begun to trust her. He had therefore thought she would be around for a while and was going to catch her out on her big sting. However, suddenly she had sent him a note to say she had to go away unexpectedly but would be back in touch. Now it appeared at least this part was true. It also appeared that she had no idea that Eduardo Solares/Oscar Ramirez and Juan de la Rosa, the old man she had swindled, were related.

The distant voice continued

"I'm probably going to be visiting Italy first. I'll contact you when I know my flight details."

"I'll have my driver meet you at the airport."

"Gracias. Hasta luego."

In London Susanna Sanchez, or Eleanor Ellis in her London persona, leaned back on her pillows and started fantasizing about nights with Eduardo again, and how she was going to give him back his money but then sting him again for much more. She did not need the money. As a genuine heiress, she had more than enough money to keep her in luxury. It was the adrenaline and loneliness that made her live her triple life. It was a much more exciting life than living alone in a huge mansion, trying to fill empty days with luxuries and vacuous social events. It was also cold-blooded revenge against all men who were being made to pay for the treatment she had received from her husbands, all of whom had been gaslighting narcists, and who had paraded her as a "trophy wife." However, she was beginning to get weary of trying to remember who she was in various people's lives. It was exhausting trying to keep up with different personae and each time she did a sting, although highly elated initially, she felt very deflated afterwards. Maybe after her trip to Spain, she would revert to who she really was – Rachel Robertson, and maybe buy the mountaintop ranch in Colorado she had had her eye on for many years. She would then spend her time painting landscapes and riding her piebald stallion who was currently on loan to a friend.

Meanwhile in Madrid, Oscar Ramirez sat with his mobile phone on his paunch staring into space, with a massive grin on his face, unable to believe his luck. He leaned forward and dialled from his office phone.

Esteban Vallejos, chief of Fraud Detection and Money Laundering in the Madrid office of Interpol, answered his phone on the second ring.

"Si? Oscar?"

"Hi, Boss. You will never guess who is returning to her own vomit?"

He waited with a dramatic pause, before continuing.

"La Perra. The Bitch."

Oscar could tell from the exhalation of breath at the other end of the phone that he too was stunned.

"And this time, Ramirez, you are not to let her get away again. You had her under surveillance for long enough before getting into bed with her. Which was right out of order and beyond the call of duty. Then she flitted. Still don't know why."

"Don't forget that my alter ego, Senor Solares, has a driver who will pick her up from the airport. And I will be ready and waiting for her."

For the first time that day Esteban Vallejos smiled.

"Well done. She is not in the bag yet, but I am hopeful."

After they had rung off, Oscar leaned back in his chair and smiled to himself. Things were not so bad now. He quite enjoyed the thrill and danger of the chase, something his wife would not understand, and if she knew, would spend every day worried sick until he arrived home at night. She certainly would not understand his wish to stop via a small, secluded hotel to reacquaint himself with Susanna before arresting her. However, that might just have to stay in his fantasies as he knew he could not risk her escaping justice once again.

SEVENTEEN

Sebastian appeared at about six o'clock and made suitably paternal noises over his son. He did not offer to pick him up when he was crying but stood looking helplessly at his bawling son. Serena quickly picked him up and started crooning to him. Immediately, he snuggled into her neck and started trying to suck it.

Serena noticed that Sebastian had a lighter air about him, and he spent much of his time gazing into thin air. She mused that maybe he was planning his exit from his family. This was exactly what he was doing. A quick session earlier on his laptop had transferred money from a savings account in the joint account and a regular monthly standing order was set up to cover more than enough housekeeping money. With the house already in Claire's name for financial reasons, he hoped that the divorce would be quick and smooth. Claire and the children would be more than taken care of, so she would have nothing to complain about. It was as he was thinking of all this that a sudden cold fear gripped him. How would Roger react? In his whirlwind affair, he had not for one moment stopped to think that he was going to abandon his business partner's daughter and family.

"Shiiiiit!" he muttered to himself.

"Pardon?" said Serena, who was sitting sorting laundry for Claire with one hand whilst rocking St John in her other arm.

"Nothing," he replied quickly. "Just forgot something."

He hurried up to his office and flopped down in his luxurious leather swivel chair and put his feet up on the footstool.

"Shiiiiiiiittttt!" he muttered again.

Surely Roger would understand. He too had walked out on his family, but in Sebastian's case it was more complicated as it was the same family but at a different stage in life. Roger only had one child when he left Jayne/Serena. Claire had been five years old. Sebastian had three children, all under five years old. However, Roger knew how difficult Claire could be. Sebastian would blame the pressure of having Serena around for making him have an affair, as well as Claire's frigidity. He would make them both the culprits. Nevertheless, he still had a nagging worry that Roger might put family loyalty above their business partnership and make life exceedingly difficult for him. What if Roger cut him out of the business? Roger had slightly more invested in it and had the casting vote in any decisions. He then started to think about his own parents. His father, in his role as a Bishop, wanted to ensure his grandson was going to be baptised, and he and Sebastian's mother were due to visit within the next few weeks to discuss the baptism and to see the baby. He knew they would disown him totally, especially if it came to light that he had run off with a thrice-divorced woman. He could imagine his parents cutting him out of their wills and leaving it to their grandchildren, as he had no siblings. They had always liked Claire, after initially branding her as a "hussy" for falling pregnant before marriage. His father had to maintain strict moral codes within his family, and this was why he had insisted on Sebastian marrying Claire. Suddenly Sebastian's financial security felt very insecure. He began to wonder if he was rushing into things and if he should slow down with his exit from his home. The thought of staying with Claire and the "Brats" filled him with immense gloom. Her frigidity (although maybe her mother could teach her a thing or two now!) and permanent state of exhaustion did not bode well for his sex life. Gradually his mood sank lower and lower as he consumed more whiskey,

"Bloody hell. I feel like I'm in prison," he muttered to himself.

His mood immediately lightened when his phone rang, and he saw who the caller was.

"Hi." He tried to sound casual, whilst his heart was racing. "I was just thinking of you."

"Hi Honey. How's things? Any chance of us taking a little trip to Rome in a couple of weeks' time – my treat for your wonderful financial advice?"

"That would be amazing. The old bat has moved back in so I can't wait to get away from here."

There was heavy breathing down the phone.

"I can't wait. I am back from Oxford tomorrow. I will be back in my hotel by five. If you want afternoon tea…."

"Ooooo yes. With my pinkie raised…."

She burst out laughing.

"Aw you Brits……. Afternoon tea in my room it is. Until then…."

Sebastian hung up and smiled. He decided he would have to prepare the ground with Roger before leaving Claire, telling him how difficult she was and very uncooperative in the bedroom. Roger was a man who was driven by his sex drive and would understand, so would not condemn Sebastian for looking elsewhere. Regarding his parents, he would drop hints during their visit about just how awful his marriage was and how miserable it made him feel. This would be followed by a couple of emotional phone calls to his usually doting mother about how unbearable Claire was now and how desperately depressed it made him feel, to the point of feeling like "doing something silly". This might be enough to allay too severe a reaction when he did leave. However, his parents must not know he was moving straight out into another woman's bed. On reflection, he did not fancy living in a hotel. Part of the excitement of their affair was meeting in the hotel. Living there would be hugely different. Maybe he should wait until she got her cottage, and they could continue with the excitement of their affair in the meantime. The next hurdle was to mend fences with Claire, who was now expecting him to move out soon. Sighing he wobbled to his feet and gingerly made his way downstairs to find Claire and Serena in the kitchen preparing dinner. The girls had eaten and were watching a DVD in their bedroom. Sebastian sauntered into the kitchen and much to Claire's surprise and bemusement planted a kiss on the top of her head.

"Dinner smells good," he said.

Claire looked at him suspiciously and moved away from him, still managing to stir the sauce on the stove. Serena looked aghast.

He sat down tentatively on the kitchen bar stool and looked at Claire.

"I don't realise just how lucky I am. I'm a fool. Why do I mess about with other women when all I need is right here, in my own home? I am so sorry. Please forgive me. I have phoned her and finished it. I will ask someone else in the office to take her portfolio over. Will you forgive me?"

He gave Serena a look which made it obvious that he did not want her in the room. She stopped chopping the vegetables and made her excuse, saying she would check on St John who was asleep in his cot. However, she went and sat in the living room, feeling extremely ill at ease, and tried meditating. She did not trust Sebastian and felt it was just another of his ploys. She was not surprised when, half an hour later, he and Claire appeared in the living room, his arm around her. Claire told Serena that he had come to his senses and apologised for his appalling behaviour. He wanted to stay. He was done with having affairs. He wanted to be with his wonderful family.

He then asked Serena to forgive him for his attitude towards her and Satish, asking if they could start again. Serena felt deceit and negative energy swirling around him but could do nothing but accept his apology and agree to wipe the slate clean. All the time he kept his arm around his wife and somehow it looked and felt wrong.

"Let's celebrate. I will get some bubbly."

He tottered off to sort it out.

Serena looked straight at Claire. "Is he for real? Do you believe him?"

Claire sighed and sat down next to her mother on the sofa.

"Mum. I don't know what to do. I've been here so many times with him. Apologies, make-up – but I am not going to get pregnant this time – but then he does it all again. I just don't know."

She put her head in her hands and sighed deeply.

Serena put her arm around her daughter.

"Only you can know what you want."

"That's the problem. I don't know what I want. Part of me just wants to see the back of him. But the thought of being a single parent with three under five-year-olds……"

"But I am here," interjected Serena.

Claire looked her mother direct in the eye.

"But for how long? No doubt once Satish comes back, you'll both be off again. I'll just have to hope that this is the last time he is playing his games. But I have been here so many times before and it has always been one lie after another. Has he really come to his senses? We can only wait and see."

Sebastian's reappearance with a bottle of champagne and three glasses cut short their conversation. Serena decided she would not cause any ill-feeling by refusing the drink but asked for just a small glass. As he handed round the glasses and toasted the future, he beamed at them both.

"Oh. While I think of it. I have a business trip to Rome coming up in a couple of weeks."

Satish's journey to Birmingham had been difficult. He hated the crowded train and the man next to him shouting into his phone. Noise, negative emotions, bad smells, and the occasional sideways glance at him had made him feel extremely uncomfortable and once again he longed for the tranquillity of Thailand. Cows on the line stopping the train for half an hour did not add to his mood. Trying to withdraw into himself and meditate proved fruitless as he was sitting on an aisle seat and was constantly being battered by passing passengers or deafened by the man shouting into his phone. Eventually, the train disgorged its passengers at New Street Station and Satish was immensely relieved to see the familiar face of Anish peering impatiently at the disembarking passengers. They greeted each other with a long hug.

"Satish. Having a lady in your life is doing you well."

Anish stood back and looked his cousin up and down.

"You look happy."

"Normally, yes I am. Except when travelling by train. And…. things are not easy where we are staying. But enough of me. How are you?"

With a hesitancy in his voice, Anish replied

"Mama is not too good. We fear she is nearing the end. Would you mind if we went straight to the hospital? I can take you home if you would rather. But…. I fear we do not have long…"

The two cousins chatted as Anish led them out of the station and to where he had parked his car. Satish insisted they went straight to the hospital and ten minutes later they were parked and making their way to the ward. Satish's aunt and Anish's mother lay unconscious with an oxygen mask around her face. A slim dark-haired young woman was holding her hand, and although she had her head bowed, she had clearly been weeping. Tears could be seen on the tops of her cheeks. There was something familiar about her. The round of her back, a mole on her neck, and the shape of her ears. Satish's heart skipped a beat as she turned a tear-stained face to them.

"Shanthi!" he exclaimed.

She looked at him in total surprise.

"Sati. My god. How different you are."

She stood and they quickly embraced. He held her at arm's length and looked her up and down. He remembered the last time he had seen her. She had a tear-stained face then. She was eight years old, as he was then, and about to leave the beachside house she had always called home to move from Sri Lanka to England with her family, only to be followed two years later by Anish's family. He remembered watching her as she climbed into the battered car that was taking her family to the airport, and waving until it disappeared, and then spending the rest of the morning staring down the road, willing her to return. Every day for a week he had returned to the same spot. Watching. Waiting. Praying for her return. As Satish's second cousin, she and he had spent their childhood together, running naked up and down the beach and plunging, laughing, in and out of the sea, trying to catch fish or scampering up coconut trees. He also remembered that they had been betrothed to each other as young children but that that betrothal was broken when Shanti's father moved his family to England, and the letters between the families became fewer and fewer until they had stopped altogether. As he thought of this now, he felt his face burning. Hurriedly he looked away and at his aunt.

"How is she?"

Shanthi sat back down and took the old lady's hand again.

"Fading. We have said our prayers and made offerings."

As if in affirmation of this, the old lady stirred slightly and made a grunting noise. Satish and Anish pulled up chairs and sat down. Shanthi looked at Satish again.

"I can't believe you're here. I thought I would never see you again. When Anish said you were coming, I thought he was teasing me. I thought you were still in Thailand."

"No. It is a long story. I am here for a few weeks, maybe a few months. I don't know yet."

Shanthi looked him up and down and then suddenly noticed the thin silver ring on his hand.

With a slight crack in her voice, she asked

"Are you married now?"

Satish hesitated. He was not sure how to describe his status. Although having declared his commitment to Serena, it was not a legal marriage as such, and the relationship was always on the understanding that this commitment might have to change due to spiritual forces or changed circumstances beyond their control. Karma, at any time, could force them to part. Ruefully he replied

"Not exactly. More promised to someone."

Shanthi forced a smile and said

"Congratulations."

A change in his aunt's breathing brought their focus back to the bed. Her breathing became rattling, and Anish went to look for a nurse.

"And how about you Shan? How are you?"

She turned a sad face to him.

"Anish's family have been good to me. After Papa died two years ago, they let me move in with them. Mama died ten years ago. My sister Chandrika married an English man and moved down to London last year.

She's away on holiday at the moment. She doesn't know about Mammy. That's what I call her."

She looked lovingly at the old woman and stroked her hand.

"She has been like a mother to me. I work in the hospital in the admin department. Anish has told me a bit about you from time to time. How you're getting famous in spiritual circles."

She gave him an admiring smile. A sudden increase in rattling sounds cut short the conversation. Anish reappeared with a nurse who immediately checked the old lady over. Sadly, she shook her head.

"Prepare yourselves. It will not be long now."

Satish's aunt, Anish's mum, and Shanthi's Mammy died twenty minutes later

EIGHTEEN

Serena awoke the next morning and for a moment had forgotten she was alone in her bed. The bedclothes had scrunched up next to her in the night and as she sleepily reached out across the bed, she was shocked to find the heap was empty. Satish was not there. A sudden hollow aching filled her heart and body. Fighting back tears she got up and pulled on her yoga pants and tee shirt to do her morning ritual and crept downstairs to the dining room.

As she sat in the sunlight humming to herself, she found the whole ritual empty and meaningless without Satish with her. Tears slid down her cheeks and she wiped her eyes. Trying to refocus on her ritual, she heard the dining-room door creak open behind her. The twins quietly came in and sat down, each one on either side of her. Olivia looked at Serena's tear-filled eyes and said

"We wants to do your morning thing too."

Abigail added

"Cos Satish isn't here to do it with you."

Serena smiled through her tears and put her arms around each of the little girls and squeezed them.

"Thank you," she whispered. "I would love you to join me."

Together they sat in the early morning sun, crossed-legged, eyes shut, heads back, humming a single note. Afterwards, Serena showed them some easy yoga poses. Just as Serena was showing them a downward-facing dog pose Claire came in, St John tucked in her arm.

"What do you think you are doing?" she asked irritated.

"We's keeping Serena happy."

"We's learning yoghurt."

"I think you mean yoga. And Mother I don't want you filling their head with any of your stupid *woo woo* stuff. They are far too young."

"Satish was three when he first started yoga. The younger they start the better," Serena replied, stinging from her daughter's rebuff.

Once again Serena felt the ache of missing him.

"We liked it," Abigail interjected. "Yoghurt stops people being cross."

"Yoga," Claire snapped.

"I think Mummy needs yoga 'cos she is always a grumpy pants," sulked Olivia.

"Olivia! Don't you dare talk about me like that! I will smack your bottom if you are not careful," Claire snapped at her daughter.

St John started crying at the sudden angry voice next to his ear. Claire shot an angry look at Serena and turned away to take the baby away to calm him down.

"Go and brush your teeth," she ordered the girls.

Olivia crossed her arms and put her head down into a deeper sulk. Serena gave the girls a rueful smile and gently suggested they did as their mother told them, and she would show them some more yoga later as she was going to look after the twins while Claire went for a medical check-up with St John. As the girls scampered out of the room Serena sighed and once again felt the emptiness in her heart, missing Satish. She wondered how she would bear their being apart and started visualising him coming back quickly. She also wondered if she had made a mistake coming back to Claire's house, especially now that Sebastian was appearing to want to be the family man.

In Birmingham, Satish was also feeling lonely and bereft. No longer used to awaking alone in his bed, he ached for Serena's warm embrace. Over the distance, he felt her longing too. Exhausted physically, emotionally, and spiritually he felt something he had not felt for more years than he could remember. A cloud of heavy depression was descending on him as he remembered the previous evening.

There had been a mourning wake held at Anish's house immediately after his mother's death and Satish had found himself sitting on the settee, wrapping his arms around Shanthi as she sobbed onto his chest. He had suddenly become aware of her trembling body and how she had grown into a very desirable woman. She was no longer the little girl he had innocently played with so many years ago. Had things gone as originally planned he would have been married to her by now and probably a father of several children. He had not wanted to push her away in her grief, but he had begun to feel uncomfortable and had tried to keep his mind focussed on Serena, willing his body not to respond to Shanthi. It had been a struggle.

As he reflected on this in the hard morning light, it was a harsh realisation that he still could be unfaithful despite all the inner work he had done on himself. This realisation was adding to his feeling of hopelessness, but he decided he needed to fight against it, so he got up and began his morning ritual. It felt empty without Serena by his side, but he persevered and felt more at peace with himself by the end of it. Once dressed he went down to the kitchen where the family was congregated. Anish was sombre, and Shanthi was red-eyed from crying most of the night. She lowered her eyes when Satish entered, and he saw a slight colour rising in her cheeks. Anish filled them in with funeral plans and told them several other cousins were due to arrive. Food had to be prepared and beds found for the night, so the three began what seemed to be endless preparations to say farewell to a woman they all loved so deeply.

It was halfway through the morning before Satish realised he had not spoken to Serena since his arrival. His dark mood descended again as a stab of guilt entered his heart. Excusing himself from the preparations he hurried to his room and phoned

Serena. His mood immediately lifted when he heard her voice.

"Beloved," he said. "How are you?" I am so sorry I haven't phoned. Auntie died last night. It has been non-stop since then."

"Missing you," a trembly voice replied. "I'm so sorry about your aunt. I miss you so much it hurts."

"I know. I feel the same. I'll be busy with the funeral and with family here for a while, but I want to be back as soon as I can."

"I must go. I can hear Claire screaming at the girls. I think they have done something. Not sure what but Claire is really shouting at them. Must go. I love you. Speak later."

"I love you too." Satish felt heavy-hearted as he rang off and prepared himself mentally to re-enter the frantic preparations for the arrival of the extended family.

Serena was in her room when she answered Satish's call and she could hear Claire screaming at the girls in their bedroom. Hesitantly Serena went to their bedroom and peered around the door. The sight that confronted her made her immediately want to burst out laughing but also made her feel extremely guilty.

Claire was standing just inside the door with her back to Serena, her hair scraped up into a bun on her head, so Serena could see the tips of her ears were bright red, showing she was extremely angry. The twins were both sitting cross-legged in the middle of the floor with fearful faces but also trying to suppress giggles at their mother's rage. Abigail had Claire's dressmaking scissors in her hand. Piles of blonde hair lay around them. Bright marker pens lay strewn around the floor. Both girls now had very ragged short haircuts that vaguely imitated Serena's haircut. To make matters worse they had coloured each other's hair with rainbow-coloured marker pens. Serena held her breath.

"But we wants to be like Serena," said Olivia defiantly. "She's not a grumpy pants. She is fun and nice."

Serena then noticed the snaking marker pen lines drawn crudely around the bottom of Olivia's legs and halfway up them and wondered if Claire had noticed them yet. She decided that, as none of the others had seen her, she would slip away quietly and return to the sanctuary of her room and wait for the fall-out.

It was not long before Claire was hammering on her door. Reluctantly Serena opened it to find a furious-looking Claire and two sheepish-looking girls standing outside.

"Look. Just look. This is what you have made them do!"

Claire pointed angrily at the girls.

"What the hell am I supposed to do with them now? This is all your fault. I can't take them back to ballet looking like this."

Serena thought she saw the brief glimpses of smiles on the girls' faces as they suppressed their giggles, but they quickly looked brow-beaten again as Claire spun around and glared at them.

"I'm sorry," Serena began.

"Sorry!" Claire shouted. "Sorry. All you have done is caused chaos since you have come back. God how I wish I had my old mother back. I have somehow got to get this marker pen off them and get them to the hairdresser to get a proper cut."

Claire turned and started to push the girls back towards their room, but they both turned and gave Serena a big smile and blew quick kisses at her. Serena smiled back and retreated to her room.

"Oh Satish," she sighed "What have we come back to? I do wish you were here."

Sebastian went to the office but just after midday told his staff he had an external meeting. Shortly after he was slipping between the sheets in Eleanor's suite, ready to make up for lost time. She had been a little cool with him at first, but suddenly her attitude changed, and she was all over him again. She had been doing some deep thinking as she was worried things were moving too fast, but her steel resolve had kicked in and she had her plans ready for her sting. After a couple of hours of passionate lovemaking, she got up from the bed and looked at her phone.

"Damn!" she said.

Turning back towards Sebastian, who was lying flat out exhausted, she smiled at him sweetly and said

"Honey. Could you lend me a couple of hundred pounds until tomorrow? My bank card has played up again and I need to make a cash payment today for something. I need to transfer some money to my other account and then I can pay you back straight away."

Sebastian sighed and heaved himself upright.

"Of course. Pass me my jacket."

Without hesitation, he opened his wallet and peeled off four fifty-pound notes.

"No rush to return it."

As he lay back down again, he reflected on how much more he had had to pay out for high-class women in the past who had not given him anything like the experiences that Eleanor had given him. It was money well spent.

Serena decided that she would stay out of Claire's way and spent the morning meditating in her room. Claire hammered on her door at midday and said she was taking St John for his check-up later that afternoon and could she look after the twins and not cause any trouble. Like a naughty child, Serena emerged from her room with a downcast face. Inwardly she knew she had done nothing wrong but felt Claire did not need her standing up to her. As she had meditated it became clear to her that Claire was on a knife-edge. The traumatic birth, possible post-baby blues, dealing with the twins and the ongoing shenanigans with Sebastian were all causing more stress to someone who was already highly strung. As she raised her head Serena saw that Claire's eyes were red-rimmed from crying. Without hesitation, she put her arms around her daughter and pulled her close. Initially, Claire tried to resist but then melted into her arms and started to sob again.

"Their hair was so pretty. I don't know how I am going to get it looking nice again. And Seb will go insane."

Serena stroked her daughter's hair and said

"It'll grow again. There is no long-term harm done. Shall I take them to the hairdresser while you are out with St John?"

Pulling back and snivelling, Claire nodded.

Serena continued "Okay. Tell the girls to get ready. Shall I ring round some places?"

Again, Claire nodded and wiped her eyes.

The hairdresser had to hide a smirk when Serena and the two girls arrived for their appointment at five o'clock. It was obvious what had happened, especially as, try as she could, Claire had not managed to remove the multi-coloured marker pen from their hair. Claire insisted Olivia wear leggings to hide the pen marks on her legs. Each twin sat in resentful silence as the hairdresser did her best to cut their hair into something that resembled a decent style. They both ended up with pixie cuts like Serena's and they both beamed with delight when they saw that they looked even more like her now. The hairdresser said

"That will be £120 please."

Serena gasped in shock. The hairdresser looked at her as though she were stupid.

"We did fit you in as an emergency despite being fully booked. And we are into evening appointments now."

Reluctantly Serena handed over her debit card and prayed that there was still enough money in her account to cover it. She would have to ask Satish to transfer some money to her later.

The girls skipped alongside her, holding her hands as they walked down the main road. Serena stopped at a cash point to check on her balance and found that Satish had already deposited money from their joint account into hers.

"Bless him," she muttered to herself, and once again a wave of loneliness swept over her.

"Hurry back. I need you so," she whispered.

Pulling herself together, she smiled down at the twins

"Okay how about going to Yummies for a hot chocolate?"

They squealed with delight and ten minutes later they were sat in the glasshouse at the back of the teashop with hot chocolates and cookies. Serena had been delighted to find they did vegan hot chocolate and a range of delicious vegan cakes and cookies. She felt she needed something to boost her mood.

Abigail looked at Serena with her big blue eyes, full of sadness.

"Don't be sad. We love you," she said.

Serena smiled.

"I love you too. I miss Satish."

"I miss Satish. I want to hear him tell us about Ellies," said a sad Olivia. "When is he coming back?."

Serena sighed. "As soon as he can."

When they got home, they found Claire was already home and St John was fast asleep in his Moses basket in the living room. Claire looked brighter and seemed happy enough with the girls' haircuts. She was dreading Sebastian's reaction and had phoned him to tell him so it would not be a shock and a source of another flare-up when he got home. However, his mobile was turned off and when she phoned the office, they said he was out at a meeting. She hung up with a sense of foreboding. Not giving up she decided to text him. At least he would see the message when he turned his phone on again.

"Hi, Seb. Just for info. The girls have cut all their hair off. Really mad at them. Love you xxxx"

The message dinged away.

Shortly after Sebastian turned his phone on and read the message. He snorted loudly, and Eleanor turned round to look at him from the dressing table stool where she was sitting, doing her make-up.

"My bloody domestic bliss. The twins have chopped all their hair off. Claire has gone ballistic. Delights of suburban life."

He flopped back on the bed only to have Eleanor come over and straddle him.

"Come on Big Daddy, let me take your mind off of it," she said as she started to undress him once again.

NINETEEN

The next week passed uneventfully. Serena was relieved at the break in the dramas that plagued her daughter's household. Even Sebastian seemed to be a little nicer towards her and was back early one evening and said that he would treat them to a takeaway to save the "girls" from having to cook. Eleanor had had enough of him for the day and had told him she had a meeting with an old friend from her days when she was trying to be an actress. Her height had gone against her, and she was constantly turned down for roles. However, her training was now being put to effective use in playing her different personae.

The general shape of the day was Serena helping look after the girls until Maria came to clean and do the washing and ironing. Serena would then either take the girls out to the park or do something creative with them. In two weeks, nursery would start again, as essential building work was being done over the Easter holidays. The twins were becoming better behaved now they had something to do that interested them. Claire spent most of her time looking after St John, who was now beginning to flourish, especially with the cuddles and love showered on him by his grandmother. Even the weekend went happily. Sebastian suggested on Saturday that they went out for the day so the whole family plus Serena spent the day at the zoo. Claire had to reprimand the twins when she realised when they were in the Monkey House that they were trying to guess which monkey was called St John. Sebastian had to reprimand them when they were in the reptile house and Olivia whispered to Abigail that the grumpy-looking giant tortoise looked like Mummy and Abigail said she wished that she had a shell she could hide in when Mummy was being a grumpy pants.

During the week various friends of Claire's dropped in to see her new baby. Some from her pre-birth class were heavily pregnant still, and Sophia and a couple of the mothers were friends from the twins' ballet classes and three others from their nursery. They were all intrigued by Claire's mother and after initially being taken aback by her appearance, they enjoyed talking to her and hearing about the Lotus Light Community. Several of them independently said how they wanted to do yoga to get their figures back and enquired whether Serena could help them. Serena initially felt reluctant to use something so precious to her for vanity reasons, but a group of four of them showed interest in the deeper aspects of yoga and the way of life that Serena was living. Eventually, Serena agreed to meet in a small group at Sophia's house in a couple of weeks when Sophia and her family got back from their ten-day holiday in their house in France. Claire began to realise that her mother had quite a celebratory status among her friends. They had clearly been talking amongst themselves as most of them knew each other. One morning two of the mothers from nursery dropped in to see Claire, and also to check Serena out. Shona gushed about how she had heard about Serena and asked if it was true she was into Tantra. Claire coloured at this, realising her mother would now know she had gossiped about her to her friends. Her discomfort was made even worse when Britney, who was never up to date with the gossip and news and had not understood the relationship between Satish and Serena, blurted out to Claire

"And when are we going to meet Satish? You said he is a real hotty, especially in his loincloth. I really like the strong, silent type. I need a new man in my life. And some Tantra!"

Serena did not look at her daughter but quietly replied "Satish and I have studied Tantra and put it into practice."

At this point, Britney went bright red and choked on her peppermint tea.

Unfazed, Serena continued "We get great peace, pleasure, and enlightenment from it. However, there's a lot more to it than the popular press makes out. It is not just about sex. It is a whole spirituality of life and how we relate to others. It is just a part of our way of life. I'm willing to talk to people about it if they wish."

An uneasy silence fell over the room.

On Sunday Sebastian said he had to collect some paperwork from the office and would drop in on a colleague. Claire was very sure that this was a cover for Sebastian to be doing something else but did not want to upset the relative peace that was over the household, so let it pass. He returned home after three hours in a very exuberant mood, having had two hours in Eleanor's bed. Claire ignored the scent of another woman on him. She was enjoying the calm in the household too much to upset it, and she knew that if he ended this affair, he would only start another one.

Despite her mixed feelings about missing her "old Mum," Claire began to appreciate Serena's presence more and more, not just for the practical help that she gave but for her peaceful and gentle aura. She recognised the positive effect it was having on the twins and also on herself, finding herself becoming calmer and less worried about inconsequential things. When Maria burnt one of Sebastian's shirts when she was ironing it, Claire just shrugged and said

"Never mind. He has a wardrobe full of them."

Maria looked shocked, having expected a tirade of angry abuse at her. Serena too was taken aback at the more laid-back Claire. Claire had been doing some deep thinking and had realised that her mother had the peace of mind and steadiness that she wanted for herself.

"Maybe I should learn from her," she had said to herself one morning. "She has come back for a reason. I must appreciate her while she is still here."

There was a growing, nagging dread in Claire's heart that one day her mother would return to Thailand. All the time Satish was up in Birmingham she knew this would not happen, although part of her longed to see him again.

Serena spoke to Satish several times a day, and she found that after each call she felt more and more distant from him. The bed still felt too big and empty without him, and she longed for him to return, but the memory of their life together in Thailand was fading fast. He too was missing his partner. After the funeral, there had been a massive amount of paperwork to go through and his aunt's estate to be sorted out. Anish had inherited a substantial amount of money plus his mother's house, which he said he wanted to sell to help finance and launch the community in Sri Lanka. Satish had been overwhelmed by his generosity. Anish had said he felt there was nothing for him now in Birmingham but then had stopped short when he realised that he was selling Shanthi's home from under her. She had looked at him with her deep and gentle eyes and said hesitantly

"I have always dreamed of going home. I've nothing here. I have financial skills. May I help to set up the Community?"

Anish had taken her in his arms and hugged her.

"That would be wonderful. We must celebrate the birth of our new community."

Satish suddenly felt very homesick for his community in Thailand, but he too had said he wanted to help found the new community.

"We will all be back in our birthplace. It feels so right," he said, feeling the most positive he had felt since he had stepped foot in England. However, he wondered how Serena would feel about not returning to Thailand long-term but going to stay with the extended family of Anish, Satish, and Shanthi while they looked for the right property in Sri Lanka.

Anish had to go out to meet a friend and left Satish and Shanthi to talk over ideas for the community. Eventually, their talk got around to their own lives.

"Will you marry Serena?" Shanthi asked with a slight tremor in her voice.

"We are committed to each other," he replied slowly. "I suppose we are kind of married but there is no legal paperwork. It is not a legal union. It is much more of a spiritual union. If we were to part, it would be because spiritual forces call us out of our relationship. Or, of course, if one of us died. We are completely faithful to each other and love each other deeply."

"I see," Shanthi replied looking down at her hands. "And no children yet?"

Satish hesitated before he replied. He found he did not want to admit to Serena's age and felt guilty about that. Instead, he said

"She cannot have children."

Strangely Shanthi felt relieved at this, but she said

"I'm sorry to hear that. You would make a good father."

Satish suddenly realised how hollow he felt when he thought about never having children with Serena.

"I have a quest which I must fulfil. My karma is not to be a father," he said, suddenly feeling unconvinced about everything in his life, and whether his life was indeed going in the right direction regarding his relationship with Serena.

Shanthi quietly said

"I remember we were to be married. How we used to pretend we were in the temple at our wedding. I put flowers in my hair. And you puffed your chest out to look like a big man. And how I said I wanted eight children. Four girls and four boys." She smiled to herself, "Although now I would probably only want two. One of each, that is plenty."

An uneasy silence fell between them as they pondered what might have been. Shanthi stood up and went to make tea and as she walked out of the room Satish found himself admiring her slim figure and youthful gait. Mentally he chastised himself for having unfaithful thoughts, but he was also aware of a new and different passion stirring within him. He was also aware of how he dreaded returning to the chaos of the house in London.

As the days passed and Serena felt more and more distant from Satish, she suddenly found herself craving for other deep and close relationships. She felt a strong relationship was developing between her and Claire, and she loved her grandchildren. There still felt to be a large hole in her life, and gradually she realised how much she missed her own mother. Although she had not seen her for twenty-five years, she still remembered her as though it were yesterday. A deep longing was developing in her for reconciliation with her mother. By Thursday it had become so overwhelming that she asked Claire if she could cope on her own for one day as there was something she had to do. Claire looked puzzled but immediately realised from the intense expression on Serena's face that her mother had something difficult to undertake, although she did not know what it was. Serena had decided not to tell Claire what she was going to do in case it went wrong.

"By all means Mum. You deserve a day off. And it is better this week as I won't have to be taking the twins to nursery. It is easier to amuse them here than having to go backwards and forwards. Go and have a lovely day, whatever it is you are doing."

Serena smiled her thanks, went to her room, opened her laptop, and searched for "Cheap train tickets to Stroud." She went to bed that night full of excitement and trepidation.

Dorothy Allwood stood at her kitchen window, a cup of rapidly cooling tea in her hand, staring down her garden at the last of the daffodils being flattened in the Spring rain. She felt a great affinity to them, feeling bashed down herself and increasingly unwilling to spring back up again. Normally, as it was Friday, she would be attending the Women's Institute tonight. However, she was still smarting from being unseated as Chair of the WI two weeks ago. The flamboyant forty-year-old Charlotte Bingsby had won a landslide vote and, despite Dorothy's twenty years of challenging work as Chair, she did not receive a single vote in her favour. Setting her face like flint, she had received the sycophantic thanks from the Committee for all her dedication, and their saying how they hoped she would now finally be able to enjoy a long-overdue retirement had been a blow to her heart. The tone had been that her work there was now finished, for good. Since then, her usually busy phone had been eerily silent. Even Beth Baines, her closest friend, had not been in touch. Last Sunday at church had been equally painful. Suddenly her name had been removed from the flower rota, and people seemed to be in too much of a hurry to stop to talk to her. She had been reduced to talking to the new vicar, whom she detested. She was a divorcee in her mid-thirties, having taken on her first parish, including three small village churches, and to Dorothy's utter disgust there were rumours that she had a girlfriend in another local parish. She constantly sported a rainbow in some form or another. Dorothy had fought hard not to show her total disdain for the woman but felt she had not succeeded.

"Another example of standards slipping," she had muttered to herself as she was leaving the church. "I wonder how long before we get electric guitars and go Happy Clappy."

Slipping over on the church path had been the final insult. Her dignity had been bruised more than her body, but after helping her to her feet, the stragglers of the congregation had left her to walk home alone. Previously the strong alliance between the church and the WI had worked in her favour. Now it was the opposite. It felt as though everyone was closing ranks against her. Dorothy had never felt so lonely since Geoffrey died.

Putting the now cold cup of tea down on its saucer she turned back to the room. Her eyes alighted on the photo, now going brown with age, that was on the sideboard. She and Geoffrey were sitting holding hands on a low wall, surrounded by sunflowers, and Kristina and Jayne sat on either side of them. It was taken when the girls were teenagers when they all went on holiday to France. She picked the photo up and stroked it absentmindedly. They were still living in the old house at that point, and it was before Geoffrey had sold his lucrative property development business just before a property crash in the 1990s. They moved to her current house after Kristina's death. She had succumbed to meningitis in her final year at university. Dorothy sometimes wondered if her death had been the cause of her younger sister "going off the rails." However, Jayne had already decided she wanted to live in London and had moved into a bedsit in Earls Court and found a job as a secretary for a financial consultancy. Within a year she was pregnant by her boss and Geoffrey had insisted he and Dorothy disown her. With no children to house Geoffrey and Dorothy had their cottage in the country to themselves. Sadly, Geoffrey did not live long enough to enjoy it as much as they had hoped. At first, they had been happy here, but Dorothy always felt envy at the closely-knit families around them in the village, and she hated the pity in people's eyes when she talked about Kristina and the puzzlement when she said she was not in touch with Jayne.

Dorothy reflected that she had no family to help her. Her older sister, Babs, was now in a dementia home and her brother Percy had died ten years ago. She now had no one who cared about her. Even her niece, who had lived in her village for so many years, had now emigrated to Dubai with her money-mad husband.

Sighing she put the photo back and went to the kitchen to make herself another cup of tea. She had just sat in her armchair in her front room and opened a copy of "Country Homes" when her doorbell rang. She peeped round the front room curtain, but the caller's face was hidden under the hood of a raincoat. Ensuring she put her safety catch on the front door she opened it. The visitor pushed her hood back. Dorothy took a sharp intake of breath when she found she was looking into the face of the daughter she had not seen for twenty-five years.

"Hello, Mother. Please don't shut the door. I just want to talk."

She had put out her hand to stop her from shutting the door.

Dorothy stared in amazement at the woman on her doorstep. Despite a quarter of a century passing, she recognised her daughter immediately. She had a radiance about her, and Dorothy liked her pixie haircut, although she was not sure about the rainbow colours, or the thick black tights, Doc Marten boots, and tie-dyed purple skirt. For a moment she considered shutting the door on her daughter, but suddenly the loneliness she had been feeling building up inside her exploded and she realised she desperately wanted company. With a wobbly voice, she said

"Just a moment. I have to shut the door to release the chain."

Her arthritic fingers were fumbling, and Dorothy was worried that she would open the door to find no one there. That it would all have been a dream. However, when she re-opened the door and held it back, her daughter was still there, dripping and looking relieved.

"You had better come in. You look soaked. Hang your coat there."

Dorothy's mind was darting all over the place. Should she hug her daughter? Kiss her? Remain detached? What could she say to her after all this time? She felt a surge of conflicting emotions. Guilt. Anger. Shame. Discomfort. Comfort. Shock.

She realised her daughter was speaking.

"This is a lovely cottage. I only saw it before you had it done up."

Dorothy was suddenly overwhelmed with sadness at how much time had passed since she and Geoffrey had disowned their only remaining child.

"Come through. Would you like a cup of tea?" Dorothy felt awkward, not knowing how to treat her visitor.

"I have my own herbal teabag. Here, just put boiling water on it."

Cups of tea were made in silence and five minutes later the two women were sitting in two armchairs next to each other in the front room.

"You are looking well, Mum. Can I call you that? Mother sounds very formal and I think I am too old to call you Mummy."

Dorothy always thought Mum was common but did not object. She was still trying to believe her daughter was here.

"Good cleansing and moisturising routine, no junk foods, and daily walks. Not hard to do. You look…. different. You have obviously been somewhere sunny."

Dorothy could not keep the edginess out of her voice.

"I have been in Thailand for three years. I got back a couple of weeks ago. I am staying at Claire's. You are a great-grandmother again."

"Again? Oh. Yes. Your daughter had twins, didn't she?"

Dorothy could not keep the frostiness out of her voice as she desperately searched in her memory for her granddaughter's name, but it eluded her.

"Yes. They are beautiful. Here. I have a photo. And of the new baby St John."

Serena handed over her phone with a photo on it she had taken the day before. Dorothy immediately saw Geoffrey's blue eyes and her blonde hair in the twins. They looked just like her two girls did when they were that age. A lump grew in her throat.

"St John? A bit of a weird name."

"He could have been Percival."

"Nothing wrong with Percival. Your uncle was called Percival."

Once again Serena felt the wrath of a mother who could never be pleased. Sadly, Serena put her phone back in her bag.

"I am sorry about Uncle Percy," she continued.

She had heard about his death from her cousin. Hesitantly she said

"And of course, Father. You must miss him."

Dorothy could see her eyes were full of genuine compassion and empathy, even though he had been cruel to his daughter at times. The lump in her throat increased and she felt tears pricking in her eyes.

"Of course," she said primly, fighting to control her emotions. She continued

"Why are you here Jayne? Are you after money or something? You are not on drugs or anything?"

Serena did not feel at that very moment that it was the right time to say she had changed her name. She calmed herself before answering in a slow, measured tone.

"No, I am not. That is not why I am here. Can't we put the past behind us? I want you back in my life. I always hoped and prayed you might want me in yours. I've learnt so much over the past three years. I'm a different person now. I want to heal all the wounds in my history. In my family. In my relationships. I want to have a mother again."

Her voice was now wobbling.

"I know I was a disappointment and a cause of shame for you and Father. I'm sorry. I realise how much hurt I caused you. I felt so bereft after Kristina's death......I shouldn't make excuses. I was alone in London. Young. Foolish. Naïve. Swept off my feet by an older man. But I feel I have made something of my life now. And all this past stuff, all my mistakes and difficult times, well they are just stepping stones on the path to this point. I'm where I'm meant to be now. Life is short. We should be helping each other. We should not be split apart as we have been."

Serena cradled her teacup and looked down into it in silence as her words ran out, heart thudding, awaiting her mother's reaction with a sense of dread. Dorothy felt her heart thudding as well and her eyes were filled with tears. She realised just how foolish she had been in her constant rejection of her daughter. It had been more on Geoffrey's part. He was extremely old-fashioned in his views and was furious that she was "up the spout" by some greasy businessman in London and had wanted nothing more to do with her. Dorothy had gone along with it because she could not stand up to him, although her heart had been broken at losing her second child so quickly after Kristina's death. Quietly she put her cup of tea down on the side table and leant forward to take Serena's hand. Hesitantly she said

"I have so often wondered about you. Where you were. What you looked like. Whether you were happy or not. What my grandchild looked like."

She was silent for a while, cradling Serena's hand in her own wrinkled one.

"As time went on it got harder to try to contact you again. I should have opened the door to you when Geoffrey died, but somehow it felt dishonouring to him. He was so furious with you. You know how unforgiving he was."

Dorothy smiled. "Do you remember when you lost his lucky golf ball in the lake? You had the nerve to tell him all golf balls were the same."

"And I know he couldn't really tell one from another," replied Serena.

The two women smiled at each other in mutual remembrance of family times. They squeezed each other hands and leant forward and embraced each other.

TWENTY

Serena returned to London with a new deep peace within her heart. She told her mother about her last twenty-five years but in a way that did not make Dorothy feel guilty. It was only after Serena had gone that Dorothy realised just what a wonderful, mature, sensitive woman she had as a daughter. Serena decided, as they had continued talking, that she would tell her mother about her name change from Jayne to Serena and the reasons for it. Dorothy accepted the fact, but she still kept calling her Jayne to herself. However, her memory was beginning to fail her, and quickly the details of her daughter's life over the past quarter-century got muddled in her mind. Provisional plans had been made for her to visit and stay in London to meet her granddaughter and great-grandchildren. Claire was delighted at the reconciliation and looked forward to Dorothy's visit. The twins were very confused to learn that they would have an even older granny coming to visit them soon. Olivia stuck her thumb in her mouth to think it through and Abigail asked

"Will she be really old and wrinkly and smelly and like a real granny?"

Serena found the new relationship with her mother helped to fill the emptiness in her heart with Satish's absence. She spoke to Dorothy every day and still spoke to Satish several times a day. She longed for his return, but he was embroiled in helping with paperwork following his aunt's death and was helping to put the house in order so that they could sell it. His frustration at not getting his writing done was carried in his voice as he talked to Serena two days after she had visited her mother.

"Beloved," he said "I feel my life is running away from me. I need your stability to ground me again. I miss you. So much is happening. It is so good. We will have enough money to start our new community. Shanthi is so competent at administration that I believe she will be a huge asset to us. She is fluent in four languages, all that we need. Anish is ready for a change. The energies are good. I feel great positivity."

Serena had noticed how much Shanthi's name had crept into Satish's conversation every time they spoke, and she fought against feelings of insecurity and jealousy. However, Satish told her how he loved her in every phone call and how he longed to be with her again. Nevertheless, she began to wonder if they would be together again, and in her spirit, she knew that any parting would be their karma. Her heart would still break.

When Claire found her mother sitting staring at the silent phone after this conversation, she sat down next to her and asked her what the problem was. Serena was hesitant to share her fears but eventually told her that Satish seemed to be getting very close to his second cousin.

"She is his age. They were children together and once were betrothed, although that was broken off when her family moved to England. They have links I can never have. And she could give him children."

Hastily she wiped a tear from her eye and her daughter squeezed her hand. Claire felt guilty when she realised how much she dreaded the thought that Satish might not be with her mother much longer, not just for her mother's sake but because she would not see him again. She enjoyed the feelings that he evoked in her and did not want them to end, but she reddened again at remembering the embarrassment Britney has caused her. She decided she would take matters in hand. When Serena went to the bathroom, she quickly looked up Satish's number on her phone and made a note of it. When Serena returned to the room, she found her daughter looking self-satisfied. When asked why she was looking so pleased Claire replied

"Wait and see. I am going to plan a surprise for you."

However, life was busy, and Claire quickly forgot about her plans to surprise her mother and only remembered it days later.

Another pleasant weekend was spent with Sebastian playing the father role. Eleanor had other plans for the weekend, and he felt he was gaining Claire's trust again by spending time with them. He also had a long phone call to his mother moaning about how impossible Claire was to live with, and that he even suspected she had eyes on another man. Her lingering glances at Satish had not gone unnoticed, and he had decided he would embroider on this to his advantage. His mother was angry and complained that Claire did not know how lucky she was to have such a devoted and hardworking husband. She always knew deep down that she was a hussy. Sebastian sat listening to her tirade with a big smirk on his face. He felt his plan was slowly coming together. He cemented it by asking her when she and his father were coming to see St John and discuss his baptism. Although Sebastian was an atheist, he knew he had to get St John baptised to keep his father off his back. His mother agreed to arrange a visit very soon. Sebastian knew their visit would be a chance to show them just how dysfunctional his family life had become.

Over supper on Sunday, it was agreed that Dorothy could come and stay the following week, arriving on Wednesday and staying until Thursday. Serena said that she would sleep on a fold-out bed in the twins' room so that Dorothy could have her bed. Sebastian suddenly remembered that he had an overnight business trip so he could leave the women to get acquainted in peace. The thought of a whole night with Eleanor made him feel so excited that he had to leave the room for a while. A quick phone call to Dorothy and everything was arranged.

The next week started peacefully but things quickly turned around for Sebastian. He arrived at Eleanor's hotel room late on Tuesday afternoon and asked to shower as soon as he got there. He had spent the afternoon with a client who had insisted on smoking a large cigar. Sebastian could not object as they were in the client's own house, but now he stank of pungent, stale cigar smoke.

Before he had a chance to get to the bathroom, Eleanor told him of her travel plans for their weekend away in a couple of weeks. They were going to fly to Rome on Saturday afternoon and were booked into a discreet but luxurious hotel in the centre of the city, near the Spanish Steps. They had adjoining double rooms as the owners of the hotel were strict Catholics and did not allow bookings from unmarried people in their double rooms.

"Never mind," she breathed into Sebastian's ear as she slowly started unbuttoning his shirt "There is a door between them. It is divine there."

Sebastian insisted again that he showered first before their usual afternoon of lovemaking but suggested she order champagne and lobster as he was starving.

He let the hot water blast away the smell of cigar smoke and then he flipped it onto cold to give an enlivening torrent over his body. Slipping into a thick towelling bathrobe, he went back into the bedroom. At that moment there was a knock on the door and Eleanor answered it. She too had changed into a thick, towelling bathrobe. As Eleanor answered the door, Sebastian heard a familiar voice say

"Hola Madam. I have your order here."

Eleanor stepped back and nonchalantly said

"Just put it on the table by the window."

Maria, dressed in a black and white maid's outfit, walked into the room, holding a silver tray with an ice bucket with the champagne, glasses, and two plates, covered with silver covers. She glanced at Sebastian and then froze and looked back at him, her mouth dropping open.

"Mister Jackson!" she gasped and nearly dropped her tray.

Eleanor looked at her in shock and then back at Sebastian, who had turned bright red and was pulling his robe tighter around himself.

"Maria. What the hell are you doing here?"

"I am working, Mister Jackson. I told you I had another job at a hotel when you hired me. It is the only way I can pay my rent. I work for you in the morning and here in the afternoon and evening."

She wanted to ask what he was doing here as well but the answer was so blindingly obvious.

"Look. This is very awkward," Sebastian blustered. "You haven't seen me. Okay? If you value your job…. Or should I say *jobs*."

"Yes, Sir. I understand. I never saw you. I go."

Tears were springing into her eye as she placed the tray on the table, and scurried out of the room.

"Well! What was all that about?"

Eleanor threw caution to the wind and lit up a cigarette, despite the no-smoking policy of the hotel.

Sebastian sank onto the bed.

"Our bloody useless maid. That's all I need. Her blabbing to Claire."

Eleanor snaked her way to the window and opened it to let the smoke out. She stood there for a moment and then turned towards Sebastian "Well everyone has their price – if you're willing to pay it. Maybe she needs to move on from being your skivvy. I am sure there is plenty of other work out there for her. How much do you pay her?"

"Two hundred pounds a week cash in hand."

Eleanor thought for a moment.

"A couple of grand should keep her happy. Unless that is too much for you….."

Her doubtful voice filled Sebastian with unease, and he proudly said

"That's nothing to me. It would be worth it to keep her quiet. Don't worry. I will sort it. The trouble is I don't know where the cow lives. Buzz down and ask for her to come back up."

Eleanor sat on the bed and rang down to Reception.

The girl in Reception was not helpful. She told Eleanor that Maria had just gone on her break and that she was then going to be helping in the kitchen. She enquired if they had had a problem with her, to which Eleanor felt she had to reply

"No, none whatsoever."

If Maria got into trouble with the hotel, then she might feel vindictive and tell Claire what she had seen. Eleanor continued "We just wanted to give her a tip. Never mind. We will drop something into Reception for her later." She hung up.

"Shit," Sebastian breathed. "What a bloody complication that is."

Eleanor rolled over on the bed and slowly let her robe slip off her.

"Come here and let's forget about Maria."

However, the moment had been ruined for Sebastian and Eleanor had to work hard to get him to respond to her caresses. He went home that night feeling very unfulfilled.

When Sebastian got up on Wednesday morning, he seemed very edgy. He wanted to know exactly what plans Claire and Serena had for the day and whether Maria was due to come and at what time. Claire looked at him puzzled and said

"Maria comes every day. Why? Dorothy is coming about mid-day. So Maria is going to be busy making up beds and cleaning. Why?"

"No reason. Just wondered what you're all doing."

Serena studied him and she could tell he was hiding something from Claire. She suggested that Claire have an easy morning and have a bath and she would take the girls to nursery and pick them up, and in between would do some baking. Sebastian thought this was a good idea. He realised that he could not delve any further into their plans. He felt stumped about what to do about Maria. He had to stop her from coming to the house, but he did not know where she lived, and he did not have her phone number. Only Claire had it and he could not access her phone without raising her suspicions. Eventually, he decided he would have to intercept Maria on her way to their house. He went up to his office upstairs to fetch some papers and make phone calls. Serena took the girls to nursery which took twenty minutes, as the nursery was only a couple of streets away. When she got back at about quarter past nine, she made Claire and herself a hot drink. Sebastian came down twenty minutes later. He appeared nervous and twitchy.

"Okay," he announced. "I must go."

He kissed Claire and smiled at Serena.

"Have a good day. I will see you tomorrow as I am away overnight. Don't worry, I have everything packed."

Serena watched him go with a sense of foreboding. Claire watched her carefully.

"He is up to something isn't he?" she mused, nursing her cup of tea.

Serena sighed.

"He appears muddy again."

"What is it that you seem to see about people? You seem to be able to see things I can't."

Serena sighed again and reluctantly said

"I sometimes see energy fields around people. The colours change according to their emotional or spiritual states. It was something I learnt at the Community."

She waited for the snort of contempt or comments about it all being *woo woo* stuff, but Claire just sat thoughtfully staring into her now empty mug. To Serena's utter amazement, she said

"I wish I could see what you see. I would know when I am being lied to."

Serena felt a surge of empathy and sadness for her daughter and leant across the breakfast bar and took her hand.

"Sometimes it is a curse and not a blessing. The truth can hurt."

Claire looked up at her and said

"And someone once said that it will also set you free."

Serena's jaw dropped in amazement.

Sebastian drove his car to the next road and parked and then walked back towards the bus stop where he knew Maria would be alighting. Just as he thought at five to ten, she got off the bus and started to make her way towards his house. Fortunately for him, the bus stop was three roads away from his road. He caught up with her.

Surprised she stopped as he skipped in front of her.

"Mister Jackson. Don't worry. My lips are steeled."

"You mean sealed."

"I will not tell the Mistress anything," she hastily continued.

"It would be very unfortunate if you did. You would not want to upset her after such a difficult time with the baby. Now I think this might help you to keep quiet."

With that, he drew out from his jacket two thousand pounds, made up of fifty and twenty-pound notes, and held them out to Maria. She gasped and stared at them. It was more money than she had ever seen. Hesitantly she took it, and counted it, looking at it in disbelief.

"It will help you while you find another job."

Slowly it dawned on her what he was saying.

"Are you sicking me?"

"You mean *sacking*. Not exactly. Just a payment to help you find a new job…. Immediately. I will give you a very good reference should you require it. You just happened to be in the wrong place at the wrong time. And I want you to phone my wife right now and tell her you are no longer coming to work for her. Okay? Tell her you have family problems. Anything. Just let her know you won't be going today, and you won't be going back."

Maria hesitated for a moment and Sebastian took the gamble of going to take the money back from her. Her mind was working rapidly. She knew there were loads more shifts coming up at the hotel and there was the chance of being promoted to the Under Manager of one of the floors. She could request not to be on the floor where Eleanor had her room. Confidently she stuffed the money into her bag and took out her phone. Trembling she phoned Claire's number.

"Hola. Missus Jackson. I am sorry. I cannot come today. I have a family emergency. I must leave my job. Immediately. I am sorry."

Sebastian could hear Claire's voice at the other end of the connection.

"Maria! No! I am sorry you have problems. What has happened? If you need time take it, but please come back. This is awful. Why? You can't just leave me like this."

"I am sorry Missus Jackson. I must go. Thank you. Adios."

She hung up and put her phone into her bag. Looking Sebastian straight in the eye she said

"Okay?"

Sebastian breathed a sigh of relief.

"Here is my card. If you need a reference, please let me know. Have you left anything at our house?"

Maria thought for a moment and then replied

"Only a pair of shoes I use when I clean. I can get some new ones."

She suddenly realised she had a free morning and two thousand pounds she was not expecting to receive. However, it was the thought of never having to go into the chaotic and dysfunctional house ever again that filled her with the greatest joy. She decided she would treat herself to something nice.

Claire stared in disbelief at her phone after Maria had hung up.

"Shit. That is all I need. Maria chucking in her job. Says she has family problems. But she doesn't really have any family. Something doesn't add up."

Claire was sitting shaking her head slowly.

"And your mother is due here in a couple of hours. And we have beds to make up and cleaning to do."

Tears started to fill her eyes, but Serena quickly put her arm around her and told her not to worry and that they would get it done between them.

"And we have to get the girls from nursery."

"I'm doing that," offered Serena. "Come on, let's get to work."

When the women started cleaning, they found they had run out of kitchen cleaners, so Serena offered to go to the shops to get some. Claire quickly wrote a list for her, and Serena almost ran to the row of shops about a quarter of a mile away. She had told Claire to have a quick soak in the bath while she was out and not to worry. As she hurried past the tea shop, she suddenly espied Maria sitting in the window with a large piece of cake and a cup of coffee. Hesitantly she went in. Maria's eyes widened in shock when she saw her, and her face reddened.

"Missus Serena!"

Serena sat down opposite her and said how sorry she was to hear of her family problems, already knowing it was all lies. Maria dropped her gaze in shame. Serena could see confusion, shame, and guilt swirling around Maria's energy field. Tears glistened in her eyes.

"Missus Serena. I am sorry. I cannot tell you. I cannot work for Missus Jackson anymore."

"Why? We depend on you."

Maria started sobbing.

"I cannot tell you. I should not have come here. Please….. don't tell anyone you saw me. I beg you."

Serena took her hand.

"Please tell me. I will keep your secret."

Maria squeezed her hand in return.

"I cannot. It would break the Missus's heart."

Serena sat back and withdrew her hand.

"Something to do with Sebastian? Has he made a pass at you?"

Maria looked confused.

"What means a pass?"

"Has he tried to seduce you or kiss you or touch you?"

Maria looked up with her eyes wide.

"Oh no. No. But….."

She looked down again.

"But it is to do with Sebastian?" Serena pressed on.

Silently Maria nodded.

"But I didn't tell you anything," she said quietly. "Now I must go."

With that, she got to her feet, went over to the till, and thrust a twenty-pound note into the hand of the cashier, and hurried out, without waiting for change. Serena sat dumbstruck for a few minutes before the waitress came over and first asked if she had finished and then cleared the half-drunk coffee cup and half-eaten cake away. With a heavy heart, Serena went to the shops, returned to the house, and was glad to hear Claire running her bath. She could process what had just happened in peace, before collecting the girls from nursery.

When she got back to the house after collecting the twins, she found her mother had just arrived by taxi from Paddington. Claire was sitting with her in the front room and Serena was relieved to see that they seemed to be engaging with each other. The twins feigned shyness and tried to hide behind Serena when they entered the room, but Dorothy reassured them with a smile that she would not bite. This seemed to amuse the girls and they went and sat down on either side of her on the settee.

"Are you Serena's mummy?" asked Abigail.

Dorothy was confused for a second but then replied

"Yes. But I always call her Jayne. That's her proper name."

Olivia wrinkled up her nose and said

"I like Serena better."

"And you are more like a granny than Serena is!" added Abigail.

"Do you have a boyfriend as well?" asked Olivia. "Can he do headstands like Satish?"

Serena suddenly had a feeling that the next twenty-four hours could be very testing.

TWENTY-ONE

The afternoon was spent with the three women catching up on family history. Dorothy spent a lot of time cuddling St John and he seemed to like her. She suddenly realised she regretted deeply not spending time with her daughter, granddaughter, and two great-granddaughters. The twins for once were well behaved and were slightly in awe of their perfectly manicured, heavily made-up great-grandmother. She did smell a bit of lavender and they were intrigued by the thick layer of powder on her face and the deep creases around her always slightly pursed mouth. They also had to work out what she was saying through her "Queen's English" pronunciation. Serena could see deep hurt as she talked about her church life and all the things she had done with the Women's Institute, making it sound as though they were still the centre of her life as if to try to impress her granddaughter. However, when Serena had visited her, she had let slip that she had been cut out of this and Serena could see the hole it had left in her life.

"And when am I going to meet the father of my lovely great-grandchildren then?" beamed Dorothy mid-afternoon.

Serena felt uncomfortable, still processing the conversation she had had with Maria and still wondering what Sebastian had done to make Maria resign.

Blithely Claire said

"He is away on business."

"What a shame!" replied Dorothy. "I do so want to meet some of the menfolk of my new-found family. And what about your husband Jayne? Was it Hamish you said? Or Roger? Sorry, I am getting forgetful. I get muddled."

"Roger is Claire's father. I divorced him. He ran off with his personal trainer."

"Oh. Sorry. I vaguely remember your cousin telling me something about that.," Dorothy flustered.

Serena continued

"Satish is away. He will be back sometime, but I don't know when."

"Satish. That is an odd name. I thought it was Hamish. A lovely Scots name. I would love a Scottish son-in-law. Such a lovely race of people. I was sure it was Hamish."

"No. Satish. He is from Sri Lanka."

"Is his family from colonial times?"

"No. Native born Sri Lankan."

A look of horror spread across Dorothy's face. She went to say something but thought better of it.

Serena saw this and continued

"He is the loveliest, kindest man I have ever met. He is younger than me."

"How much?" Dorothy sounded scandalised.

"Twenty years."

Serena realised that her careful conversation with her mother when she had visited her had not registered. Although she had told her about Satish, at the time she felt it had not been heard.

"That's, that's…. a bit disgusting. You are a mature woman. He is a youth still."

Dorothy's mouth pursed in disapproval and the lines around it appeared to turn into cracks.

Serena would not be phased.

"He is mature beyond his years. He is a well-known spiritual author and teacher. He has many followers around the world."

"I do hope you are not getting involved in a sect. Once you are in you can't get out, and they take all your money. Jayne, what have you done?"

The twins were looking uneasy at the increasingly heated conversation and Serena quietly suggested to them that maybe they would like to go to their room and draw Great Granny a picture. Once the twins had disappeared, Serena turned back to her mother.

"I have found my life purpose. I have learnt so much and what is important in life. I have felt loved more than I have ever felt loved. I have healed and I have forgiven, and now I feel I have something to offer the world. I have done what my soul has been calling me to do. Nothing and no one is going to take that away from me."

Serena was surprised to find herself standing up to her mother for the first time in her life.

Dorothy snorted her disapproval.

"And where does the church come into all this mumbo jumbo? I hope you haven't become an atheist – or even worse – a pagan."

"No Mother. I have found a deeper spirituality than I ever had before and have found some deep truths. I was an atheist when I went to Thailand. I was very angry, bitter, and damaged before I joined the Community. There I found acceptance, deep healing, and forgiveness. Whilst I do not believe exactly what you believe, both our beliefs are based on love. I respect your beliefs. Mine are just rather wider. I told you about it when I visited you. I hope you can respect my beliefs as well."

Dorothy looked defensive.

"I was in shock when you visited. I didn't really take in any of what you were telling me. It sounds mumbo jumbo to me."

Although Serena had since then talked to her mother every day it had not been at a deep level. She realised that only now was her mother understanding the deep change that had taken place in her. She said

"I wish everyone could find the deep peace I have found through the Community and with Satish. I realise the true worth of things now. Our love, my child, and grandchildren. And now having you back in my life."

Dorothy looked uncomfortable and deflected it all by asking for another cup of tea. Just as Claire went out of the room the doorbell rang and she went to open it. Serena and Dorothy were sitting in awkward silence. Claire came back into the room, looking slightly flushed and uncomfortable.

"I have a surprise for you Mum."

Satish stepped into the room behind her.

For a moment time froze for Serena. She registered the look of shock and disapproval on her mother's face. Her spirit immediately leapt with joy at the sight of Satish's outstretched arms and his broad smile.

"Beloved!" he said.

Satish's eyes shone with love as he held out his arms to Serena. However, that momentary hesitation on Serena's part was disastrous. She did not immediately leap out of her seat on the sofa and go to him. Satish realised her hesitancy and withdrew his arms with a look of surprise and hurt. Serena got to her feet, went to his side, and took his hand, and gently pulled him into the room.

"Mum. This is Satish. Satish, this is my mother, Dorothy."

"Pleased to meet you," he said, bowing his head and putting his hands together in greeting, and then went to shake her hand. Dorothy forced a smile but did not take his proffered hand. For the second time, he withdrew from a rebuffed gesture of affection and greeting.

"Pleased to meet you." Her voice was hard and brittle. Serena felt her mother's eyes boring into her, her disapproval stabbing her.

Demurely Satish sat on the edge of the sofa next to Serena.

"I am sorry I did not phone you. Anish had an urgent meeting in London with his solicitors and I came with him. I could not phone you because my phone had died. I thought I would surprise you. I hope I did not inconvenience you."

The hurt still burned in his eyes. He did not tell her of the phone call from Claire telling him how desperately Serena was missing him and could he possibly come down for a surprise visit.

Serena realised she had to recover ground with him and try to heal his hurt.

"It….it….it was such a surprise. I am so pleased to see you. I have missed you so much."

She kissed him on the cheek.

She heard the squeals of delight from the twins, who had heard the doorbell and had peered down the stairs and seen him. They thundered down the stairs shouting his name. However, they stopped in the doorway, having sensed that something was awry. Satish spotted them and waved them in. They skipped up to him and hugged him. Abigail skipped over to Dorothy and gave her two drawings they had done.

"We did these for you."

One was of elephants and two people who were obviously Serena and Satish hugging each other, and the other one was of all the family except Sebastian doing what appeared to be different yoga poses, but Satish and Serena had hardly any clothes on. Dorothy looked shocked and started to cough so violently that she nearly spat out her false teeth. Abigail backed away and went to stand next to her sister who had Satish's hand in hers and was swinging it backwards and forwards.

"Have you come back now?" asked Olivia.

"Are you going to make Serena happy again and make her make squeaky gaspy noises?" asked Abigail. Serena stifled a laugh and Claire reddened. Dorothy looked even more horrified.

"If I can stay tonight that would be helpful." He turned to Serena and continued

"I am sorry Beloved, but I need to go back to Birmingham tomorrow. I miss you so much. Things are moving fast with the possible new Community. Once Anish has the money released from his mother's will and sold her house, we can buy some land in Sri Lanka."

Claire and Serena were exchanging glances.

"I am sleeping in the girls' room as Mum has our bed for tonight. I am sure we can find you somewhere."

Serena's body ached at the thought of having Satish under the same roof but not in the same bed as her. The disappointment on his face was heartbreaking. Dorothy was watching their exchange with eagle eyes and disapproval. Claire felt the colour rising on her face and a warmth spreading through her body.

"I could sleep on this sofa. It is long enough," he said.

Serena smiled at him weakly. Claire could see the longing the couple had for each other and knew that, somehow, they would find a way to be together. As she bent down to pick up Serena's cup from the coffee table, she hissed at her in a low voice so that Dorothy would not hear

"Just make sure you keep the squeaking down."

Gradually over the evening, the atmosphere warmed between Dorothy and Serena, and Satish. He was able to win Dorothy over with his skilled storytelling and had her chuckling at the escapades of the elephants and funny stories of situations when things had been "lost in translation." when volunteers had come to work in the Community. The girls would go to bed only if Satish would read them a story. Claire sorted out bedding for him to sleep downstairs, but as she was hunting through the linen to find a single duvet cover, she suddenly felt guilty.

She found Serena in the kitchen washing the plates and said

"You two have my bed tonight. Sebastian is away on business. I can put St John in his Moses basket. I'll sleep downstairs."

Serena turned to her, smiling, her eyes soft with gratitude. "Are you sure?"

Claire nodded, although the thought of Satish being in her bed was making her burn with desire.

Serena dried her hands and hugged her daughter.

"Thank you. It means so much. And there will be no squeaking."

Bedtime could not come quickly enough. Fortunately, Dorothy went up early and she had not been informed of the change of sleeping arrangements. Both Claire and Serena intuited it would be better for her to think that Satish was asleep downstairs, and Dorothy had said that in the morning she would keep to her bedroom until "The coast was clear" and he was up and dressed.

Once Claire and St John were set up in the living room, Serena and Satish slid into Claire's king-size bed and each other's waiting arms. For one night they felt life was normal again as they desperately made up for lost time apart. When the cold morning light woke them and for a minute they had to remember where they were, a feeling overwhelmed both of them that life from then on would never be the same again.

They managed to get dressed and downstairs before Dorothy appeared, and she was none the wiser of the change of sleeping arrangements. She seemed at ease with her newfound family and offered to make tea for them all. There was a slightly embarrassing moment when she put cow's milk into Serena's peppermint tea, but Serena managed it with her usual gentleness so as not to hurt her mother. Dorothy started to dread going back to her empty cottage, but she needed to go home as she had the plumber coming the next day to service her boiler. She had booked a train for two thirty so they could have lunch together before she took a taxi to the station. Mid-morning Satish had a phone call from Anish to ask if he minded staying another night in London as Anish's visit to the solicitor had needed more paperwork which had to be signed the next day. He also asked if he could come to meet up with Satish as he needed him to read some paperwork and give him a second opinion on it. Satish put him on hold while he asked Claire if he could stay another night and whether Anish could come over with the documents. Claire felt her colour rise at the sight of her mother almost bursting with excitement at the thought of having him for another night.

"Of course. He can come for a meal if you like."

Satish clicked off hold and relayed this to Anish. When the conversation had finished Satish said

"I forgot to say. Our cousin Shanthi is also down here with Anish. I hope you don't mind if she comes as well."

Serena suddenly felt a stab in her heart and dread at the thought of meeting her.

Serena and Satish walked to the nursery to collect the twins, barely speaking to each other, and he realised that she had been very subdued since his conversation with Anish. He tried to find out what was the problem. but she seemed to be closed to him. It did not occur to him that the woman he loved so much was feeling insecure and jealous.

The girls bounded out of the nursery and asked if Great Granny was still at home.

"You are a coolerer Granny than she is!" Olivia said.

"You don't look old and painted," Abigail added.

"And that's why she doesn't have a boyfriend like Satish."

Serena asked the twins not to say such hurtful things in front of Dorothy.

They had lunch and made plans for Dorothy to visit again, and for Serena to go down to her mother's again in a few weeks. Fortunately, the twins behaved themselves and seemed sad at the thought that their newfound Great Granny had to go home.

Dorothy left by taxi and Satish and Serena sat with the twins, telling them stories, and making them giggle, and it began to feel like nothing had changed. Whenever Satish was sat next to her, Serena felt her body tingling and her breath stilted. Whenever he looked at her, she could see warmth and passion in his eyes. They were both longing for the night again back in their own room.

At six o'clock the doorbell rang, and Claire answered it. Serena heard her say

"Oh, you must be Anish."

She heard Anish introduce Shanthi to Claire and they came into the living room. Claire followed behind, her breath having been taken away by the sight of Anish, who was almost the twin of Satish, with sensuous lips and warm, deep eyes. He was dressed in tight jeans, and a leather jacket left open, and she could see he had a well-sculpted body under his tight tee shirt.

Unlike Satish, his hair was cut short and he smelt of cologne. Claire felt a warmth in her body.

Serena was too busy studying Shanthi to notice the effect Anish was having on her daughter. Shanthi lit the room up with her smile and dazzling white teeth. She was wrapped in a white sari to indicate mourning, and it highlighted her dark, almost black, skin, and lustrous black hair. Serena noticed how Satish swallowed hard when he saw her, and he stood up and demurely kissed his cousin on the cheek.

"Anish, Shanthi. Please meet my beloved Serena."

Serena noticed Anish's resemblance to Satish and then realised her daughter was staring at him. The colours swirling around in her aura told Serena that she no longer need to worry about her daughter's lustful feelings about Satish and she could see Anish had picked up quickly on Claire's attraction to him as he kept smiling at her. Serena quickly processed all this, and graciously greeted both Anish and Shanthi. They said they were delighted to meet the woman who had made Satish so happy. She turned to Satish beaming, but her face fell when she saw the expression on his face as he gazed longingly at Shanthi.

Anish, Satish, and Shanthi went into the dining room to go through the paperwork, and Claire pulled together the sliding doors to give them privacy in their financial discussions. Meanwhile, Claire and Serena ordered takeaway. They had decided that would be easier than cooking, especially after having entertained Dorothy. While they were going through the menu

Claire was trying to pump Serena for information about Anish. She had to admit she did not know much about him, but she knew he was not married and was Satish's closest relative physically and emotionally. Satish had brothers and sisters still in Sri Lanka but had very little to do with them. He and Anish were like twins, despite Anish's worldliness. He acted as a balance to Satish's deep otherworldliness. Both men had a deep love and respect for each other. Serena had gathered from talking to Satish over the phone during the previous fortnight that Anish was looking for a deeper meaning in life and this was why he was eager to help start the new community. Claire suddenly found herself fantasising about running off to Sri Lanka and starting a new life. She was gazing into space when she realised her mother was asking her a question.

"Do you want Sag Aloo as well?"

Claire returned to reality with a jolt.

"Yes. Yes. Order whatever you want."

Serena went to the dining room to tell the others that food would be delivered in half an hour, but she stopped in the doorway to take in the sight before her. All three were deep in conversation as they poured over the paperwork spread out on the dining table. However, it was the glances that went between Satish and Shanthi that shook her to the core. The lingering looks at each other and slightly shy smiles told her all she needed to know and feared.

The takeaway arrived and the paperwork was hurriedly cleared away so they could sit at the dining

table to eat. Claire had impressed both Anish and Satish
with her financial acumen when they started to pour
over some figures and could not make sense of them,
and, overhearing their problem, she had offered to
help. Anish joked that she should join the team and
move to Sri Lanka with them. Claire beamed back at
him, and Serena saw that life was returning to her
daughter once more. Her eyes were sparkling, and she
seemed to glow under the gentle teasing of Satish and
Anish. Once again Serena's heart was bursting with
love for Satish as he seemed to know just how to bring
out the best in people, and he was making Claire shine
in front of Anish. Studying Anish, she could see that he
liked Claire, and she was strangely reassured by this.
She felt that she had lessened the threat to Satish from
one woman, but what of her other rival? Her over-
active mind had her imagining Satish and Shanthi
falling in love and believing that maybe now he was
feeling trapped in his relationship with her. She
watched every interaction between them to see if her
worries had a foundation and a couple of times noticed
that their glances at each other lingered slightly longer
than normal. However, her fears were allayed when
they sat down to eat for it was not long before, under
the table and out of sight, Satish's hand was on Serena's
thigh and gently stroking the inside of it, signalling they
were in for a night of passion. Having to control her
breathing she smiled at him in acknowledgement.

After the meal, there was another session of
scrutinising paperwork, and it was at this point

Sebastian returned. He paused in surprise at the sight of everyone around the table, calculators in hand. Claire jumped up and drew him into the room, and quickly introduced everyone. Even Sebastian noticed the look that went between Anish and Claire as she introduced him. However, Sebastian did not care. After his overnight stay with Eleanor, he was now on count down to their weekend away at the end of the following week. He hung around for as little time as he thought he could without appearing rude and then make his apologies to go and continue his work in his attic office.

Around ten o'clock Anish and Shanthi gathered up all the paperwork and made plans to get a taxi back to where they were staying. Anish informed Satish that if he wanted to stay in London for a bit longer then he was not needed immediately in Birmingham as they had made such substantial progress on the paperwork.

"Thanks to the mathematical genius of Claire." Anish beamed at her. Claire blushed and muttered that she had not really done that much.

"But you have," Anish insisted. "We did not understand half of these final accounts of my mother. You have made them make sense. Even better, we realise we are to inherit more money than we ever thought we would. We can go ahead with our new Community."

As they left Anish and Shanthi kissed Claire, Serena and Satish, Serena noticed that Anish lingered a little longer over kissing Claire, and she responded to him by pulling him close. Although not a vindictive soul, she felt a sense of satisfaction that maybe Sebastian had some karma coming to him.

TWENTY-TWO

With Dorothy gone Serena and Satish were back in their old room and Satish felt he was temporarily home again. He knew he would have to go back up to Birmingham before too long but for the time being, he was going to enjoy being back with Serena, but not so much with her family and its negative energies.

Serena had arranged several private yoga sessions at the beginning of the following week for some of Claire's friends, some at their houses and some in Claire's house, and, at Claire's suggestion, Satish joined in so that he could give deeper spiritual teaching. However, it soon became obvious that the students only wanted to know how to be able to stay slim and supple and were not interested in broadening their minds and spirits, and both Serena and Satish picked up on the sexual vibrations emanating from them. The women busily eyed up Satish and kept looking at Serena in disbelief at her fortune in "having caught" such a desirable man. One of them even asked in a low voice what her secret was as she needed to find herself a toy boy to keep her on her toes. Serena decided that, in the future, she would teach the yoga lessons alone.

It would also give her an independent source of income from Satish, who was doing well with the sales of his books and was therefore happy to support her, but she wanted her financial independence. Satish seemed happy with that and suggested

"Maybe you should advertise to find more clients."

"I would need to get properly certified first, but maybe I will see if I can find more people," Serena mused. However, one potential student was going to prove to be a disaster.

Roger stared at himself in the mirror. He had to admit that he was still very handsome, with his silver-peppered hair and brooding Latin looks inherited from his Spanish father. At least Arabella, the wife of one of the Directors, and Amy in accounts both thought so. He suspected that Melanie had more than a professional relationship with one or two of her clients, so it was only fair and just if he played the field a bit wider as well. However, he was getting tired of having to keep tabs on when Arabella's husband was out of town, and Amy's bedsit in Harringay was dreary. At first, he had enjoyed "slumming it" with her as it was an escape from the high-maintenance life of so many of the women in his life, but, lately, it had felt a little bit too tacky. It was time for a new adventure. He straightened his tie and decided it was time to try another conquest. He was determined to show that child that his ex-wife was shackled to that he, Roger, was the true man. He could not believe Jayne had fallen for Satish's mumbo-jumbo spiritual nonsense. Roger refused to call her Serena except in her presence as she had made it clear she would not answer to Jayne. To him, she would always be Plain Jayne, despite having been extremely attractive when he first married her. Single parenthood had changed that, so she had become Plain Jayne. Although now she was no longer plain. He ran his hand through his hair and smirked. Melanie was away for a couple of days supporting a friend who had just gone through a messy divorce. He had nothing in the diary so perhaps he could drop in to see his grandchildren. Checking his watch, he saw that it was now nearly two o'clock and the girls would be back from nursery.

Half an hour later he was knocking on Claire's door. She was so surprised to see him and immediately blurted out that she hoped everything was okay and what was he doing there.

He smiled his teeth flashing smile and said

"Can't a grandfather come and visit his grandchildren?"

"Of course."

Claire felt nonplussed. She did not understand why Roger should be showing an interest in his grandchildren after virtually ignoring them for so long.

He found Satish and Serena in the front room with the girls practicing yoga positions. They were all surprised to see Roger.

Abigail was on all fours arching her back.

"I's a cat."

She then rose up with her legs straight, her hands on the ground, forming an upside-down V shape.

"Now I's a dog."

Olivia was sat with her legs in a semi-lotus position.

"I am being meditateful," she said.

"Oh. How interesting."

Roger sat down on the settee. Satish and Serena were both doing shoulder stands and gently returned to upright positions.

"Can you does yoga Grandad?" asked Abigail as she stood up.

"I expect so," Roger replied with a touch of superiority. "There doesn't appear to be much to it."

Serena and Satish exchanged glances.

Olivia grabbed his hand and tried to pull him off the settee.

"Come on then. Show us. Can you do a shoulder stand? Satish is so clever he can even do a headstand. I bet you don't know how to do that."

Roger realised that he was being backed into a corner and the look of sympathy on Satish's face was more than he could bear.

"I am not in the proper clothes for yoga."

Olivia, always one for pushing boundaries, said

"I don't think you can do it. Satish can. He's clever."

The gauntlet had been thrown down. Roger got to his feet and flashing his best smile at Serena, took off his shoes and socks and said

"Okay Satish, show me how it is done. Maybe start with a shoulder stand."

Satish was hesitant.

"Are you sure Roger?"

"Absolutely."

Satish slowly lay down on the floor and extended his feet into the air. He then lifted his whole body until he was in the shoulder stand.

"Easy peasy!" said Roger smugly.

He lay down and tried to copy Satish. It took several attempts to get his legs into the air, and then as he raised his whole body there was the sound of ripping material as the back seam burst in his expensive Italian linen trousers. This made him lose balance and he toppled over with a crash onto the ground, where he started screaming in pain.

"Bloody hell I have knackered my back."

He grabbed at the lower part of his back.

"I can't move. Get me an ambulance."

Both girls looked wide-eyed at their grandfather writhing on the floor, a large rip in his trousers, exposing a pair of silk Superman boxer shorts. They both burst into giggles. Seeing Grandad's underpants was the funniest thing they had ever seen.

Serena rushed to Roger's side and tried to move him.

"Get off you stupid cow," he shrieked. "I've slipped a disc."

Claire was already on the phone with the paramedics, who said they would be there in five minutes. Serena had to admire their professionalism in not laughing when they arrived to find a very late-middle-aged man rolling around on the floor, with expensive ripped trousers that cost more than they earned in a week, and the explanation that he had toppled over doing a yoga position. However, one of them spotted his boxer shorts and had to stifle a snigger. Roger was not amused when the paramedic said, "Come on Superman, it is off to hospital for you to check you out."

They took him to hospital for a scan to make sure there was no serious damage. Fortunately, Roger had not slipped a disc but had merely badly pulled a muscle, which would soon heal with rest. However, his pride, and his expensive trousers, were damaged beyond repair.

A phone call with Anish on the following Wednesday meant Satish would catch a train back to Birmingham the next morning. Serena was, once more, sad to see him go but felt reassured of his love for her, but she still had a niggling feeling of jealousy knowing he would be back in Shanthi's company again. However, he assured her he would be back the following week and that everything was nearly finished in Birmingham. As he stroked her hair in bed the previous night he had whispered

"And then we can really be together again. We can start our plans to return to our proper home – well for a short time, and then we can start our next adventure together. I feel good energy around a community being formed in Sri Lanka. We will have the money for it. It will be a new adventure for us."

Serena smiled back at him, and she felt his hot breath on her face. However, she was not sure whether she felt sad or excited about this. The thought of leaving her family in England made her heart ache, and she suddenly realised that she did not really know where she called home now.

As she waved Satish off, Serena still felt a deep conflict within her. She decided she would make herself a tea to calm herself but discovered her frangipani tea had finally run out, so she rummaged in the cupboard and took out the jar of tea she had bought in Southall. Sitting cross-legged on the settee, feeling lost without Satish, she started sipping it but wrinkled her face up in disgust. It tasted more bitter than her frangipani tea and it made her head spin. Putting the tea down, she sat back and started reflecting on the past few days. She was enjoying being with her daughter and family, despite the tensions and drama. St John loved her and although he was too young to smile yet, he did seem to beam at her. Serena felt a deep bond with him. She had a deeper bond than Claire appeared to have with him. Claire robotically mothered him, merely meeting his needs for food, clean nappies, and warmth. She was continuing the pattern of mothering that her mother and grandmother had followed. Serena suddenly became aware of this and wanted to break the cycle of robotic and almost loveless parenting. She spent lots of time talking to him, cuddling him and propping him on her shoulder and walking him around, showing him things. Claire was oblivious to this and was in a world of her own. Serena lost count of the number of times Anish's name came up in conversation. Claire was eager to know if he was going to visit again. Serena did know that they were friends on Facebook now, and Claire, who previously seemed disinterested in it, was suddenly spending time with her face buried in her laptop or phone. Serena felt a niggle of concern that her daughter might be setting herself up for heartache.

As Serena was sat meditating Claire burst into the room.

"Bloody Sebastian," she spat. "He only invited his parents to lunch today and forgot to tell me! They are due at midday! What the hell am I going to do? I don't have Maria to clean anymore, and I haven't done a shop for a while. I have two and a half hours before they arrive."

Claire sank into her armchair with her head in her hands.

"And the twins will need collecting from nursery."

Serena stood up and said

"Come on. Let's see what there is in the kitchen already. I can nip out and get some groceries and I can collect the girls. We can do a quick blitz between us in the living room, kitchen, and bathroom. When is Sebastian back? I take it he is going to be here with his parents?"

"Half twelve. I will have to entertain them for a bit on my own." Claire's tone showed her resentment.

A quick rummage in the cupboard turned up half a dozen eggs, flour, half a Roquefort cheese that Sebastian had bought, new potatoes, and some limp salad.

"Right!" Serena said. "If I remember correctly quiches are standard fare for church people. We can do potato salad and I will buy some fresh salad when I go and get the girls and I will grab a cheesecake from the deli for afters. And also some of their samosas for me. You start the food, and I will get cleaning."

The two women worked extremely hard over the next hour and a half. Serena cleaned the living room and bathroom while Claire made pastry, and boiled potatoes, and cleaned the kitchen. At eleven-thirty Serena left to get the shopping and collect the twins and Claire continued cooking the quiche. She whisked the eggs and milk and then to her annoyance discovered that she had run out of mixed herbs to add to the Roquefort in the quiche. She decided she would phone her mother and ask her to get some. Spotting Serena's phone still plugged in, charging on the worktop, she cursed. Then she remembered the jar of what looked like herbs she had seen out on the top earlier. Opening the jar, she smelt it and there was a slight almost musty, oregano smell about the leaves. Shrugging her shoulders, she spooned two tablespoons of the dried leaves into the egg and milk mix and poured it over the quiche. Just as she had put it in the oven, the doorbell rang, and she went to greet her in-laws.

She was taken aback to see her tall, pot-bellied, and balding father-in-law in his purple Bishop's shirt and big silver cross and her immaculate, tall, thin mother-in-law dressed in a pale mauve suit and white hat.

As he kissed his daughter-in-law Sebastian's father, indicating his purple shirt, explained

"Got to see the big boss this afternoon. The Archbishop has called a meeting of several of us bishops this afternoon. A bit unexpected. Hence the garb."

Serena and the excited girls arrived ten minutes later.

"Hello, Anthony and Georgina," Serena said warmly to them. They were surprised at the sight of their daughter-in-law's mother. They had not seen her since the baptism of the twins four years ago. Afterwards, they had confided in each other how they were worried about her as she had seemed so low in spirit and looked unwell. However, they could see that a positive change had taken place within her and as they sat and talked, Anthony was interested to hear about the Community and its plans.

"Strictly off the record," he confided, "I think anyone of any deep spirituality basically wants peace and love on earth. I think we have a lot to learn from other spiritualities, and we have good things to offer as well. I would love to hear about your new Community once it has been started."

Claire's phone rang and her expression darkened as she listened to Sebastian explaining how he was held up but would be back as soon as possible. She rang off and scowled. He was already annoyed himself as he wanted to have some time telling his mother how awful Claire and Serena were and how unhappy he was, and wondering if his marriage could survive. He wanted to "sow the seeds" about a potential split before his trip to Rome.

Lunch was a relaxed affair. Serena had samosas and salad and the twins had chicken nuggets. The quiche was well received. A bottle of champagne was opened to celebrate St John's birth.

As Serena was telling them about the elephants in their Thailand community Georgina started giggling uncontrollably. Serena stopped, puzzled. At this point, Claire started giggling, which set Anthony off chuckling. With tears running down her face, Georgina asked

"Did I spot some rainbow elephants in the hall to go with your wonderful hair?"

This started the girls off laughing. They proudly told their grandparents about their Elly train in the hallway and grabbed their hands and dragged them out to see it. This set Georgina off laughing even more and she was doubled up clutching herself as the twins told her how Daddy nearly exploded, he was so cross when he saw it.

"I'm going to wet myself," she cried, crossing her legs. The twins exchanged glances and burst into giggles at the thought of their immaculate grandmother doing such a thing. Fortunately for Georgina, there was a small toilet next to the kitchen.

Anthony too was doubled up with laughter and unable to contain himself.

He roared with laughter when Serena told him how Sebastian had reacted.

"Stuck up idiot," he laughed. "I think they add a little *je ne sais quoi.* You can't buy wallpaper like it in Liberty's."

Serena was bemused. She wondered what had got into them all. Claire too was laughing uncontrollably, and the twins were laughing at the adults laughing. She felt a little left out, although she could see the funny side of it all.

"This one," Anthony pointed to the first one in the line, "this one has got to be Nellie. I know a song about her."

With that, he burst into song with a booming voice. "Nellie the Elephant packed her trunk…."

Georgina joined in with her operatic voice, making up a descant. They stuck their arms up in front of their faces and started waving them around like trunks. This started the twins off laughing hysterically, which encouraged Anthony and Georgina to sing even more loudly and wave their arms more frantically.

At that moment, the sound of the front door key in the lock was heard and Sebastian came in. He stopped in his tracks at the sight of his father, in his clerical shirt, his pectoral cross swinging wildly from side to side, stomping up and down the hallway waving his arm in front of his nose, singing Nellie the Elephant. His pristine mother was following, waving her arm as a trunk and trilling away to her husband's baritone. Claire, the twins, and Serena were doubled over laughing and trying to sing the chorus.

"What the hell…." Sebastian did not know how to react.

"Come and join in," Anthony sang.

Sebastian stood staring for a minute in disgust and then ducked into the living room and made his way to the dining room to avoid the flailing arms, He saw the remnants of the lunch still laid out, with a plate of quiche left for him. Angrily he sat down to eat, knowing that with his mother in this ridiculous mood, he would never be able to talk to her about Claire and Serena. It would have to wait until after his trip to Rome. He was even more annoyed when his parents snaked and stomped their way into the dining room, with Claire, Serena, and the twins in tow, still singing, and then to be told that they would have to go shortly, and a taxi was picking them up to take them to Lambeth Palace. He had only had one mouthful of the quiche and almost spat it out in disgust.

"What the hell have you put in this? It tastes like compost."

Normally Claire would have been stung by his remark, but she just laughed.

"We enjoyed it."

The sound of a horn outside announced the arrival of the taxi. Anthony and Georgina hugged Claire, Serena, and the girls, which was unusual for them as they were not normally demonstrative people. Anthony clapped his son on the back.

"Chill out old boy. You have a cracking family here. And your wife makes a bloody good quiche."

Anthony and Georgina set off down the path with Anthony still singing Nellie the Elephant, and Serena was sure she saw him skip a couple of times. She wondered with trepidation how his meeting with the Archbishop was going to go. A few minutes later she heard a heated exchange of words coming from the kitchen.

"So, this is what you put in the quiche?"

Sebastian sounded angry.

"Yes. I thought they were mixed herbs."

"You stupid mare. It is weed. You have just sent my father off to meet the Archbishop, and he is stoned out of his mind, never mind how mother is."

Serena quietly crept away into the sanctuary of her room and tried to work out how she would explain what had happened.

Once over his initial anger at the situation, Sebastian began to see the funny side of it and was relieved to have a phone call from his mother later to say that the Archbishop had been highly amused at how animated and jovial her husband had been and how he had ended up in a giggling fit as well when Anthony told him about the Elly train and started humming Nellie the Elephant. However, they did not go so far as to do the elephant trunk impressions. She also told him how they thought Serena had turned into such a lovely woman and how pleased he must be to have her supporting Claire. They had vowed not to leave it so long before visiting again and said he really was so lucky to have Claire and the children.

Despite this, Sebastian seemed to improve in mood and as the week drew to a close, he kept reminding Claire of his business trip to Rome. He was not sure how long he was going to be away. Claire did not care. When she walked in on Sebastian packing for his trip and realised he was packing his black silk briefs instead of his usual white cotton boxers, she still did not care. Her mind was too full of fantasies about running away to Sri Lanka with Anish, although she realised the absurdity of it. She kept telling herself that her fantasy was the one thing that was keeping her sane in the middle of her loveless marriage and the drudgery of looking after three small children.

As Sebastian pecked his wife on the cheek and walked down the path to the waiting taxi, on the way to the airport, Claire had a strange feeling of finality. Serena too had a strong feeling that the following week was going to be very turbulent. She vowed she would make the weekend a haven of peace and tranquillity for Claire. With some of the money collected from her yoga classes, she paid for Claire to have her hair cut, and she felt very affirmed when Claire returned with a new, short hairstyle, not dissimilar to her own. However, Claire's hair was now a deep, shiny chestnut colour with no signs of grey. Claire told her mother she had decided to treat herself to the "full works" as she had a feeling her life was about to change for the good but did not know why or how. Serena spent more time in meditation, with a gathering feeling of the calm before the storm. Even the twins picked up on this and seemed a little subdued. They even seemed to be worried by Sebastian's absence, although they were so used to having an absent father.

When Serena expressed her sense of unease to Satish on the phone, he replied that they were both walking the paths they were called to and that she was a warrior and could face anything.

"I wish I had you here to stand with me," she whispered down the phone to him.

"Beloved, you have journeyed long and hard and your soul has grown in so many ways. Whatever is going to happen will be to strengthen you further. You do not need me. I will hold you in my prayers and meditations, but you need to walk this path alone. Be brave. I will be back at the end of next week. Probably Thursday. Then we can be together again."

Serena smiled.

"Thank you. I don't know what I'd do without you."

"And I without you," he replied.

Serena realised that he had not mentioned Shanthi once in their hour-long conversation.

TWENTY-THREE

Sebastian could not wait to get on the flight to Rome. Eleanor had gone ahead of him by a couple of days as she wanted to do some clothes ordering from some of the exclusive boutiques she liked to frequent.

When she met him at the airport, she was wearing a skin-tight red dress with a slit up the thigh, which enhanced every curve of her body. Sebastian found himself bursting with desire, eager to get to the hotel and unable to control his impatience at the slow-moving Rome traffic. Eleanor did not help matters by breathing suggestive ideas into his ear. Once they got to the hotel, he had to cool himself down as Eleanor introduced him to the hotel proprietor as her "cousin from England". Sebastian remembered how puritanical Eleanor had said the hotel owners were, but "they could have a high level of luxury without too much expense". However, when Sebastian saw the price of the rooms, he had to suppress a gasp. They went to their rooms. Each one was a suite, with a living room and bedroom with an enormous bed. Between their rooms was a door, which Eleanor had asked to be unlocked. She suspected that the owners knew more than they let on, but they were happy to have her custom as she had been a regular over the years, visiting with her various "cousins" and "brothers." They knew she had an expensive taste in room service as well.

Wasting no time, they tumbled into Sebastian's bed, but not before Eleanor had shown him some items she had brought with her that would "spice things up" – a couple of sets of handcuffs, and a packet of blue pills. She did not show him the sleeping pills she had also brought with her.

For four days they spent the daytime wandering around the sights of Rome, being tourists and savouring the culinary delights. Sebastian had visited Rome on a school trip when he was fourteen but did not remember much about it. He had been too busy eyeing up the Italian girls, who were interested in his blond hair and blue eyes. He got sent home early from the trip after being caught climbing out of the hostel window on his way to meet one of the signorinas he had picked up. His parents had grounded him for a month and cut his allowance. Now he was too taken up by Eleanor to look at the Italian women who were blatantly giving him the eye.

Eleanor taught him a vast range of new experiences in the bedroom, doing things that he knew Claire would never experiment with in a million years. He felt he was living his dream. He was with a gorgeous, sexy, passionate woman in a luxury hotel in one of the most romantic cities in the world. He could not imagine a better life.

However, suddenly on Wednesday Eleanor seemed to change. She became introspective and all through breakfast she seemed to force her usual cheerfulness. Sebastian asked her what was wrong. She assured him she was fine and just had a little bit of a headache. Sebastian picked up a certain sadness about her and it seemed as though she was looking at everything in a very observant way as if it were the last time she would be seeing it. That afternoon she seemed back to her normal self and the moment they got to his room after lunch to have a "siesta" she had her hands down his trousers and breathing suggestions into his ear. Just as he was on the point of losing control and was hastily tearing off his trousers, her phone rang.

"Ignore it," he panted as he undid her bra and pulled her down on the bed.

However, the caller was persistent. After ringing off, the phone rang again almost immediately.

Eleanor got to her feet, half-naked, and said

"It must be urgent. We should be exchanging contracts on my cottage today."

Sebastian sat up, a fuming heap of frustration while Eleanor rooted in her bag and found her phone.

"It's Freddy, my solicitor," she said as she dialled back.

Sebastian sat on the bed trying to cool down his passion as he listened to Eleanor.

"Hi, Freddy. Is it done?"

A long silence ensued, with Eleanor's face changing from the sweaty glow of passion to a deathly pallor. Finally, she spoke in a shocked voice

"What! Can they do that? No. No. I can't lose it. It's perfect." She had sat down on the dressing table stool running her free hand through her hair. She continued in a desperate voice

"Freddy there must be something I can do to save the situation."

By now Sebastian was on his feet and he wanted to sit next to Eleanor but there was not quite enough room on the stool for the two of them. More than anything he wanted to be next to her, holding her close as he could see her dream tumbling down before her. He could see tears forming in the corners of her eyes. Suddenly she brightened a bit.

"OK so if I increase my offer they will exchange today. How much?"

Sebastian could just about hear the voice at the other end of the phone but could not make out the words. Eleanor was biting her lower lip.

"Sixty grand. Wow! That is a huge increase."

Sebastian could hear the garbled voice at the other end of the phone increasing in urgency. Eleanor sighed.

"OK. It is less than five percent of the price. I am away at the moment. I am not sure what I can do. Let me get onto it. How long have I got? OK. We are an hour ahead here, so it is two-thirty here. One thirty in the UK. I have an hour and a half you say before the deal is off. I will get back to you."

Eleanor finished the call and slumped with a look of total defeat on her face. Sebastian felt irritated that the blue pill he had taken at the end of lunch was now fully working, but it was highly inappropriate at this moment.

"I need to raise sixty grand in an hour and a half. I'd transferred the full, agreed price to my account and now they have upped the price. They have another cash offer fifty grand above my offer. If I can find sixty, they will exchange contracts today. Oh, Sebastian."

She turned to him with her eyes full of tears.

"I had such a dream for us in that place. It is so perfect. You can get to London easily. I'm near my dear friends."

She put her face in her hands and began sobbing in an act that would gain an Oscar. Sebastian decided to squeeze next to her on the dressing table stool, but it was not built for two people and instantly there was a loud crack as one of the legs broke. They tumbled onto the plush carpet and Eleanor quickly had to regain the momentum of the moment. She got up and threw herself down on the bed, sobbing into her hands.

"I need to give forty-eight hours' notice to draw down that sort of money," she sobbed. "Of course I have it. I could buy that dinky little place ten times over. I just don't have access to my money right now."

Sebastian was now sitting next to her on the bed and stroking her hair, aware that his dreams too were crumbling.

"Maybe I should just give up and go back to the States," she sobbed. "I can't go through all this again."

Sebastian sat thinking. He got up and went to his luggage where he kept his laptop and returned to the bed. Logging into his online banking for his offshore account he sat and crunched some figures. Opening his calculator app, he sat and did some sums. Eleanor lay watching him, a smile creeping over her face which was still hidden behind her hands, but she kept giving a stifled sob and sniffing heavily. Sebastian stretched and turned to her.

"Honey. I can lend it to you. I will need it back before the end of the month, but if it means you get the house of your dreams, that's fine by me."

Eleanor sat up and wiped her mascara-streaked face with the back of her hand.

"Are you sure? It's a lot of money to ask for. That's why I didn't ask you immediately."

Sebastian took her face in his hands and stared into her eyes.

"I know I can trust you. I know you have the money to pay me back. Now. What are your account details again?"

Eleanor had to stop herself punching the air in delight.

An hour later there was a phone call from Freddy to say contracts had been exchanged and all was well. Sebastian ordered a large bottle of champagne to celebrate. Eleanor insisted on going back to her room to change into something she knew he would like.

Once in her room, she quietly locked the door and went to her bathroom with her mobile phone. She had almost to lean out of the window to get a signal as she tapped in a London number. After a couple of rings, a surly voice answered.

"Yeah?"

"Dwayne. Well done. You did a perfect posh solicitor. He fell for it. The two hundred pounds will be in your account tonight. I am going dark for a while. Things might get a bit too hot for me here so I will be out of touch, but I won't forget you."

"Yeah. OK. See Ya."

The phone went dead. Dwayne was not a man of many words. However, he felt he had just done one of the easiest jobs he had ever done. Two phone calls that cost him nothing under the phone package he had, and he had made two hundred pounds. That would get him some more white powder for that night.

Eleanor felt a twinge of sadness as she realised that she was probably not going to use Dwayne's services ever again. Eleanor Ellis/Susanna Sanchez had one more outing before they would cease to exist, and she would regain her real identity. She would become Rachel Robertson again and give up the excitement and stress of her multiple personae.

Sighing she opened her suitcase and took out a black lace basque and soft leather thigh-length boots and put them on. She needed to exhaust Sebastian, so she took out the small riding crop that was stashed in the lid of the suitcase and went back into his room.

He was laid back on the bed with his eyes closed.

"OK," she purred as she slunk across the carpet towards him. "You have been such a good boy. Time to be a bad boy now."

With a spring she was onto the bed and straddling him, snapping the crop in her hand. She started licking his chest and neck and making passionate noises. His response was immediate.

TWENTY-FOUR

Sebastian felt as though he was floating, with his arms and legs outstretched. Was he floating in the sea? No. He felt the soft linen beneath him, and his memory began to return. He found it hard to open his eyes. His head was thumping, and his groin was aching. Through the fog of half-remembered things, he pictured himself being chained with handcuffs to the bedhead and being fed another blue pill. Things after that were a bit blurred. It was a muddle of champagne, black lace, riding crops, Eleanor at her wildest and enjoying the power she had had over him as he was chained to the bed.

He went to move but it felt as though he was still chained to the bed. He also had a piece of material crammed in his mouth which stopped him from speaking. He tried to roll over but could not. Eventually, he forced his eyes open to see that he was still chained, naked, to his bed. The curtains were drawn. By straining his head he could see the bedside clock said two-thirty. He was confused for a minute. Then he realised the sun was peeking around the corner of the heavy curtains which meant it was two-thirty in the afternoon. He wanted to gag with the cloth in his mouth and he tried to dislodge it with his tongue. After twenty minutes he managed to get it out and he started coughing. There was no sign of Eleanor. He shouted her name. No reply. He knew the door between their rooms was fairly soundproof, but he shouted anyway.

"Okay. Enough of the joke. Eleanoooooooooor."

He started pulling at the handcuffs around his hands and feet, but they were too strong and did not give. He shouted even louder. When he realised Eleanor was not coming, he started shouting for help in Italian and jerking the chains of the handcuffs, so it made the bedhead thump against the wall. It hurt his wrists to do so but he had no other option. After screaming himself almost hoarse for half an hour, the connecting door opened, and a maid came through. She had seen the "Do Not Disturb" sign on his door to the corridor but in cleaning the Signora's room she had heard the cries for help from the adjoining room. Stopping dead in the doorway she stood wide-eyed at the sight of the tall, blond English man, stark naked, chained to the bed, and with the effects of the blue pill obvious still. She let out the longest and loudest scream.

The owners of the hotel were not impressed. Having calmed Venetia down from her discovery, they sent her home for the day. They then went to Sebastian's room and first threw the bedcover over him to regain some dignity. The husband looked at the handcuffs and realised he would have trouble getting them off, without cutting the bedhead to pieces. The alternative was to call the fire brigade, but he decided against that because of the scandal it would cause. He, therefore, went to find himself a saw, returned, and set about sawing through the antique wood bedposts. The wife went into Eleanor's room and came back shrugging. In Italian, she informed her husband that the Signora had left a few clothes, but it would appear she had taken essentials with her. She had left early that morning with a large bag saying she was going shopping but please leave the Signor to sleep as they had been celebrating her buying a house and he had overdone the champagne. On reflection, the wife realised that the bag the Signora was carrying was the size of a cabin bag. She put her head in her hands and sighed.

An hour later Sebastian was free. Once the chains had been cut free of the bed there was the problem of the handcuffs around his ankles and wrists. It was only at this point that the owners realised that Eleanor had shown a little kindness. She had left the keys to the chains and the handcuffs on his dressing table, with a little note saying

"Sorry. It was a gas. Thanks for everything. Chau."

Sebastian sat staring at the note in disbelief until the sound of the hotel owner clearing his throat brought him back to reality. The hotel owner was not happy that he had just sawn through an expensive wooden bedhead when the keys were there all the time. Sebastian profusely thanked the couple and told them that of, course, he would pay for the cost of a new bedhead. Little did he know that it was an expensive Baroque bedhead that costs thousands of pounds. He still could not take in what had happened, refusing to believe that Eleanor had gone.

"I am sorry Signor," said the wife in broken English "but her perfume has gone. She has completely gone."

The couple left him to get dressed.

Sebastian sank back into the bed in despair. Then he sat back up exploding into expletives as he remembered the sixty thousand pounds that he had transferred to her account. He got up and went to his wallet. His credit cards were still there, so he breathed a sigh of relief. However, this was short-lived as he saw that his mobile, on silent, had several missed calls and five text messages. Hesitantly he opened the messages. They were from his credit card companies asking him to call them urgently.

Shortly after, he was sitting on the bed, staring at the phone. His credit card accounts had been all but maxed out. Such a sudden burst of activity in a foreign country had alerted Security in the credit card companies and a stop had been put on all his cards. However, it was not before they had been used to buying all manner of expensive designer clothes and shoes. All this had been done that morning while he was still comatose.

He opened his laptop and crunched in numbers. She had also emptied his onshore bank accounts. At least she had not accessed his offshore account, so he still had plenty of money. He could transfer some money onshore but with all his cards frozen he could still not access any money and it was going to take a couple of days to get new cards. He nearly hurled his laptop across the room in frustration but stopped himself in time. It would just be another unnecessary expense, even if it felt good at the time. Suddenly he thought of his passport, and, just as he feared, that had gone too. A passport was worth quite a lot of money on the black market. Sighing, he realised he had to sort out travel papers as well. He buzzed down to reception and asked for a very strong black coffee and some toast, while he examined his options.

Eleanor had a very busy morning. Leaving the hotel at eight-thirty, she first went to a busy public toilet where she went in as Eleanor Ellis and came out as Susanna Sanchez, having put on her brown wig, and inserting brown contact lenses in her eyes. She pushed her Eleanor Ellis passport into the flip-top sanitary bin, knowing she would be long gone before anyone found it, if ever. She lingered in the cubicle for a long time until she guessed all the people who saw her go in would have left. Hurriedly she exited and was relieved to see that the caretaker was on her break, so even she would not notice or remember her change of appearance. The next stop was the designer shop where she had ordered her clothes and she checked the fittings before paying for them on one of Sebastian's cloned cards. She then visited several other shops, each time racking up the credit cards. The bag she had taken out from the hotel was not big enough for her purchases, so she bought a crocodile leather suitcase in one of the shops, into which she put her purchases.

One of the cards was declined, but another one was accepted, so Eleanor realised it was time to stop shopping, especially as it was now ten-thirty and she needed to catch the flight at one-thirty. She would have to hurry as she was cutting it fine to get through security. Hailing a taxi, she set off for the airport. She was longing to see Eduardo again. Of all the men she had experienced, he was one of the most interesting. She had phoned him earlier in the week with her flight details and he was going to collect her from Madrid airport. He had said he could not wait to see her again.

Her excitement was mounting as the plane flew over the coast of Spain. This would be her last sting. Then Susanna Sanchez would go the way of Eleanor Ellis. She would make the most of her time with Eduardo. She would enjoy their nights together and then would enact one last sting to get back at all the men who had treated her badly over the years. She would fly back to the States and take on her proper identity again. This gave her a sense of relief. She was getting bored of trying to remember who she was, and who knew her as which persona. She had never needed the money. She had just wanted the excitement of the affairs and the stings. The heady mix of pheromones and adrenaline had kept her going, but it was exhausting. She was tired. She was craving normality. She was on her usual post-sting slump and decided she had had enough. The thought of living a "normal life" seemed almost exciting.

The plane landed and taxied to the gateway. The captain came on over the intercom and asked for everyone to remain in their seats. No one was to deboard the plane until instructed. People sat back down looking puzzled. "Susanna Sanchez" was booked in first class, so she was one of the first people to see the door of the plane swing open and, to her surprise, Eduardo Solares aka Oscar Ramirez of the Fraud Department of Interpol stepped into the plane and walked straight up to her.

"Hola," he said to her coldly as she looked at him with her mouth wide open.

"Susanna Sanchez. I am arresting you for theft, fraud, and money laundering."

From out of his pocket, he took a pair of handcuffs and snapped them on her wrists, just as Sebastian was being released from his, just over eight hundred miles away.

TWENTY-FIVE

Satish returned to London on Thursday, arriving at Claire's house about the same time as Sebastian was being released from his handcuffs. Serena was delighted to see him and when he pulled her close and pressed into her, she had no doubt he still had a lot of passion for her. Claire took the girls into the kitchen to allow the couple space to catch up in the living room. Satish assured Serena that the bulk of the paperwork was now done. and they were waiting for a purchaser of Anish's mother's house. He added that Anish had been quite taken by Claire and her financial ability. There was no mention of Shanthi.

Serena and Satish decided they would cook dinner together and would do a favourite Thai dish for the whole family. The girls were sitting at the island in the kitchen colouring, St John was asleep in his Moses basket next to the window. Claire had poured them all a large glass of wine to celebrate Satish's return, and she was glowing inwardly at the messages that Satish had passed on from Anish. She was just topping up her glass when her phone rang. It was plugged in and charging on the worktop. She looked at it with puzzlement.

"It's Sebastian. He never normally calls me when he is away."

She picked the phone up and answered it. By the poor signal and crackly connection, it was obvious that he was still in Rome. Gradually her face went through the widest range of emotions that Serena had ever seen on her daughter's face, as Sebastian told her everything that had happened, down to every last detail. Initially, it was slight annoyance at his interrupting her glass of wine, then slowly her face turned angry, then to stone, then she burst out laughing in a cold, brutal laugh when he admitted to being chained to the bedpost, but her final expression was one of total disgust. He was begging her to help him. She slowly shook her head. Then with utter finality, she said

"No. You got yourself into this mess. You get yourself out of it. I think it is called karma. And don't bother coming back here. Your stuff will be at the office."

Claire slammed the phone down on the counter but had to check quickly that she had not broken it.

"Bastard!" she spat at it.

Serena and Satish had both stopped what they were doing and were watching mystified. Fortunately. the girls were too absorbed in their colouring to realise that their family had just completely and utterly broken up. Satish went over to the twins and suggested he took them into the living room to read them a story, which they accepted as a brilliant idea and squealed with delight. They ran past their mother without a glance, or they would have seen an expression of such rage and hatred on her face that they would probably have had nightmares for a long time after.

Claire slowly sat down on one of the bar stools and ran her hand through her hair.

"Bastard!" she repeated. "He's still in Rome, with no passport, credit cards, or money, having been totally scammed by that American slut he was shagging. Serves him right. They say karma is a bitch. Well, it has come dressed up as a rich American scammer bitch. He's not coming back here."

Claire burst out laughing in a callous, harsh laugh.

"And she chained him to the bedpost and force-fed him Viagra and sleeping pills, and then she went out and blew his credit cards. I wish I'd been a fly on the wall when he woke up and realised."

Serena's imagination veered away from the thought of Sebastian chained naked to a bed.

A new determination set itself on Claire's face.

"First things first. Tomorrow I am getting the locks changed. I own this house, so he has no right to come in. Then I am packing his stuff and dumping it at the office. Boy, is the shit going to hit the fan when Father finds out what he has done. I doubt he will keep him on. And I doubt his Bishop Father is going to welcome him back with open arms. Tough. Serves him right."

Serena's mind was whirling with all of this. She was amazed at the toughness of her daughter. She had always expected her to dissolve into tears and incapability when the inevitable split came. However, the opposite had happened. Claire had a strong resolve about her and seemed freer in her spirit than Serena had ever seen her. Serena realised that this was the best thing that could have happened to her. Taking her hand, she pulled her daughter close.

"Don't worry. We will get through this together. Everything will be okay."

However, Claire was not in the mood to be mollified. She pulled away.

"I own this house outright. I have my own income from my stocks and shares, plus I could do some freelance work. I will go for him for maintenance, although I don't think I will get much to begin with because I doubt Father will want him working with him anymore. Of course, I will have to let him see the children, but strictly on my terms. I've been waiting for him to screw up big time for so long now. I knew he would one day. He just couldn't help himself. I can live my life now. I'm not worried. I will survive." She hesitated for a moment. "No, I am not going to survive. I am going to thrive. I am finally free to do what I want. Without his constant criticism."

She grabbed her glass of wine and held it up in a toast.

"Freedom!"

Serena smiled with relief and asked Claire if she minded if she told Satish what had happened.

"What about the girls?" Serena asked.

"Oh, just leave them for now. They are happy at the moment. No need to upset them tonight. They hardly ever see their father, so if we just carry on as normal, let's see how long before they miss him."

Serena felt this was unfair but did not want to argue with Claire. Serena went into the living room where Satish was sitting with a twin on each side of him. She asked if they minded watching television while she talked to Satish in the dining room. Happily glued to Peppa Pig, the twins would be no trouble for some time. Once she had relayed everything she knew to Satish he sat looking thoughtful. They were sitting at the dining room table, and he leant across and took her hand.

"This complicates things," he said sadly, "as I was hoping we might head back to Thailand soon and then go to Sri Lanka. I expect you want to stay here for now until everything is sorted out with Sebastian. I suppose she will divorce him."

Serena nodded.

"She has good grounds."

He nodded too.

"Any relationship break-up is sad. They are mismatched. They were together for the wrong reasons. It was always going to fail. I am sorry."

Serena could see the deep and genuine pain he was feeling. A true empath he could pick up on the deeper levels of the feelings of people. At this moment Claire was too angry to feel hurt and deep disappointment, but he knew there would come a time when the fact her marriage had failed would become a huge pain in her heart. He looked into Serena's eyes and said

"No one wants their relationships to fail or to end. Even if they start going wrong, we always hope they will come right in the end. Sadly, sometimes they don't. Parting is inevitable. Sometimes it is needed to set people free to follow their right path in life. We might start a path with someone but then our destiny calls us to another path. Sometimes it is through one person's selfish actions. Sometimes it is because life is calling us in a different direction. They are both painful."

Serena felt a chill go through her soul as she felt Satish's words had a strangely prophetic ring for their own relationship. Despite this, he spontaneously leant forward and kissed her on the lips, and stroked her hair. She forced a smile back at him.

Going back to the kitchen they found Claire had been busy. Already she had left messages with two locksmiths asking if they could let her know if they were free to come and change her locks in the morning. She had phoned her father and briefly filled him in on what had happened and informed him she would be bringing Sebastian's clothes and other belongings to the office. Roger had initially been furious at Sebastian's treatment of his daughter, but as she continued speaking, he realised she was glad to be seeing him gone. He felt conflicted because Sebastian was a good, hard worker who had a nose for making money. In loyalty to his daughter, he could not continue to have him working under the same roof.

However, he could always give him some freelance work…. Obviously, he would not let Claire know this.

The three adults made dinner together and they all sat down with the girls to eat dinner. Unfortunately, halfway through dinner, Abigail asked the question they were dreading.

"When is Daddy coming home?"

Serena and Satish exchanged glances. Claire took a deep breath.

"Daddy is going to be away for a long time."

"Oh. OK." Abigail shrugged her shoulders and carried on tucking into her Pad Thai. "What's for pudding?"

That night in the shelter of their room Serena and Satish talked about what the evening's developments meant for them. Serena realised that she could not leave her daughter at this challenging time. Even though Claire was relieved that Sebastian would not be coming back, she had many things to organise, starting in the morning.

Claire was up early the next morning and was already busy on her laptop when Serena and Satish went down to do their morning ritual. Firstly, she had to ensure that she had enough money to tide her over until she started getting maintenance from Sebastian, or she could secure or release some income herself. Serena reminded her that she was getting money from her private, ad hoc yoga classes which were gaining in popularity. Serena was now thinking about becoming certified so she could teach openly and professionally. Claire had substantial savings, but she did not want to dip into these if possible. After some number crunching, they realised they could survive without Sebastian's wages.

"Maybe it's a good thing Maria isn't coming anymore," mused Claire.

Serena gently suggested the girls gave up their piano and ballet lessons. It was obvious to her that the girls did not enjoy them. She was surprised when Claire agreed.

"Sebastian wanted them to do them. I think they brag in the office about all the different activities their kids do. *My Portia does the flute. Oh really, my Clarence does the French Horn. The flute is so passe.*" Serena laughed at Claire's impression of the pompous staff at Roger and Sebastian's firm.

Claire hestitated for a moment and then asked

"Would you mind if I joined you in your morning ritual? I can finish all this later."

Serena beamed at her in delight.

"Of course we don't mind."

After breakfast, Claire set about her tasks once again with renewed energy and optimism. Once everything that needed doing was done, Claire, Serena and Satish waited for the inevitable return of Sebastian, who they knew would not take his expulsion from the house lightly.

Sebastian returned to the house the following Tuesday. It had taken him several days to sort out an emergency passport, negotiate the bill with the hotel owners, try to arrange for money to live on, and eventually rebook his flight home. He had not believed Claire when she said he would find his stuff at the office so arrogantly decided he would go to the house first.

Satish, Serena, and Claire were all sitting in the front room after delivering the twins to nursery, having a morning drink when Satish saw a taxi draw up outside and Sebastian get out.

"Oh dear me," he said. "I think we are about to have some trouble."

Claire sprang to her feet and looked out the window. With a wry smile, she said

"Bring it on."

They heard Sebastian try his key in the lock. They then heard him swearing loudly when it did not work. He then started thumping on the door. When this did not work and he got no reply, he rang Claire's number. She let it ring several times before picking it up.

"Yes?"

"Claire. I am outside. Let me in."

"So we heard," she answered calmly and coldly.

"Well let me in then."

"What part of *your things will be at the office* did you not understand?"

Another torrent of expletives was heard.

"Claire. Stop being so unreasonable. Let me in and we can talk about it."

Now all three of them were standing looking out of the window, but they were obscured from Sebastian's sight by the voile curtains that allowed them to look out but no one to see in. Sebastian was pacing up and down the front path, and a small group of intrigued neighbours, who had been alerted by his shouting, were now gathered on the opposite side of the road. Nothing like this had happened before in their leafy suburbia.

"Sorry, dah-ling." Claire used the darling word with such contempt in her voice she surprised even herself. "Things are way past the *let's talk about this* stage. It is over. I am divorcing you."

Another round of expletives.

"Claire. I will get my solicitor on to you straight away."

"No worries. Mine is already in touch with her. See you in court. Chau – or was that rather tactless of me to remind you of Rome?"

She cut off the call and burst out laughing.

"I rather enjoyed that last comment," she smirked. "Good riddance to bad rubbish."

They could see Sebastian standing staring at his phone. He looked once again at the front door and they thought he was going to start hammering on it once again, but he decided against it and slowly made his way down the front path, scowling at the gossiping neighbours on the other side of the road. He strode off down the road to go to his office, where the reception was going to be equally frosty.

A letter from Sebastian's solicitor arrived the next day, acknowledging receipt of the letter from Claire's solicitor. Thus started the heated exchange of increasingly vitriolic correspondence and ended in a costly divorce settlement. Sebastian was, as he feared, disowned by his parents because Claire phoned them and told them what had happened. They had so enjoyed their visit recently that she and Serena were "in their good books" and they were very sympathetic towards them both. Sebastian's father was furious about his son's disgusting behaviour and told Claire that he would not get a penny from either of them, but to let them know if she ever needed any help. They asked if, "when the dust had settled" they could visit again as they were so delighted with their grandchildren.

Sebastian went to live in their North Devon cottage, where he began pottery classes and attempted to surf, paid for by work that Roger sent him on the sly. He soon found himself some female admirers, along with one special male one.

TWENTY-SIX

Claire's divorce came through in the middle of July. Spring and early Summer had been a turbulent time as Sebastian tried to wriggle his way out of any financial responsibility for his children, even saying that he was not totally sure that they were even his children. A quick paternity test proved they were. Despite having been stung so severely by Eleanor he was still very wealthy and managed to continue to hide his money offshore. Although he had to report being scammed to the Italian Police to get a crime number and to be able to sort out a new passport and credit cards, he was too embarrassed by the incident to continue pressing for an arrest and conviction once he was back in the UK. He thought he would never be able to track her down anyway and get his money back. Fortunately for him, he could still live a comfortable lifestyle with the money that remained and with some freelance work, as well as the work from Roger. Claire was willing to negotiate regarding access to the children, but he challenged it, wanting to have joint custody, even though it was impractical. This was denied and it was agreed he would visit once a month from his cottage in Devon.

Serena saw a transformation in her daughter. No longer having to put up with constant sniping criticism from Sebastian, Claire grew in confidence. She began to lose weight and joined Serena and Satish every morning in their morning routine, along with the twins. If ever she missed a session, she said that she felt the day had not started right. She also became happier and calmer. She was in regular contact with Anish and although Serena was concerned that this friendship was developing too rapidly, especially in the light of it being so close to Claire's split with her husband, she felt it was overall a positive relationship and was boosting Claire's confidence.

Serena felt happy again as Satish was now permanently back in London. The house in Birmingham sold quickly and there were several meetings between Anish, Satish, and Shanthi to make further plans. Satish had managed to arrange speaking engagements at various retreat houses around the Southeast, which were usually sold out. His books were gaining in popularity, but he had to be paid via the Community in Thailand as his six-month English visa did not allow him to work in the United Kingdom. During July he had started talking about going back initially to Thailand in September and then going to join Anish and Shanthi in Sri Lanka a month later. Serena realised that very soon she would have to decide whether to go with him or stay to support her daughter. Generally, however, Claire was coping well. The twins were upset when they were told that their Daddy was not going to live with them anymore, but they were astute. When he visited them, bearing large and expensive gifts, and took them out to the Zoo, they quickly realised they were going to be spoilt each time he visited, and they ensured they milked him for everything they could. There were a few tears every time he left but they soon stopped if Satish offered to read them a story.

Serena had found great satisfaction in supporting Claire and being with her grandchildren. The twins were a constant source of amusement and St John began to flourish. It usually fell to Serena to give him his bottle and he would stare at her with a hypnotic intensity as he slurped away, his chubby hands reaching out towards her face. Never had she felt such a deep maternal instinct as when she was nursing him. She knew there was a deep soul connection between them. Serena was also enjoying the luxuries of London life and began to take for granted the fresh, clean water from the taps and the luxurious soaks in the bath, with or without Satish. Regular weekly phone calls with her mother increased her sense of rootedness. Satish, however, was becoming increasingly homesick for the simple life of the Community. He began withdrawing into himself more and more. Serena was basking so much in her newfound domestic bliss that she did not see this. She kept putting off the decision about their future together, as every time she thought about having to make the decision, she felt overwhelmed. She was torn between her love for Satish and longing for

Thailand and her love for her daughter, grandchildren, and mother. It was a decision she did not want to have to make, as whichever way she decided she knew she would be heartbroken for those she would not be with and would miss. However, a phone call in the second week of August changed everything.

Serena was cooking lunch when her phone rang. Turning off the hob, she answered.

"Is that Jayne Allwood?" a female voice asked.

Serena was taken aback. It was a long time since anyone had called her by that name.

"Ah yes. Yes. Sorry, I have changed my name."

"Is your mother Dorothy Allwood?"

A sudden dread clutched Serena's heart.

"Yes. Why? Who is this?"

"I am a Ward Sister at Cheltenham Hospital. Your mother has had a stroke. She is doing well but we need to keep her in for a few days. She asked that we phone you."

Serena felt the world crumble around her.

"Yes. Thank you. Can I visit?"

Still in a state of shock, she looked around for a pen and paper, but Satish was already handing her one, as he immediately realised there was bad news. With a shaking hand, Serena wrote down the details of the ward.

"Please tell Mum I love her and will be down to see her tomorrow."

She finished the phone call and burst out crying.

"Mum has had a stroke. I must go and visit her."

Satish gathered her into his arms and stroked her hair.

"Of course, Beloved. It is too late today. Go tomorrow."

Claire had come into the kitchen and stopped in her tracks to see her mother in tears. She sent Satish and Serena into the front room to sit down while she finished preparing lunch. They booked train tickets for them to go together down to Cheltenham the next day. Satish said he wanted to be there as support for Serena but would leave her to visit her mother alone.

The journey the next day seemed never-ending. Eventually, they arrived at the hospital and Satish went to the café while Serena visited her mother. She was in a small sideward and immediately Serena could see the effects of the stroke on her mother. Her face was distorted, and her right arm lay limply on the bed. As she tried to speak her speech was slurred and her vision seemed to be wandering everywhere, and she was hooked up to monitors and a drip. Serena suddenly realised how much she had grown to love her mother. Taking her hand, she kissed her, and Dorothy looked at her slightly bewildered. Suddenly she recognised Serena and tried to pull her close and through slurred speech gave thanks that she was there. It was a difficult visiting time as Dorothy struggled to speak and seemed to want to say a lot. Serena was aware she needed to rest. A nurse came to check her and having ascertained that Serena was next of kin, asked if she could speak to one of the medical staff before she left.

Serena saw that her mother was tiring so after half an hour, she said she had to go but would be back and not to worry about anything. Already her mind was buzzing about the practicalities of having her mother in hospital so far from London. She realised she and Satish needed to stay locally overnight so she could visit her mother again the next day and bring in some things that she needed. It turned out that Dorothy had collapsed during a shopping trip to Cheltenham and so all she had with her was what she was wearing at the time. Serena assured her she would buy her some nightclothes, underwear, and toiletries, kissed her, and left the ward. She found one of the doctors outside the ward. He took them to a small office where he explained that the stroke had been severe but already Dorothy was making substantial progress, but it was too early to say how much permanent damage there might be. However, she would probably need physiotherapy and it would not be advisable for her to live alone for the immediate future. Serena felt stunned. She felt her plans to return to Thailand crumbling. There was no way she could abandon her mother as well as her daughter and grandchildren.

It was decided that Satish would return to London and Serena would stay overnight in a bed and breakfast in Cheltenham, so she could do what she had promised. It was with a heavy heart that she said goodbye to

SUE CEE

Satish and started to buy the goods on the list that she had written. Once back in the hospital, she could see an improvement in her mother already. Her eyes were focussed and even seemed brighter when she saw Serena. She nodded her approval as Serena showed her the items she had bought. Dorothy took her hand and stuttered

"You are such a good girl. I do not deserve you."

Serena smiled.

"I am glad I can help."

She spent two hours with her mother and then spent a lonely evening and night in a bed and breakfast close to the hospital. The doctor's words that Dorothy could not live alone echoed in her mind. She knew the conversation she would have to have back in London.

When she visited her mother again the next morning, she could see further improvements but knew she had a long road to recovery before her. The train journey home felt bleak and lonely, with Serena's mind churning with all that this latest incident would mean for her own future.

Claire missed her mother over the two days she was away and realised just how much she had come to depend on her. Feeding St John alone was a chore to her, and she suddenly really appreciated Serena. Satish's return eased the situation, but when he told her about Dorothy's state her reaction was immediate.

"She can come and live with us here. If necessary, we can put a stairlift in. Now Seb hasn't got his office

312

upstairs we can make that your room if you and Mum don't mind, and we can put Dorothy in your present room. I can't see her managing the stairs to the attic."

Serena did not have to broach the subject of where Dorothy could live when she got back. The moment she arrived back in the house, Claire offered to give Dorothy a home, should Dorothy be happy with the idea.

Dorothy was in hospital for a week and then was allowed home. Serena hired a car and drove down to fetch Dorothy back to Twickenham. First, she went to her house and got together a list of items that Dorothy requested and shut the house down for the time being. It was hoped that Dorothy might at some stage be able to live back in the cottage, but, for now, she had to be living with someone in case she had another stroke. However, the consensus was that it should be sold, and Dorothy move to London. As Serena shut the front door of her mother's cottage behind her, she was already compiling a list in her head of the selling points of the cottage and wondering how quickly it might sell, if that was what Dorothy did want to do eventually. As she was walking up the garden path to the front gate an elderly man stopped at the gate and went to open it. When he saw Serena, he stopped in surprise.

"Oh! Good afternoon," he said. "Is Dorothy in?"

Serena studied him. He was tall and well-dressed, with a kind but sad-looking face. She immediately picked up a sense of loneliness and grief from him. By now she had reached the gate.

"I am Dorothy's daughter, Serena."

The man looked surprised.

"Oh! I thought she lost her daughter." Then he looked embarrassed. "I am sorry that is a tactless thing to say."

"She did. That was my older sister. I am the daughter she probably didn't talk about. I haven't been in touch with Mum for a long time. Long story. Can I help you?"

The man looked her up and down and thought to himself that he was not surprised that Dorothy had disowned her, looking at her rainbow hair, piercings, tie-dye long skirt, and Doc Marten boots, to say nothing of her strange round black and white pendant around her neck which he suspected was a Pagan symbol. However, she appeared to be a kind and helpful soul, and who was he to judge? He continued

"Well, Dorothy hasn't been to church for a couple of weeks, and I wanted to see if she is all right. Sorry, my name is Bernard Weathers. I am the Church Warden at St John's. I noticed your mother has been absent and I wanted to check that she is all right."

Serena told him what had happened to Dorothy, and he looked shocked.

"Dear me. And you say she is going to come and live with you in London?" He looked disappointed at this.

"For the time being. I have just shut up her house for now."

"Would you like me to keep an eye on it for you?"

Serena could see the genuine concern on his face. "Thank you."

They exchanged phone numbers and email addresses. He then confided that he would miss Dorothy. He had always admired her and her flower-arranging skills had been outstanding.

"A very valued member of the choir when we had one," he added sadly. He continued

"Please give her my love and best wishes for a speedy recovery."

They said their goodbyes and Serena set off for Cheltenham in the hire car to collect her mother. Dorothy was ready and waiting when she got there. Serena relayed Bernard's message and Dorothy looked sad and thoughtful.

"Bernard is a very kind man. He lost his wife last year…." she tailed off, but then added, "One of the few at St John's that I trust now."

Serena heard a touch of anger and bitterness in her mother's voice.

The journey back was slow, partly because Serena was still not used to driving again after so many years without a car. Dorothy sat staring out of the window and Serena's heart went out to her. Her life was changing beyond her control, and she was being uprooted to somewhere she did not know. However, she did now have a family who would love and care for her.

When they arrived at Claire's she was greeted by two excited girls who had made cards under Claire's strict supervision. No glitter, paint, or glue. Just coloured pencils.

"Satish has gone to do some talking," Olivia pouted. "We had to make boring cards."

Dorothy assured the girls they were lovely cards.

To Serena's annoyance, she found Roger was there, "visiting his grandchildren." He went into charm overdrive when he met Dorothy. They had met briefly when Dorothy had visited London on a shopping trip before Serena told her she was pregnant with Claire. They had gone for lunch together at Fortnum and Mason's. Dorothy had clearly shown her disapproval of him then, despite his paying for the meal. Now he knew he had to put on a charm offensive to impress her. He helped to take Dorothy's bags up to her room and then sat down next to her on the settee in the front room. Claire went to make a pot of tea.

"How lovely to see you again Missus Allwood. Still looking as elegant as ever."

Dorothy seemed to lap up his attention. Serena even wondered if she had forgotten who he was but concluded that maybe she was just going along with his flattery to keep the peace. Somehow, to Serena's annoyance, he was able instantly to relate and engage with her mother and she felt more and more pushed out as they sat chatting and laughing together. Claire came back in with the tea tray and looked at her mother with raised eyebrows. She too was surprised at the

KEEP KARMA AND CARRY ON

chemistry between the two of them. She too felt like an outsider as Roger held court with Dorothy.

Roger left the room to go to the bathroom. Dorothy said in a loud whisper to Serena

"He seems to be a really nice man now. What a shame it didn't work out between you two. At least he is from the same country as you and much more your age. Far more suitable for you. And I am sure he is a Christian."

Serena suppressed a snort at the thought of Roger being labelled as a Christian. In Dorothy's eyes all white, elderly, or middle-aged, middle-class men were Christians. It was the only world she knew.

Serena quietly said

"He is married to Melanie now. And I am with Satish, who I love very much."

Roger returned and sat down next to Dorothy and poured her another cup of tea. His phone buzzed. He looked at it and looked annoyed and pressed "Ignore."

Dorothy said

"I was just saying to Jayne…oh sorry Serena…. what a charming man you are now."

Roger's phone buzzed again. He looked at it and scowled.

"Excuse me. Melanie has just rung me twice."

He pressed "Answer" but also accidentally pressed "Speaker" as well.

A voice screamed down the phone at him

"You utter bastard. You have given me the clap…. again. Who was it this time? That little slapper from accounts…. or that whore you visit in Bermondsey? I want a divorce."

The phone went dead. Roger stared at it, his face red, sweat appeared on his brow and a pulse appeared on his temple.

Dorothy looked shocked. Claire looked horrified. Serena had to stifle a giggle. Roger stood up, saying "I think I had better go. Nice to meet you again Missus Allwood." Dorothy just glared at him.

TWENTY-SEVEN

By the end of August, Dorothy was established in what had been Serena and Satish's room, and they were happily situated in the attic room. It felt more private, and they were glad of this, as Satish was having to plan his return to Thailand. His visa was due to expire, and he knew he could not afford to get it extended. Serena knew she could not go back with him for the time being and hoped and prayed that, eventually, she could go back to where she had been so happy. However, for the foreseeable future, she had to concentrate on her family commitments. Once Claire had the girls settled at school and if Dorothy could find suitable local sheltered accommodation, then perhaps Serena could join him. Dorothy would need someone to be around for her, and Serena knew that Claire would be happy to keep a check on her grandmother. Dorothy had come to like Twickenham but still longed for her cottage in the Cotswolds.

Bernard had been phoning her every few days to check on her and even came up to visit her one day. He took her out to the nearby coffee shop for lunch, so she did not have to walk too far. She was making a steady recovery but needed a stick to keep her balance.

She and Bernard enjoyed each other's company and he had been saddened by the treatment she had received from the church to the point that he was, after twenty years, going to resign as Churchwarden.

"It isn't the same without you there," he admitted.

Serena noticed that her mother seemed to glow after talking to or being with Bernard. He had genuine charm and manners.

"Not like someone else I know," mused Serena to herself.

Roger had not visited them again after his embarrassing phone call from Melanie. Dorothy had finally taken to Satish and was enthralled by his tales of his travels and of the countries where he had lived. She could also see how much he and Serena loved each other, and she was glad her daughter had finally found love.

Satish was taken up with meetings with Anish and Shanthi as they planned the future Lotus Light Community in Sri Lanka. Anish and Shanthi were now staying in a budget hotel in Balham. Both Anish and Shanthi were lit up by the thought of returning to their birthplace. Satish too was looking forward to this, but he wanted to finish various commitments he had in Thailand before going to Sri Lanka. As the three of them were becoming increasingly excited about the future, Serena felt more and more excluded, and she noticed that the spark between Satish and Shanthi seemed to have reignited. Serena had noticed the lingering looks and the occasional touches that went between them. She noticed how Shanthi flushed whenever Satish entered the room after being away for a time, and how he hugged her very closely when she and Anish left to go to their hotel rooms. However, she was too busy caring for her mother and her daughter and grandchildren to be able to dwell on this for too long. She knew her present calling was in London and told herself she had to accept this. Nevertheless, when Satish announced that they had bought the air tickets for him to go the Bangkok and for Anish and Shanthi to go to Colombo, she felt a stab in her heart and a sense of dread that she was being well and truly left behind. The couple spent as much time together as they could, soaking up each other's company, staying in bed late in the morning, and going to bed early at night.

The twins were sad when they realised Satish was going away.

"Please stay," Olivia pleaded, making her blue eyes as big as possible as they filled with tears.

"You will make Serena very, very sad."

Satish smiled sadly at her.

"I have to go. Sometimes, in life, we must follow a certain path. It is the one we are called to. If we do not follow it then…." He sighed deeply. "We have to follow it to be true to ourselves and to what we are called to be. I cannot explain it to you now. One day you will understand. I love Serena and she loves me, and she understands that we must be apart. I hope one day to come back. If you will let me…."

Abigail jumped up and down.

"Yes, yes. For Christmas. You can bring us an Ellie back for our present."

The dreaded day of departure arrived. Dorothy was spending the morning with a new friend she had made at the local church, as she did not want to intrude on what she realised would be an emotional moment. Satish was preparing to leave for the airport. He had already said goodbye to the twins before they left for nursery as he would be gone by the time they got back. In the days beforehand Serena had spent extra time in prayer and meditation. With a heavy heart, she knew what she had to do. She was aware of the increasing intensity of the attraction between Satish and Shanthi, although he never failed to shower attention on Serena, and he was as passionate a lover as ever. Dorothy was so grateful for a home where she felt protected and cared for, and Claire was blooming with her newfound freedom, despite having to care for three under-five-year-olds. However, Serena's mind was made up

As Satish was putting the last of his things in his bag, she sat down on the bed next to it and patted the bed for him to sit down. She fought back tears.

Slowly she slipped the commitment ring off her finger and placed it into the palm of Satish's right hand, closing her hand around his. She lifted her head and looked at him through tear-filled eyes.

"I cannot come with you now, although I so want to. In reality, I will not be able to join you for a long time. My calling is here with my family. I am needed here. I might never be able to return to be with you. So…. I am going to release you from your commitment to me."

Her voice wavered but she continued, "I love you. I always will. You made me believe in myself again. You showed me that I can love and trust again. You helped me to heal and become who I am today. I am so torn. I want to be with you, but I know I must stay. I cannot hold you to your commitment to me. Nor I in mine to you. Maybe in time we shall renew our commitment to each other, should our paths cross again and it is our destiny. In my spirit, I feel it will not be so. I know you have a different path from me, at least for the time being. I'm granting you the freedom to walk that path, and whatever it might bring. New opportunities…."

Her voice caught in her throat

"New relationships. Maybe love."

And in a voice barely above a whisper

"Maybe your own family."

She looked down as the tears fell from her eyes, quietly sobbing.

Satish sat in silence for a long time his head bowed, staring at her hand wrapped around his. Eventually, with his voice cracking, he said

"Beloved. I will always love you. When we committed to each other we always had a feeling in our hearts that one day our paths would be forced to part. We are now at that point, though my heart breaks. My calling is back in Thailand and then Sri Lanka. Yours is here. Thank you for being so noble as to release me. I pray one day our paths will cross again. If not in this life, then in the next."

He looked up at Serena's tear-stained face, and gently stroked her face with his left hand. Then he lowered his hand and slipped his commitment ring off, kissed it, and gently placed it in Serena's hand.

"You are a remarkable woman. You have such strength. You have travelled far in your life, and in your spirit. I will never forget you. You will always have a place in my heart. May Karma bring us back together sometime and somewhere If not in this life, then in the next."

With this, he drew her close and they embraced. Suddenly the intense passion of the night before was forgotten and they were now two heartbroken people saying farewell.

Claire knocked gently on the door.

"Satish your taxi is here."

Satish and Serena had decided prolonged goodbyes at the airport were more than they could bear, but now Serena desperately wished to have longer with him. However, she knew she had to say goodbye here, where she felt safe, and where she could spend the rest of the day sobbing her heart out for the only man she had genuinely and totally loved.

"Goodbye Beloved. Don't come down if you don't want to."

They kissed long and passionately, and then Serena listened to him bumping his bag down the stairs, his goodbye to Claire, and then the final clunk of the front door shutting. Serena felt her heart break in two.

She spent two hours crying, the ache in her heart being almost unbearable. Through the open attic window, she heard Claire go out with St John in his buggy to get the girls from nursery. Half an hour later she heard the front door open. After a few minutes, there was a gentle tapping on the door. Serena sniffed and called out

"Yes?"

The door opened and the twins' faces appeared around it, both tear-stained and Abigail had a bunch of flowers in her hand. Silently they came over and climbed up on the bed, snuggled up to her, and hugged her. The sun moved slowly round as a couple of hours passed and Serena looked at her clock and realised that Satish would be boarding his plane. At that moment, her phone rang. It was Satish.

Trembling she answered it.

"Beloved. I had to speak to you before I fly. I will always love you. Until we meet again. I must go. We are boarding."

"Love you too," she whispered and dissolved into tears as he rang off.

The twins hugged her closer.

Another gentle tapping on the door and Claire came in with sandwiches and cold drinks.

"The girls didn't want lunch. They wanted to be with you. But I guess you will all be hungry now."

Serena smiled at her daughter and said to herself just how lucky she was

TWENTY-EIGHT

October arrived, with an unseasonal heatwave. The girls had started school the week of their fifth birthday and seemed to be happy there, feeling very grown up in their school uniforms. Claire appreciated the longer time free during the day to concentrate on planning what she wanted for her future. She had decided she had had enough of office work and the politics that went with it. Therefore, she decided, she would do a Reiki course and an Aromatherapy course so she could practice from home and fit in around the girls' school times. She started studying online courses which promised certificates that would enable her to practice. In the meantime, she would offer financial advice to people she knew for a small fee.

St John was now very active in his baby bouncer and was turning into a happy, placid child. He loved Serena and beamed at her every time she came into the room. He lapped up the cuddles and kisses poured on him by his grandmother and great-grandmother.

Dorothy was blossoming with the love and care she was receiving from her newfound family. Bernard made several trips to see her, and each time he left to return home, Dorothy seemed to have improved in her health. She even began talking about moving back to her cottage and going to St Edwin's church in the next village. Bernard had already transferred there, and they already had their eye on him as a potential Churchwarden. It turned out that they had both had a bit of a crush on each other since they first met at choir twenty years ago but had suppressed it as they were both married at that time.

Satish kept in touch with Serena, initially daily, phoning or messaging three or four times a day, but by the end of October it was once every two or three days and his messages became shorter and increasingly impersonal. He had gone back to a couple of crises in the Community, which he was endeavouring to sort out, before going to Sri Lanka. As he settled back into Thailand, he felt more and more disconnected from the Western way of life in which he had been immersed for six months and soaked up the peace and slower pace of life in the Community. He was also in daily contact with Anish and Shanthi in Sri Lanka.

Serena studied for her yoga certificate and passed with a distinction, which meant she could start doing professional yoga classes. She quickly established a regular clientele and even had waiting lists for some classes. They were now held in community centres and church halls around West London.

Anish was in regular contact with Claire and asked for her advice on various financial matters. Claire willingly helped them. At the beginning of November, she mentioned in passing that Satish was now in Sri Lanka. Serena felt a stab of hurt and jealousy. Why hadn't he told her he was there now? Claire tried to smooth over her mother's hurt feelings by suggesting that maybe he was so busy he had just forgotten to tell her. Serena was not sure. She knew in her heart that Satish and Shanthi were getting close, and he did not want to admit it to her. However, her connection with him was so strong still in her heart that she just knew the truth. Serena looked down at the ring he had returned to her and which she was now wearing on the ring finger of her left hand. She had vowed she would wear it forever as she would never forget him and never love another man. Somehow it felt hollow as he was so obviously already moving on, although she had to remind herself that he had been betrothed to Shanthi as a child. She began to believe that this was his karma, and that family honour was being restored. Slowly she took the ring off and put it in the pocket of her harem pants and decided she would look for a silver chain in the local charity shop and start to wear it around her neck instead.

November blew in with gales and rain. Persuading the girls to go to school became a chore. Claire and Serena took it in turns. One day, just as she got back from being blasted down the road, Serena was surprised to see she had a message from Roger.

"Can we talk?"

Puzzled she messaged back.

"Okay. Where and when?"

They agreed to meet in half an hour at the local coffee shop. Roger was looking haggard as he arrived ten minutes late. Serena had already ordered her soy latte and was sipping it. She did not want to be indebted to Roger in any way. He ordered a strong black coffee and sat down. After making enquiries about the family, he took a deep breath and launched forth.

"Melanie and I have broken up. She is divorcing me. I haven't been into work since our row…. after The Phone Call."

His reddening cheeks showed Serena that he was still embarrassed about it. Serena sat quietly waiting for him to continue. After staring at his coffee for a while, he continued

"I've been doing some serious thinking. I've been a total shit all my life. I must admit that I was ready to take the piss out of you when you first came back. I wanted to get you back in bed just to show that young navel gazer a thing or two."

He looked up at Serena and continued "I've never been turned down by a woman in my life. You annoyed me. However, I've since realised what an amazing person you have become. You have helped our daughter pick up the pieces after Sebastian did what he did. You're fantastic with the kids and especially with St John. I know Claire didn't really want him, and neither did Sebastian. He told me enough times. But like me, Sebastian is a shit. I realise now that so often women will follow the pattern set by their mum. It is like history repeating itself. I also realise I need to change. I still have time to do so. I'm going to retire. I have enough money to do so. I want to do something worthwhile. But most of all…." He looked down and then hesitantly reached out and took Serena's hand and said "I want to apologise for how I treated you. Can you ever forgive me? Can we be friends?"

Serena sat dumbfounded. She could not cope with a contrite Roger. It was something beyond her experience or understanding.

Eventually, she spoke.

"Roger, I forgave you over three years ago, when I found the Community. We had to write down all the people who had wronged us in our lives and we had to work on forgiving them. It is only through forgiveness that we can be free and healed. Otherwise, we're trapped by it. We continue to be imprisoned by the other person. I've truly and deeply forgiven you."

Roger looked up and his face seemed to beam with light.

"Really?"

"Really. You will always be the father of my child. And the grandfather of my grandchildren. You didn't treat me fairly. That I can't change. But the hurt has gone."

"Can we be friends?" he asked slowly. "I doubt either of us wants to be involved romantically again."

She smiled.

"No."

He beamed again.

"And I want to be a better support to my…. our…. daughter and grandchildren. I plan to sell my Docklands flat and find a small terrace house somewhere not too far away. I want to see more of my family. I realise they are what matters."

His face clouded over for a moment.

"How am I going to face your mother again?"

The memory of Melanie's voice shrieking down the phone and the look of horror on Dorothy's face still haunted him. He had not visited since.

Serena withdrew her hand and smiled.

"I think that might sort itself out. It turns out she and her friend Bernard have a bit of a thing going and she wants to move back to her cottage. He lives just down the road so will keep an eye on her. They're both saying that at their age they need to grab opportunities while they can…."

Roger's eyebrows shot up in surprise.

Serena continued "I think there might even be wedding bells next year. She wants to be back in her house by Christmas."

"Wow!" was all Roger could say.

They finished their drinks, and it was agreed that Serena would let him know when Dorothy had gone back to her home and he could then, without embarrassment, start visiting his family again. Serena realised that she might even enjoy the company of the new Roger.

Bernard came to collect Dorothy in the first week of December. He had hired a new car so he could "chauffeur her in the style she deserved" rather than taking her home in his aging and now unreliable small car. Serena promised she would be down to see her mother as soon as she was settled back in. Somehow, she felt her mother would be rather busy for the next few weeks as Bernard had already told them of all the activities their new church had planned over Christmas.

As Christmas approached Serena and Claire made plans for Christmas. Sebastian appeared on his monthly visit with sacks full of toys for the children, but they seemed not to be interested. They were too busy doing drawings for Grandad.

Christmas Eve arrived and once all the children were settled for the night, after much arguing and threats that Santa would not come until they were asleep, Claire and Serena sat down with a glass of red wine each. Claire looked across at her gentle mother, who was sitting cross-legged on the sofa, still looking strange and bereft without Satish by her side.

"Well, Mum, what a year it has been."

Serena smiled.

"You could say that. If you wrote it in a novel no one would believe it."

Claire laughed.

"Are you happy Mum? You must miss Satish."

Serena looked thoughtful.

"Yes. I do. But he was part of another chapter of my life. I'm in a different chapter now. Nothing can ever take away what we shared. He'll always be in my heart. I'm so grateful to him for I now know I can love and be loved in return. He's shown me this. However, I doubt I'll ever love anyone else again as I loved him. I'm lucky to have found what I did with him. And, somehow, I know we'll meet again. But maybe not in this time or life."

Claire looked thoughtful and with a slightly choked voice said

"Mum you're amazing. With all you have lived through. You're so kind, forgiving, and loving. You've even forgiven Dad. You're an inspiration."

"Thanks. And, yes, I'm happy. Now you said earlier that you had something you wanted to talk to me about."

Claire looked uncomfortable.

"I've had an email from Anish. He wondered if there was any possibility of my flying out to Sri Lanka for a couple of weeks to help set up the finances for the new Community. I just wonder if you would be able to cope with the twins and St John if I went."

Much to her surprise, Serena decided she would be happy to be left with the children. For months now she had realised just what she had missed out on with her mothering of Claire. She felt she was now making up for the lost time.

"Go. Have a holiday. You deserve it."

Claire's face beamed with joy. She got out of her seat and hugged Serena.

"Thank you, Mum. You're wonderful. He wants me to go out the first week of January."

Serena was a bit taken aback that it was so soon, but also realised that she would have several days when she would not have to take the girls to school, which would make life easier. She also knew that she was quite looking forward to having the children to herself. She immediately thought of all the baking and crafts they could do together.

Claire flew out on the second of January. At first, the house seemed so empty with just Serena and the children. However, Roger popped around every day to help look after them, and they started to enjoy his visits. Claire emailed every day if she could. The only internet available was at a local café three miles away from the proposed premises for the Community. Increasingly Anish's name cropped up in conversation. One day she made a comment that made Serena aware that things had developed romantically between Satish and Shanthi. As soon as she had sent the email Claire realised what she had said and quickly sent another one, trying to downplay their relationship. However, Serena felt a strange feeling of satisfaction. She felt in her heart that they were right for each other. Serena sent a reply saying that she hoped they would be very happy together. Claire just sent a smiley back. A couple of days later she emailed to say that Satish and Shanthi were officially betrothed again, as they had been in childhood. Now family honour was restored. Serena felt strangely and deeply happy and at peace about it.

January began icy and when the girls returned to school Serena had to cajole them into going out in the cold. However, she soon began to enjoy the routine. St John was tucked up in his buggy, they slithered the short walk to school, kissing goodbye at the school gates, then Serena and St John went back home to the warm. There was a time of playing with St John and doing the chores. Serena was very grateful for online shopping. When Roger came, he always gave some money "towards housekeeping" as Serena had to suspend her yoga lessons for the time being. Picking the girls up from school, back home in the warm, with hot chocolate and hearing about their day at school, Serena felt at peace. St John would be gurgling happily in his bouncer, as Serena heated the meal she had prepared in the afternoon. Once the children were bathed, read to, and put to bed, Serena then had time to herself to read or meditate. She had found a deep contentment that she never believed she would feel ever again. The ache of missing Satish was fading. Their life together now felt as though it was in a different time and galaxy.

The two weeks passed quickly. Towards the end of it, something in the tone of Claire's emails began to make Serena feel uneasy. There was a lot more work to do than Claire had realised, and she was so much enjoying the company of Anish, and also of Satish and

Shanthi, who were making wedding preparations for later in the year. Claire felt she could now talk about them as a couple. A deep unease and nagging feeling developed in Serena's heart. Claire hardly asked about the children, always chatting on about the funny things the two men got up to. She sent a photo of her and Anish with arms entwined, wearing wreaths of jasmine.

Then the email came.

Serena was tidying up the front room when her phone pinged. As soon as she saw it was a message from Claire, she opened her laptop and started it up. It was easier to read messages on the laptop. Serena had to admit that her eyesight was not as good as it used to be.

"Hi, Mum. Hope you are okay. Hope the kids are behaving. Tell them Mummy misses them. I'm having such an amazing time here. I love it so much. The weather, the food, the beach. I can see why you love the tropics. I feel so alive. I'm also very, very busy. The Community is coming together really fast, and we hope to open in a month's time. I can't believe our luck in getting the property. We have a big opening do planned. And that is the thing. Is there any chance you can cope with the kids until the middle of February? Pleeeeeeese. I would love to be here when it opens. If you can't cope, then tell me and I'll fly back in a couple of days. Love yoooooooo."

Serena sat staring at the message. How did she feel about it? She realised that she had all she wanted here in this house, even if it were apart from her daughter in

Sri Lanka and her mother down in the Cotswolds, but she knew they would be together again before too long. The children were no problem to her, and she had enjoyed having them exclusively. Roger was proving to be a wonderful friend and had changed from being arrogant and thoughtless to showing kindness and thoughtfulness. Money was not a problem as it seemed to appear to cover their needs as and when they arose. She was enjoying living in Twickenham and had made several of her own friends through her yoga classes and a meditation group she had joined. One friend, Patrick, was showing her a great deal of attention, which she was enjoying very much, although she still felt a loyalty to Satish and felt she could never love anyone as much as she had loved him. Patrick was widowed and a couple of years younger than her. He had travelled widely and spent time in Thailand as a young man. They had met for coffee a couple of times, and even if their relationship stayed as friends, she was grateful for male company. There was much to be grateful for and to enjoy. She felt at home here. She quickly replied.

"Of course, you should stay for the opening. I can cope very well. Your Dad has been helping out too. Enjoy yourself."

The reply came back.

"Mum. Thank you. You're a star. It means so much. Thank you."

Serena smiled. Quickly she tapped out another message.

"Just as long as you don't postpone coming back again. We would not want history to repeat itself, would we? Xxxx"

There was a short reply.

"Lol xxx"

THE END...?

ACKNOWLEDGEMENTS

A big "thank you" to all those who helped me to write this book. It would never have seen the light of day without the teaching and encouragement from the wonderful Write That Book Masterclass, run by Michael Heppell, and the support of my Accountability Groups, Legs 11 and The Dynamics. A massive "thank you" goes to Matt Bird for typesetting the book and to Sarah McGeough for her advice.

Thank you also to my family members who assisted me in various ways to do this course.

You have all helped me realise my childhood dream of being a writer.

About the Author

Sue is a writer, storyteller, traveller, explorer of other cultures and their spiritualities, artist, nature lover, and eco freak. She loves painting, and pottering in her allotment, and is involved in various local environmental groups.

Among her experiences have been traveling in 44 countries and volunteering in Bolivia for a while, living as a single parent of three children, running a charity and setting up a food bank, and writing her first novel. She has finally fulfilled her childhood dream of being a writer. Her writing experience includes articles for local papers and magazines, contributing to a prayer book, and poetry.

She was born in South East London but now lives in Somerset.